By CINDY DEES

STUD GAMES
Poker Face

Published by DREAMSPINNER PRESS
www.dreampsinnerpress.com

POKER FACE

CINDY DEES

DREAMSPINNER PRESS

Published by
DREAMSPINNER PRESS

5032 Capital Circle SW, Suite 2, PMB# 279, Tallahassee, FL 32305-7886 USA
www.dreamspinnerpress.com

Poker Face
© 2020 Cindy Dees

Cover Art
© 2020 L.C. Chase
http://www.lcchase.com
Cover content is for illustrative purposes only and any person depicted on the cover is a model.

Trade Paperback ISBN: 978-1-64405-238-9
Digital ISBN: 978-1-64405-237-2
Library of Congress Control Number: 2020933232
Trade Paperback published June 2020
v. 1.0
Previously published by Dreamspinner Press as *Ace in the Hole* by Ava Drake, July 2016.

Printed in the United States of America

CHAPTER ONE

STONE JACKSON ducked into the aggressive air-conditioning of the Miami Imperium Hotel and felt his skin tighten in the sudden cold. He'd been warned, of course, but holy hot plate, it was a cooker out there. So different from England, where he'd spent the past decade living and working. Only a favor of the highest order could lure him back not only to America, but to the South.

"Welcome to the Imperium, sir. Is this your first time with us?" a busty, Jayne Mansfield blond purred at him. He searched her impressive chestular region for a name tag. Brittney.

"Hi, Brittney. What gave me away?"

"Nobody wears wool in South Beach. Not in July."

"Just got in from London. Haven't had time to change into my luau shirt and Bermudas."

"Oooh. Sounds yummy." She made a purring noise that set his teeth on edge. In her defense, he probably hated the sound because he'd never been able to make it himself.

"Registration desk?" he asked, tiring of the game.

"To your left, just beyond the fountain and palm trees."

Because all hotels needed thirty-foot-tall live palm trees in their lobbies. He strolled toward them…. Jesus. Live parrots squawked among the palm fronds. He opted to go around the whole disaster and spied a registration desk.

A blessedly less flirtatious college coed checked him into his suite on the executive floor, and he tuned out while she explained how to use his keycard to gain access to the restricted floor. This was not his first rodeo with upscale hotels.

Identification recovered and key in his pocket, he headed upstairs. Good Lord willing, as his mother was prone to saying, his trunk had preceded him to the hotel. The specialized gear he traveled with required a crap-ton of paperwork and customs preapproval and had to be shipped ahead to most of his jobs.

The first thing he saw when he stepped into his room was the big brushed-aluminum trunk parked in a corner of the living area. And as his father was prone to saying, Praise the Lord and pass the potatoes.

The suite had a sleek, modern sensibility. Smart up-lighting and indirect down-lighting created sexy pools of light and shadow. Dark gray slate floors, frosted glass interior doors, pale blue upholstery. All in all, not bad.

Although the wet bar in the living room was pitifully stocked. He would have to get *that* fixed at the earliest opportunity. Not that he was a big drinker. But he was a discerning one.

He shed his Savile Row suit and unbuckled the custom-fit leather shoulder holster. After peeling down to his spandex trunks, he unpacked quickly and donned the promised Bermuda shorts. Undershirt, holster back on, then a custom-tailored Hawaiian-print shirt made to fit over both the weapon and his muscular shoulders.

Camouflage donned. Now he would blend in enough with the locals that the Brittneys of the world wouldn't pick him out of the crowd as an outsider.

Even though he was most definitely an outsider. His work alone made that inevitable. His job required him to disengage from every situation, stand back, and observe every single person as a potential hostile.

His mother accused him of picking security work because it fit his antisocial tendencies. His father argued that the job had made him antisocial. Chicken. Egg. Didn't really matter which had come first. The fact was, he watched life go by. He didn't really live it.

Someday he would climb off the carousel. Get a life. Maybe settle down with a nice guy. Get a dog. Hell, maybe even a house.

Someday.

Without warning, jet lag slammed into him, and he felt like hell on broken wheels. He probably ought to shave. He fingered his jaw and felt rough stubble on it. But damn, he needed a stiff drink. *Jack Daniels No. 27 Gold, come be my bitch.* Scooping up his room key, he headed downstairs to the bar he'd spotted on the way in.

It had more of an S and M vibe than he'd anticipated, with lots of black leather and chrome. Who knew Miami business travelers let their kink show like this? But then, this was practically South Beach. The place was about three-quarters full. Not even 6:00 p.m. yet. Must be a happening joint by ten. More to the point, it had high-end whiskey, and lots of it. He bellied up to the bar and got ready to make out with a Jack on the rocks.

Another man swung onto the barstool beside him.

Stone registered details out of the corner of his eye. Good-looking. Clean-cut. Hair razor cut, suit tailored, shoes polished. And staring at him curiously.

"Can I help you?" he asked.

"Sorry. I didn't mean to stare. You just bear a striking resemblance to my boss."

He'd never heard that line before if the dude was looking to pick him up. He shrugged and closed his eyes as he took an appreciative sip of the whiskey the bartender poured for him.

The guy down the bar ordered some drink called a Derby. Stone watched the bartender mix it in minor disbelief. Who the hell paired bourbon with lime juice? And Grand Marnier and vermouth? The customer, a stupidly good-looking preppie type, sipped it in appreciation.

Stone shook his head. "My granddaddy would take you out back and shoot you for doing that to perfectly fine bourbon."

"Don't knock it till you've tried it," the guy popped off.

Stone's grin widened as he assessed the newcomer. Quick on the comeback. Bit of a smartass. Had the whole Captain America thing going, though. Close-shaven, square-jawed, and blue-eyed… a walking milk commercial missing only the white mustache. Totally not his type.

Cap surprised him by ordering two more Derbies and pushing one down the mirrored bar at him. "Go ahead. I dare you. Live dangerously."

Stone grunted in wry humor. Bastard had no idea how dangerously he usually lived. "Thanks for the drink. What's your name?"

"Christian Chatsworth-Brandeis."

"Jesus. Were you born with a poker up your ass to go along with that name?"

To his credit, the guy laughed. "Pretty much. Where do you hail from? I can't tell if I'm hearing a cattle ranch in Texas or Regent's Park, London."

He knew what and where Regent's Park was? It was one of the poshest addresses on planet Earth, but low profile about it. Didn't advertise itself.

"Actually, it was a dairy farm. Georgia. And Camden, not Regent's Park."

"Isn't Camden basically next door to Regent's Park?"

"How in the hell do you know that?" Stone demanded.

"Not every American is an ill-traveled rube, thank you very much."

Stone blinked. "Lemme guess. New England born and bred. Prep school, spent every summer in Europe."

Captain America shrugged.

Nailed it.

"My condolences," the guy said aloud.

"For what?"

"Losing the war?" prep school offered.

He grunted into his whiskey. "My father would be the first to tell you the War of Northern Aggression is only at halftime. Whenever you lily-white Yankee sissies are ready to go for round two, bring it."

"Want another Derby?"

"Nah. I'll stick with my Jack on the rocks. But thanks for broadening my horizons."

"You got a name?"

"Stone Jackson."

"Wow. And you picked on my name?"

"Dad's a Civil War history buff. I was born in Atlanta. Last name Jackson. Mom wouldn't let him name me Stonewall. Stone was as close as she'd let him go."

"Were you this big as a kid, or did you get beat up a lot?"

He shrugged. He'd gotten beat up a lot but not because of his name.

They nursed another round of drinks in silence. Somewhere near the bottom of the third Jack on the rocks, it occurred to Stone that he hadn't eaten in twenty-four hours or slept in a solid thirty-six. Tossing back a bunch of booze maybe hadn't been the smartest thing he could've done. High body mass would only buy him so much relief from the alcohol. "Shit. I need to get something to eat."

"Can't hold your booze, Georgia? Big, beefy guy like you? Tsk-tsk."

He told Christian Chatsworth-Brandeis precisely what he could do with himself. And without slurring his syllables, he was pleased to note.

"You staying in the hotel?" Christian asked, grinning.

"Yeah. Key's here somewhere." He fumbled in his pocket.

"Bartender, I'd like room service to send two porterhouse steaks and a bottle of your best Jack Daniels up to—what's your room number?"

"Room 2306," Stone supplied.

"To room 2306. All the trimmings. Salad, baked potatoes, and garlic bread. Double bread."

"I thought no one ate carbs anymore," he commented.

"Helps soak up the booze."

"I'm not drunk."

"You're gonna be if you don't get some food in you soon."

"Look. I don't need a babysitter, junior."

"Never said you did. Just helping out a fellow traveler."

A fellow traveler, huh? They walked across the lobby and waited for an elevator. "Where are you visiting from?" he asked Christian.

"Washington, DC. You?"

He frowned. "Nowhere, actually. I travel from job to job pretty much nonstop."

"What do you do?"

He shrugged. "Consultant. Follow around a lot of guys in suits. Don't do anything most of the time. You?"

"Aide to an important person who shall remain nameless."

"Like a secretary?"

Christian pulled a face. "It's a little more involved than that. I advise on various decisions, interface with media outlets, write speeches, solve crises, whatever my boss needs."

"You wipe his ass too?"

"Play nice. Speaking of asses, let's get you to your room before you make one of yourself."

He'd had just enough liquor to lose that thin patina of civilization his boss had worked so hard to paint onto him after he got out of the military. "Are you propositioning me, Christian Chatsworth-Brandeis, aide and ass-wiper extraordinaire?"

The elevator arrived, dinged, and slid open, and Christian gestured politely for him to go first. But old habits died hard. While Christian reached for the button for the twenty-third floor, Stone moved to block the doorway with his big frame. Christian was tall and obviously worked out, but he lacked the bulk of someone who'd relied on his muscles to stay alive for a long damned time.

As the elevator slowed for the twenty-third floor, Christian leaned forward from behind him and murmured in his ear, "For the record, I don't wipe anyone's ass after I'm done with it."

Something hot and hungry leaped in his gut. It had been a long time. A very long time. His job required total concentration, and his clients paid for no less. But the new gig didn't start for another day. He'd come in early to get the lay of the land and sleep off the jet lag so he'd be on his A game tomorrow. But he could go for a hookup with Christian Chatsworth-Brandeis—

"You going to keep standing there, or are we getting out?" Christian asked. Bastard sounded amused. He knew he'd thrown Stone off-balance with that totally un-milk-commercial comment.

He growled belatedly, "I was checking the hall to make sure it was clear."

"Are you afraid to be seen with me? This is Miami, dude. And South Beach, to boot. No one thinks twice about that sort of thing around here."

Stone frowned impatiently. "That's not it. I don't give a shit what anyone thinks of me." It was just that he'd been in the personal-security business for so long he couldn't get off an elevator any other way.

"Really? Anyone? How about me? Do you care what I think? Or am I only a piece of meat to you?"

The guy sounded offended.

Stone sighed. "I didn't mean it like that. Of course, you're not meat. You're too mouthy for that. In my line of work, people either completely ignore me or I'm forcing them to do something they don't like or want to do."

"What the hell do you do? Tell people to quit smoking, drinking, and having sex?"

"Something like that."

"Lemme guess. You're a priest."

He snorted with laughter. "And you still propositioned me? That's some kinky shit, man. Let *me* guess. You were a choir boy and the parish priest was hot."

"No, and hell no. Only religion my family worshipped was capitalism and the holy power of the almighty dollar."

"God bless America. Thanks for reminding me why I live overseas, Chris. Can I call you Chris?"

"Only if I can call you Stonewall."

"Christian it is."

CHRISTIAN ENJOYED the view as Stone exited the elevator ahead of him, although it felt more than a little weird to be ogling a man who looked a lot like a thirty-year-old younger version of his boss. Still. The man was built like a gladiator. Even better, he didn't seem to have a dumb-jock mentality to go with all those muscles. The dude was a bit crusty, and his social skills tended toward a caveman mentality, but he was also obviously jet-lagged as hell. Given the long hours and uncertain sleep schedule of his own job, he was willing to cut the guy a little slack.

And with an ass like that, he was doubly willing to cut the man some slack. The ass in question was high, hard, and tight. Nobody got a caboose like that without working out. Often and hard.

Just the way he liked his… workouts. Yeah. Workouts. He was totally not thinking about sex when he ogled Stone's rear end.

His cock stirred with definite interest as Stone strode down the hallway in front of him, and his own ass clenched and unclenched in anticipation of the epic sex possible with someone in that good a condition.

Not that he got to have sex that often, not with his job. And let alone with a specimen like this man. Yes, indeed. This could prove to be a very interesting evening.

They stepped into Stone's suite, and the first thing Christian noticed was a big aluminum trunk standing in the corner. "What's all that?"

"My equipment."

"You in a rock band?"

"Nope."

"Major S and M dungeon master?"

"Wishful thinking?" Stone shot back. He unlocked the trunk, shrugged out of his holster and sidearm, and stowed the weapon in the metal box, which he carefully locked once more.

Christian grinned. He wasn't opposed to a little leather and pain, but if anyone was going to be in charge, it would be him. Stone didn't strike him as the type to give up control, and Lord knew he wasn't. Way too damned much of his job involved having to kiss up to his jerk of a boss. In his personal life, he wanted no part of being submissive to anyone else.

The steaks arrived quickly, and the waiter batted his eyes at Stone as he wheeled in the table and set it up. Christian mentally snorted. Jackson was way too much man for that kid to handle.

"Tell me more about your work, Stone."

"Not much to say."

"Will you tell me what's in the trunk?"

"I can, but then I'd have to kill you."

"You're not a spy, are you?"

A snort from Stone. "Hardly."

"Hmm. Not a musician. Not a spy. Is there a body in the trunk?"

That one caused Stone to stare at the trunk speculatively. "No, but I could fit one in there, now that you mention it. Would have to fold it in there before rigor mortis set in, or after it wore off, of course. But it could be done."

Christian stopped cutting his steak to study Stone intently. "How do you know about rigor mortis wearing off? That's not the sort of thing the average civilian knows about."

"How do you know about it?"

"My dad is a doctor. How do you know?"

Stone shrugged. "I was in the Army a while back. Saw it up close and personal a few times."

"God. I'm sorry. I didn't mean to bring up bad memories—"

Stone cut him off. "It was mostly enemy combatant corpses I saw. My guys and I were very good at what we did."

"And what was that?"

Stone looked up, his expression so closed it was like looking into a mirror. "We killed people."

Christian blinked. What did it say about him that he found Stone's simple declaration hot as hell? Since when had dangerous men been such a turn-on to him?

Apparently, since he'd bought a Derby for a dark stranger and accepted an invitation up to the guy's suite.

He studied his steak absently. What the hell was a person supposed to say in response to that sort of a line? Talk about the world's best conversation killer.

They ate mostly in silence after that…. Stone didn't seem inclined to share any more about himself, and Christian had little success drawing him out. Which was unusual. His smooth, blue-blooded manners usually worked on everyone.

Near the end of the meal, after yet another grunt from Stone in lieu of actual words in response to a question, he finally came right out and asked, "Why don't you want to talk about yourself? I'm curious to know more about you."

Stone laid down his knife and fork and stared at him intensely enough to actually make him uncomfortable. He finally growled, "Be careful what you ask for."

"Why? Are you an axe murderer?"

A shrug. "An axe would not be my first choice of weapon. Too much blood spatter. Hard to clean up after."

Oh. Kay. Was this guy really that dangerous or just putting on a tough-guy act? Posers tended to piss him off. He leaned back, laying his napkin down. "You gonna show me your gun?"

"You wanna see it?"

"Sure."

Stone shook his head. "If that's a come-on line, it's a bad one."

That made Christian sit back even harder in his chair, reassessing. Not interested in a cheap hookup, was Stone? Huh. He didn't misread men's signals often.

Surely a guy this hot wasn't… awkward… about sex, was he? Hell, it was the twenty-first century. Same-sex marriage had been legal for a while, and sodomy laws were history. He wasn't particularly prone to casual sex, personally, but this man had an interesting vibe about him. It was dark and hot. Intense. Not his usual brand of slick Washington politico.

"What do you want from me, Christian?"

"Funny, but I was about to ask the exact same thing of you."

"Me? I don't want much of anything from me."

"You're hilarious. Not."

Stone rolled his eyes and replied, "I asked first."

Bemused, he turned his attention to the actual question attached to his name. What *did* he want?

"Undecided," he finally answered.

Stone stood from the table, and he matched the movement as Stone announced, "I'm jet-lagged as hell, a little drunk, and you make me laugh. Would I get off on fucking you? Yeah, sure."

Truth be told, he was a little taken aback by the bluntness of that answer to his question. He wasn't sure whether to be put off or turned on beyond all reason. Maybe a little of both. "Well, okay, then. Thanks for the honesty, I guess."

"Here's another bit of honesty. I don't have the time or the patience for drama and sophomoric relationship bullshit."

"Neither do I."

Their hard stares met. They understood each other, then. Sex. Hot sex. Maybe even rough sex. No strings attached. Two ships passing in the night. Christian abruptly had such an intense hard-on, he could barely stand upright. A quick glance down revealed Stone was in pretty much the same state.

They didn't kiss so much as collided. Stone was emphatically not the slender, lithe, dancer type Christian usually went for. But then, he suspected he wasn't the type Stone usually went for either. The guy struck him as every bit as much of a control freak as he tended to be.

Which left the question hanging of who was going to take charge of the sex between them, given that they both were apparently tops by choice.

Stone's frown as they ripped each other's shirts off made it pretty damned clear that he was (a) pondering the same question and (b) registering that Christian wasn't his usual type either.

But there was something challenging about this man. Something that made Christian want to bring Stone Jackson to his knees.

Then Stone grabbed his hair, yanked his head back, and *bit* his lip.

"What the hell?" he exclaimed.

"You're telling me you like it easy and sweet?" Stone growled.

He grabbed the back of Stone's neck, pulled his head forward, and bit back. "Not bloody likely."

Their bodies plastered against each other, and Christian was assailed by impressions. Jeez, this man was like a brick wall, all hard planes, sharp angles, and bulging muscles. Make that rock-hard, bulging muscles. And *scars*. At least a half-dozen bigass "half-gutted at some point in the past" scars.

"You look like you've been through a war." He added dryly, "And lost."

"Couple of 'em," Stone muttered against his mouth. "But I never lose in a fight." His razor stubble grated on Christian's face. And it was sexy as hell. This was a man's man, and Christian was about to have all of him.

"Do you still never lose?" Christian murmured.

"Now more than ever."

"Why's that?"

"Do you always talk this much?" Stone growled.

"You gonna do something to shut me up?" he popped off.

There was an aura about Stone that brought out the testosterone in him. More than simple one-upmanship. A need to challenge and measure up to.

Stone laughed darkly, and actual intimidation flickered through Christian's gut. Was he in over his head with this guy? Just what kind of baggage did a man with that many outward scars carry around on the inside? Did he have the balls to find out? Something daring—reckless, even—flared inside him. While the little voice in the back of his head shouted at him to avoid Stone Jackson like hell, a raging fire in his belly urged him on.

He'd never had sex with a man like this and probably never would again. It would be raw and pornographic and likely leave him wrecked for a long damned time to come. But he also sensed he would regret it for the rest of his life if he walked away from this moment. This man. This one-night stand.

He would always look back and wonder what it would have been like. Could he have kept up with a man like this? How much pleasure had he missed? Worse, would he look back and brand himself a coward?

That thought tipped the scales. He had plenty of flaws and had made plenty of mistakes in his life—and would make many more. He might have to suppress his ambitions and hide most of his opinions from his jerk of a boss, but he refused to live his personal life in hiding. His philosophy was that he had one shot at life and he was going to live it to the fullest.

Eyes narrowed, he reached for the buttons of Stone's ridiculous khaki shorts. His knuckles brushed against an erection large enough to give him pause. Yup. A man's man. His belly quailed a bit at the notion of absorbing all that hardness one way or another. Or maybe he'd do the taking and let Stone hang, hard and unsatisfied on his knees. The little voice in his head frantically warned him that taunting this man would not be a good idea. Payback would be an absolute bitch.

A bitch he'd never experienced before. It would include unpredictability and, undoubtedly, loss of all control. Control of himself and control of the situation. No question, Stone would totally dominate that sort of encounter.

Domination and submission had never been his vibe. Or if it had, it was a subtle undertone of his relationships rather than the main theme of them. But with this guy, he wasn't sure what to expect. Hell, for all he knew, that aluminum trunk of Stone's was full of leather, rope, whips, and chains.

A definite frisson of alarm chattered through him at that idea. The idea of being subdued, restrained… helpless….

Nope. Not a turn-on for him.

He was all about managing every situation. He liked predictable. Liked order. Some folks even called him OCD. He might even admit to being a bit of a control freak. He preferred his life to have no surprises. Even in sexual encounters, he made sure everyone had a good time, but he called the shots.

No way would Stone Jackson go along meekly with being told exactly what to do, when to do it, and how to do it.

Speaking of the devil, how was it that his trousers were suddenly unzipped, his balls being cupped by a big callused hand plunged into his briefs while Stone's hard thumb rubbed knowingly across the head of his cock? Lust exploded through him. Holy shit.

Decision time. Back out now or jump in the last car of this roller coaster as it pulled out of the station and throw his hands up in the air.

Fuck it. He was going for the ride.

His hips rocked forward hungrily, and Stone pulled his dick through the flap in his briefs, grabbed it in a firm fist, and actually dragged him across the room by it. He reached for Stone's fly, not only to reciprocate, but also to regain a tiny measure of control of his own.

Stone casually batted his hand away.

And he actually let the man do it. A thrill shivered through him. He'd just crossed over into the unknown. Apparently, he was letting Stone take complete control of this ride.

That fist around his dick tightened rhythmically, milking his cock until his knees threatened to collapse from the pleasure rocketing through him. His entire being narrowed down to his erection and the fist holding it so confidently, the message clear. No longer his cock. Stone's cock to do with what he wished.

Dang, it was sexy being handled like this, not having to make all the decisions. He could mentally sit back and enjoy the breathless drops and high-G turns of the ride.

Stone's hand reached back until his palm cupped Christian's balls and a thick, blunt fingertip rubbed his taint. He yelped as pleasure shot through him. Swoop. And drop. He plunged off the cliff, the car racing weightlessly through space.

The fingertip reached farther back, barely intruding into his ass. Just enough to force his sphincter to release and clench, clench and release around it.

He groaned, shocked at the raw sound coming from his own throat. He was the one who made other guys groan like that. He played the instrument until it sang—he wasn't the instrument being played.

The finger probed a little deeper. Crooked forward, pressing against the wall of his rectum until it rubbed his prostate. Holy crap, that was really a thing. He practically spurted in his shorts then and there, and his knees did collapse.

Which was how he ended up on his knees with his face in Stone's crotch, his breath ragged, mind blown.

The little voice in the back of his head, his own personal commentator on life, murmured, *Interesting. You're usually the one giving pleasure, not the one taking it. Perchance you've been missing out, knucklehead.*

He'd wondered idly from time to time what it would be like to bottom. But the guys he dated were usually so intimidated by his job, his family name, his status and general classiness, that they seemed to expect him to take charge and do the honors. And he didn't hate topping. Truth be told, he'd never thought to question how he liked his sex. When no one else stepped up to the plate to dictate play, he'd taken charge and taken care of business. Pretty much like how he did everything else in his life.

Until this dark, dangerous alpha male blasted into his life.

What would it be like to let go? Not to fight to stay in control of his body and its reactions? To just feel? To live in the moment?

He leaned forward and buried his face in Stone's crotch, inhaling the musky scent and sharper tang of Stone's desire. Through his pants, Stone's erection jumped against his cheek. A surge of power flowed through him. He loved being the one to do that to this man.

Whoa. Wait. There was power in bottoming?

Fascinated by the possibilities, he stood, reaching for Stone's shorts. But then Stone kissed him roughly, all but sucking his tongue free of its moorings. It hurt a little and turned him on ferociously. Shocking realization broke over him that he'd always wanted to make love to a man like this, a man who would take charge and do exactly what he wanted, who would fuck him balls to the wall and leave him begging for more. He'd never admitted it to himself. He'd been too afraid to climb on the roller coaster and see where it took him.

The emotional risk inherent in giving up control to this man skittered through him. What if he liked bottoming? What if he wanted more of the same? Where in the hell would he find another man like this? Even an hour's acquaintance with Stone was enough for him to know men like this didn't grow on trees.

He shouldn't do this. His commentator voice warned him he was setting himself up for not only a big emotional fall, but also years of disappointment in all other men.

But when Stone released his trousers and shoved them around his ankles, the voice went completely, stunningly silent. And his breath hitched in his throat in so much excited anticipation he felt light-headed.

Stone's hand was hard and strong and shockingly gentle on the back of Christian's neck, urging him down. The roller coaster car was almost done chugging to the top of the big hill. *Hands in the air.* Time to fly.

He gave way to that guiding hand, letting himself be bent down, headfirst, over the back of the sofa, his face buried in the seat cushions. Chug, chug, chug. Only sky above now. Cresting the hill.

"Stay," Stone ordered from behind him, his voice a rough rasp.

Stone disappeared for an endless, outrageous minute while Christian stayed exactly where he was, terrified of the drop to come, amazed as hell that he was putting up with being ordered around like this, and so excited that his body, hell, his entire being, quivered with it.

Stone returned, his hairy thighs brushing lightly against Christian's ass. Muscles Christian hardly knew he had convulsed, completely out of his control.

A hand milked his cock from behind until he was dripping with precum, his balls so tight they felt like they would explode any second. He lurched when a big, blunt finger circled his anus, smearing something goopy and vaguely warm on it. And then that wonderful, invading, clever finger dipped inside his rectum once more. He reflexively lurched away from the invasion, his hipbones slamming into the sofa frame, but not far enough to escape that probing finger.

He'd bottomed a few times a very long time ago, when he was first experimenting with his sexuality. They'd been furtive, fast encounters with other teenage boys. Nothing at all like this. Apprehension coursed through him. And yet his cock was jumping and jerking wildly, banging into the upholstered back of the sofa, his glutes clenching and unclenching, and he was letting a dark, dangerous stranger spread his asscheeks and lube him up some more.

And then the blunt head of that huge rock-hard cock rested against his entrance, both a promise and a threat. The roller coaster started down, and the plunge yawned in front of him. Fear of the unknown swept over him, along with burning desire to know what lay beyond it.

Whatever madness had overcome him before swept forward now, stealing his breath and what little remaining sanity he had. The speed of the ride picked up and the pressure of an orgasm built in his groin as his entire body clenched to explode. He wanted to be impaled. Wanted to be plundered and taken and possessed by this man. His limbs went weak, his breath grew so short he panted, and his fists and teeth clamped down on the sofa cushion.

"If you don't relax, you won't be able to take me," Stone muttered. He eased that big finger through Christian's clenched muscles again. He slid it deeper this time, filling him up and then retreating almost all the way out. Again, he stroked him with appalling intimacy.

Christian felt the orgasm coming. Ripples of insane pleasure were building deep inside him, tucked up high above his balls as Stone worked his prostate, which he'd only worked on others before. No wonder his partners were addicted to sex. He was dying already.

"Jesus, you're tight," Stone ground out. "I'm going to have to be careful."

It was good to know Stone was having restraint issues too. Thing was, he rather wanted Stone to tear the hell out of him at this point. His hips pumped of their own volition as his control slipped yet another notch. Sex. He wanted sex and lots of it. Right now.

Stone splayed one hand on the base of his spine, pinning him down. The strength in Stone's palm was astonishing. Christian was not a small man, and he worked out often. And yet Stone held him still with casual ease. More of that strange intimidation/attraction tore through him.

Stone took a step forward, his thighs shoving Christian's wider apart.

He was at the man's mercy now. Loving it and hating it, he swore in a steady stream. That rock-hard cock was back at his hungry opening, poised for the coup de grâce. He felt Stone tense against him....

And freeze as a phone rang.

"Not mine," Stone snapped. "Do you have to get that?"

Son. Of. A. Bitch. It was his boss's personal ringtone. The one person on earth whose calls he had to take day or night, rain or shine, about to be epically fucked or not.

"Fuck, fuck, fuck, fuck, fuck," he muttered.

He jerked up off the sofa, yanked at his pants, and fished around in the pocket. "Yes, sir," he answered, trying his damnedest not to sound out of breath—and failing.

"Did I interrupt your workout?" Senator Jack Lacey of the great state of Texas drawled. "Or is she a hot little number willing to put out?"

It was no secret he was gay, but Lacey insisted on trying to convince Christian to date women. Hell, tonight *he* was apparently the hot little number willing to put out.

"What can I do for you, sir?" he asked, ignoring the man's questions.

"I need to go over the itinerary with you for this damned fundraising blitz Jill put together. No way in hell am I doing some of these appearances she's got booked for me."

"Why don't you take that up with your wife, sir?" He did his best to stay out of the raging battles the Laceys engaged in behind closed doors.

"Bitch isn't coming to town until Friday. Some gardening shindig came up in Texas, and she flew out to attend it. Left me to do all the goddamn glad-handing with a bunch of blue-haired Jews come South to die."

Christian winced. His boss was nothing if not an insensitive racist. He actually wouldn't vote for the man, were he a voter in Texas. But Jack Lacey was a powerful senator in Washington, and as a member of his staff, Christian had gotten a chance to help draft landmark legislation on federal prison reform, which was a personal passion of his. Privately, Christian hoped to parlay that into a job at the Justice Department working at the federal level to continue modernizing opinions within the government regarding rehabilitation, counseling, and education of incarcerated people, sooner rather than later. But until then, he was stuck wiping this jerk's proverbial ass.

He looked around the living room for Stone, but he was nowhere in sight. Probably stepped into the bathroom to relieve that massive hard-on of his. Lucky bastard.

It was beginning to look like he'd get to tuck his erection in his pants, trot down the hall like an obedient lackey, and spend the next two hours explaining to his idiot boss why this series of public appearances in Florida was good for his entire national political party and would gain him favors, donations, and endorsements in his own campaign for reelection.

He yanked on his shirt, buttoned it angrily, and tied his tie with jerky movements, using the mirror behind the bar to straighten it and comb his hair. Nope, he didn't look like a man who'd been on the verge of the fucking of his life.

Although as he walked down the hall, lube squished around sexily in his drawers, reminding him in no uncertain terms of what had almost been. His intensely dissatisfied dick leaped to attention eagerly. *Down, boy. No roller coaster ride for you.* Irritated and uncomfortable, he pasted on a facsimile of a pleasant expression and knocked on Lacey's door.

Sometimes he really hated his life.

CHAPTER TWO

STONE SLEPT for shit. He dreamed all night long of a muscular chestnut-haired Adonis who looked a lot like Christian Chatsworth-Brandeis ordering him to his knees and doing unspeakable things to him. Which was odd. He wasn't a serve-the-master kind of guy, his job as a security consultant to the rich and famous notwithstanding.

In fact, the intensely disciplined nature of his day job tended to bleed over into his personal life. He liked to be in control of everything around him during his off time. Of course, in the moments during the day job when he had to take control, he had to take total, immediate control of his principal. Often it involved tackling them, bodily dragging them to safety, and throwing them, literally, into vehicles to flee.

Why Christian provoked that response in him, tonight, he had no idea. But a need to utterly dominate Christian had come over him. Which was not like him. Control was one thing. But domination was not his jam. He was an adult and preferred adult encounters with like-minded adults.

It cut down on so much drama. He didn't do relationships, and he only had sex with other men who weren't into emotional commitments. Ships passing in the night. That was his preferred modus operandi.

Although, the ships usually ended up having actual sex. Not a phone call and his partner leaping to his feet and practically standing at attention to take the call.

Who in the hell had Christian on such a short leash, anyway? He hadn't pegged the guy as an ass-kissing lackey type, in spite of his description of his job painting himself as a Boy Friday to someone important. Christian struck him as smart, confident, and more than a little cheeky. The kind of guy who set his own agendas in life.

But that call.... Christian had visibly been irritated as fuck by it, and yet had spoken in the most deferential of tones. His boss must be a giant asshole to demand that degree of sucking up from his employees.

He knew the type all too well.

Most of the time, his clients were polite, professional, and accustomed to working with top-drawer security people like him. But occasionally he had to crack the whip with some snot-nosed musician who'd just made it big and thought having crazed stalkers was cool.

Thankfully, the client he'd come to Miami to protect should fall firmly into the former camp.

Giving up on sleep, he rolled out of bed and headed for the hottest shower the hotel could offer up. As he got naked and the water pounded out the worst of the fatigue and tension from his body, his thoughts turned to the sight of Christian Chatsworth-Brandeis bent over his sofa, mewling into the cushions, muscular thighs spread wide, and that gorgeous ass eager and ready for him.

His cock swelled and hardened, startling him with how violently it reacted. Well, then. Apparently, jacking off in the shower last night hadn't soothed the beast quite enough.

He reached for the liquid soap dispenser and planted his forearm on the cold tile wall and his forehead on his forearm. While the hot water pounded down on his back, he reached for his cock. The slippery slide of his fist on his erection pulled a groan from his throat. His hips pumped in time with his fist, and he closed his eyes, picturing what it would have looked like to see his dick plunging into that fair, smooth ass below the sharp tan line of Christian's back.

It didn't take long to bring himself to a series of short, fast thrusts into his fist and grunting completion. Good thing he'd spread his legs wide and locked his knees, though. The mental image of fucking Christian had been more of a turn-on than he'd expected.

Legs weak, he stepped out of the shower. He shaved and dressed in one of his conservative, bespoke suits that lay perfectly over his holster and sidearm.

His hair neatly combed and still damp, he stepped out of his room. Folding his hands together in front of his crotch, he set aside lust and fantasies, shutting down his feelings and thoughts to enter the cold mindset necessary for his work and headed down the hall.

By the time he reached the double doors to a large, corner suite, he'd achieved full bodyguard mode. His gaze was alert, scanning the hallway in both directions, registering details of what stood on the table opposite the nearby elevator, where the security cameras were tucked unobtrusively in the corners, measuring sightlines for a shooter, cataloging the niches on either side of the elevator bank as safe spots to shove a client in a gunfight.

He knocked on the door of the suite on time to the exact second, according to his watch, which he'd set yesterday off the international atomic clock. Precision mattered in his line of work.

"C'mon in!" a voice called in a thick Texas drawl.

He stepped into a suite easily twice the size of his flat in London, decked out like a campaign headquarters in full swing. Red, white, and blue campaign signs had Lacey's name splashed all over the walls, a half-dozen telephones sat on two tables, and at least that many more laptops glowed on various coffee tables and work surfaces. But oddly, there were no humans manning them. Which gave the room a sad morning-after-the-party vibe, actually.

The election was a solid year away. He didn't envy American politicians their lives. Fundraising was pretty much a full-time job for them. How they could look themselves in the mirror every morning, he had no idea. He couldn't do it. It was like being a whore in a business suit.

He recognized the client from the pictures included in the briefing. United States Senator Jack Lacey, from the great state of Texas. A high-profile guy—six terms in the House of Representatives, finishing up his second term as a senator.

The analysis of Lacey from Stone's bosses at Wild Cards, Inc., a British security firm, was harsh: *a loud blusterer more prone to lies than truth. An ineffective politician who compensates by thrusting himself into the public eye. The type to draw the wrong kind of attention from unstable constituents and then say something to enrage those people. Probability of his alleged stalker being real are high. Violence of said stalker: unknown.*

"You must be Stone Jackson. I've heard great things about you." A perfectly groomed and well-moisturized man around sixty years old stepped forward, smiling big enough to show off his mouthful of porcelain crowns.

"Thank you, sir." He stuck out his hand and endured the limp-rag handshake. He'd worked with enough politicians to know they perfected a soft handshake for when they met the public. Otherwise, their hands would get crushed by the hundreds of people they shook hands with when working a crowd line.

A disturbing sense of déjà vu swept over him. Looking at the senator was like looking into a mirror at a thirty-years-older version of himself. The man had the same dark eyes, olive complexion, strong jawline, and broad smile that he had. Their hair was different, but even their heights and builds were similar. It was a little freaky.

At least they were dressed nothing alike. Jack Lacey was wearing a cowboy hat and cowboy boots with his custom-made Italian suit. Stone wasn't particularly into fashion, but the getup screamed of the worst sort of crass pandering to his constituency.

A big, silent man stepped forward. Lacey said, "This is Travis Tucker, my head of security."

His skin was the true black of a person of African descent who spent a lot of time outside. Stone's brief said Tucker was an ex-Marine, had pulled a stint as an embassy guard in the Middle East, and was damned good at his job. Which was a red flag for Wild Cards, Inc. If Lacey already had good protection, why call in an expensive outfit like theirs?

In fact, it had been Tucker's suggestion that supplemental security be hired from a private firm like Wild Cards in the first place. Hence Stone's presence in Miami this morning, and hence his curiosity over what prompted his being here.

"What seems to be the problem, Mr. Tucker?" Stone asked the security man directly.

"The senator is getting death threats."

Lacey interrupted. "I keep tellin' y'all, Tuck. I get those all the time. You're bein' a nervous Nellie."

Tucker never broke eye contact with Stone and continued as if Lacey hadn't spoken. "Threats are threats. It's my job to take all of them seriously, sir."

"Y'all are makin' a mountain out of a li'l ol' mole hill." Lacey snorted to punctuate the comment.

"What's your gut feel, Mr. Tucker?" Stone asked, taking his cue from the security chief and ignoring the senator's interruptions.

"I think these threats have teeth. And call me Travis, or Tuck."

Stone studied Tucker, who was maybe ten years his senior. But they were both ex-military men. Both knew the value of intuition. He nodded once, wordlessly accepting the man's worry at face value. Tucker nodded back. Yup, they were going to get along just fine.

"I'd like an extra set of eyes on the venues we'll be visiting this week. If you could help us find security weak spots, pick out potential points of attack, maybe suggest some additional measures to beef up our protection of the boss, that would be helpful."

"No problem. And Stone's fine for me. I'll need a list of events and locations—"

"My aide can get those for you," Lacey interjected. He raised his voice, shouting, "I need a copy of my itinerary for the new security guy!"

Didn't like not being the center of attention, huh? Stone knew the type. In point of fact, many of his clients fit that description.

Of course, plenty of rich, powerful people were quiet and unassuming. Didn't go out of the way to draw attention to themselves. They were the ones who rarely needed his services. It was these loud, blowhard types who had to be the star of the show who ended up at risk from the crazies.

An aide walked in from the next room, presumably to deliver the demanded itinerary. Stone glanced over at the flunky. And stared, stunned.

Light brown hair, faintly chestnut in tone. Square jaw. Piercing blue eyes. All-American good looks. Perfectly tailored suit.

Aww, fuck me.

Christian Chatsworth-Brandeis.

And he was looking every inch an aristocrat this morning. America might not officially have royalty, but if it did, this man would be part of it.

The silent horror was mutual as Christian stared back at Stone. Oblivious, Jack Lacey boomed, "This is my new bodyguard, Stone Jackson. And this is Chris Chatsworth-Brandeis, my main bitch."

Stone blinked, startled at the senator's crudeness. For his part, Christian's gaze hardened into chips of blue ice. The man did *not* like his boss. At all. Stone couldn't say he blamed the guy.

Christian held out a stapled sheaf of papers, and Stone took it with a mumbled word of thanks while Senator Lacey wandered away and sat down on the sofa with a remote control to cruise through the news channels.

"If you have any questions or need me to walk you through the senator's usual routine, let me know," Christian said.

"I will. Thanks." Good God, the awkwardness of it.

Last time he'd seen this man, he'd been half-crazed with lust, so hungry to have a lover with intelligence and breeding and class that he could hardly stop himself from coming all over the guy's backside. Christian Chatsworth-Brandeis represented everything he'd ever craved in life and been denied by the circumstances of his birth.

Farmers were not technically poor people. But all their wealth was tied up in land and equipment and animals. Success and failure were determined by the whims of global warming, and food on the table was often a direct result of grueling, backbreaking labor. He was glad for the work ethic and the physical strength his youth in rural Georgia had given him, but he'd always wished for more.

He'd wanted a college education at a top university. Travel. Worldliness. But there hadn't been money for it. Instead he'd enlisted in the Army, seen the world from the back end of a Humvee, and put himself through college online. He secretly liked to watch Ivy League university lectures online when he wasn't putting his body on the line to catch bullets for people with the cash to pay for his life.

And then his mother had gotten sick, and his parents had to move to England—his mother's birthplace—to get her the expensive medical care she needed. Her health had stabilized, but she had to stay in England for continuing care.

He was an only child, born late in his parents' lives, and as they aged, he felt an obligation to be closer to them to look out for them. Hence, when his stint in the Army ended, he'd relocated to England as well. He'd been lucky as hell to land a job with a start-up security firm called Wild Cards, Inc. They were a top-drawer outfit all the way and provided their people with the very best equipment, training, and support. They were one of the top personal security firms in the world.

His boss, Peregrine Cardiffe, founder of Wild Cards, Inc., was upper-crust British all the way, and he had helped Stone file off a few of his social rough edges. Taught him how to wear a decent suit and where to buy one and get it properly tailored. Pere also taught him how to drink brandy. How to act like a gentleman. *Act* being the operative word, though. It was all learned behavior. A layer of silver over lead.

Whereas a man like Christian Chatsworth-Brandeis was a gentleman all the way down to his DNA.

And now they worked for the same bastard boss. Which pretty much took a repeat of last night off the table.

Goddammit. He never mixed business and his personal life. No bodyguard did. It was impossible to achieve the cold, calculating focus necessary in his line of work if feelings of any kind intruded.

Speaking of work, he asked the senator's security chief, "Is there anything we can do to get cameras installed in the hotel stairwells, like today? Anyone can get into or out of this place undetected using the fire exits. And while the hotel is installing cameras, the south end of the loading dock is camera blind also."

Tucker answered sourly, "I had to change floors when we got to the hotel to even get us hallway cameras. The hotel manager informed me that the Imperium caters to clients who value their privacy and do not want the kind of invasive security I was suggesting they install."

Great. Nothing like parking a high-profile and controversial politician with a lot of enemies in a hotel that prized secrecy for its customers above all else. Places like this were dens of drugs, wild parties, and underage groupies a certain clientele was willing to pay top dollar to hide from public scrutiny.

"Who picked this hotel?" he asked.

Christian answered that one, irony rich in his voice. "That would be the senator."

A world of information was packed into that dry answer. Lacey was a player. Had vices he needed to hide from the public. Was using the absence from Washington to indulge. Which geometrically increased his exposure to a would-be killer.

"Any chance we can convince him to move to a more secure hotel?" Stone fielded.

Tucker and Christian answered simultaneously and emphatically, "No."

"Poison of preference for the senator?" he asked quietly.

"Arsenic, if I had to choose. But rat poison would be fine if it did the trick."

Stone grinned. Yeah. No love lost between this guy and his boss. "Does he know you're plotting his demise? Should I be watching you?"

Christian's gaze snapped to his, and all of a sudden heat sizzled between them. Belatedly he murmured, "Hell, even his wife is probably plotting his demise. To know him is to despise him."

"Well, isn't this going to be a fun assignment." And the sexual tension was back, thick and heavy between them. They had unfinished business to tend to, but it was strictly off-limits, and they both knew it. Dammit.

"You didn't answer my question. Why does your boss insist on being here? What's his vice?"

Christian frowned and didn't volunteer an answer. But surely he knew. He lived practically up the guy's butt. Metaphorically, of course.

Stone sighed. "I'm going to find out for myself anyway as soon as I'm on the guy's detail 24-7. You might as well go ahead and tell me. I've signed all the nondisclosure agreements your people shoved at me. You can have my balls and firstborn child if I go to the press with anything I learn about the senator."

Christian still hesitated, so Stone added, "Wild Cards, Inc. is an elite personal security firm to the world's richest and most famous. Discretion is our primary hallmark. That and keeping our clients alive and safe."

"Women," Christian murmured so low Stone had to step closer to hear him. Close enough to smell the man's aftershave. Of course it was as classy as the rest of him. Stone's knees went a little weak at the clean, expensive-smelling cologne.

"And booze."

Sensing that Christian was avoiding sharing something shocking, he murmured for Christian's ears only, "Trust me. I've seen it all."

"I get the feeling he'd like to do more… party harder, but so far, his wife and I have managed to keep him in line."

He blinked but didn't miss a beat. "And why do you work for him if he's such a douchebag?"

"He happens to support prison reform, and in addition to my law degree, I have a master's in public policy, specializing in prison reform. He's my best chance to make a real difference for a whole lot of incarcerated people."

"Irony, much?" Stone murmured.

Their gazes snapped to each other. Awareness, hell, *sparks*, flew between them for just a second. Then, simultaneously, they both firmly and regretfully tamped down on the incendiary attraction flaring between them. *Irony, indeed.*

Stone stepped back to a safer distance, clear of that sexy-as-hell aftershave. He made a mental note to find out what it was. Someday when he grew up, he'd like to smell that classy.

He leafed through the senator's busy itinerary for the next week. Holy crap. There were close to a dozen appearances booked. No way could he properly assess every single one and furthermore fix the security flaws at each. He would need a month, or a team of a half-dozen Wild Cards security experts, to do the job right.

He looked up at Tucker. "Have you scoped out all these locations already?"

The man rolled his eyes, a flash of bright white in his grim face. "I've seen each venue, but that's about it. I've only had time to do full security inspections on about half of them. Hence bringing you on board to help out." He added under his breath, "It's a fucking mess."

"And he won't cancel?" Stone responded.

"His wife booked this whole junket, and he's scared shitless of her. If she says to appear in all these places, he'll complain up a storm, but he'll do it."

"Is she trying to get him killed?"

Stone was startled when Tucker seemed to consider his rhetorical question seriously.

"Wouldn't put it past her. She thinks he's a moron."

"And they're married why?"

"Oh, she likes the political power his job gives her."

"Does she interfere with his actual career, or just ride his coattails?"

"I don't understand the question," Tucker replied.

Ahh. Perceptive guy. He sensed that Stone was going somewhere with the line of questioning. "I'm asking if she's included in the threats against the senator. Or if she's perhaps the reason for the threats."

Tucker swore under his breath. "It's possible that the answer is yes to both. I don't think we can rule it out. The good news is she's in Texas and not our problem for the moment."

Stone glanced surreptitiously at Lacey, who was currently swearing at the TV and reaching for his cell phone. The senator commenced yelling at somebody on the other end. Beneath the din, he asked Tucker, "Is it possible she's the one anonymously sending the threats?" It wouldn't be the first time he'd run into the spouse of a rich, powerful asshole who'd tried to off said asshole.

"Ms. Lacey?" Tucker blurted. "Nah. She's good people. She'd divorce him and take him for all he was worth before she'd bother killing him. She'd get a lot more satisfaction out of humiliating him."

"Yikes."

"Don't get me wrong. I like her just fine, but I wouldn't want to tangle with her in a dark alley. She would fight like a junkyard dog."

"Sounds like a great politician's wife," Stone commented dryly.

"She's the only reason he's gotten anywhere in politics."

Stone nodded. Interesting. Thankfully, his job wasn't going to include having to dive into the middle of the apparently contentious Lacey marriage. He glanced back down at the list of places Jack Lacey was scheduled to appear this week. "Which venue are you the most worried about, Tuck?"

"Hotel ballroom where the big casino-night fundraiser will be held. More sight lines than you can count, multiple access points, huge crowd, huge staff. It's going to be a nightmare. The public is going to have full access to the senator. Not even rope lines to contain the crowd."

Stone winced. If it was even half as bad as the guy described, barring a full-on Secret Service-style team of a dozen guys or so, no way were they going to be able to guarantee Lacey's safety. "How many warm bodies can you put on the job?" he asked Tucker.

"I've got two security guys from the hotel lined up for Saturday night. And now you. The boss hates bodyguards and refuses to use them most of the time."

"Are you kidding me?"

"Wish I was, man."

They were so screwed.

Wild Cards, Inc. couldn't possibly take responsibility for this client under these circumstances. He crossed the living room to address the senator directly. "How bad do you want to stay alive, sir?"

"Whaddiya mean, son? I like being alive plenty."

"Enough to cancel your appearances this week?"

"No way."

"Can I at least convince you to cancel the casino-night appearance, sir?"

"I get a third of all the donations from this damned shindig. It'll fund my television ads for months to come. I'm not fucking canceling nuthin'. I'm paying a fortune for you to keep me safe and make this event happen. You do your job and we'll all be fine."

"You are, indeed, paying a fortune for my services. And this is me giving you my extremely valuable advice. Cancel your appearance at the casino night. I don't even need to see the venue to know you will be wide open to an assassination attempt."

"Isn't it your job to take the bullet for me?" Lacey asked coldly.

A faint, strangled noise made Stone look up. Christian had just stepped into the room from beyond the senator. Apparently he'd heard Lacey's last remark too. Christian's jaw clenched so hard that the rippling muscles in the guy's perfect face actually caught Stone's attention.

He pulled his gaze back to the truculent senator and answered evenly, "My job is to keep both of us alive, sir. I will not have done my job if I have to take a bullet for you. That is the last-ditch act of a failed security detail."

A shrug from Lacey. "Not my problem."

He glanced over at Tucker, who rolled his eyes eloquently. The bastard had better be paying Tucker a fortune to put up with this shit.

"Tell you what, sir. I'm going to go downstairs and take a look around the ballroom. I'll report back to Mr. Tucker after I've seen it."

"Whatever." Lacey picked up a laptop computer, opened the screen, and hit a key on it. The computer commenced emitting the groaning, moaning, and flesh-slapping sounds of porn reaching its exquisitely unclassy cinematic climax.

Well, okay, then. Add an unabashed porn habit to the senator's list of vices.

"I'll show you the ballroom," Christian volunteered.

Stone swore mentally. He'd told the guy last night that he had no time for drama. He'd meant it. He did not have time for flirting, for innuendo-laced snide comments, or wistful, lover-wannabe banter in the damned elevator.

Irritated as fuck, he spun and headed out. Christian fell in beside him. He lengthened his stride, emphatically not interested in conversation. Christian kept up easily, matching his stride, and he moved with the supple strength of a man who worked out vigorously. *No doubt about it. We would have been a great fit physically.*

The elevator arrived, and they stepped into the empty space, alone. Here it came. Stone braced himself.

Christian spoke with contemptuous precision. "Lacey's an asshole. Demands the impossible and throws hissy fits when he doesn't get what he wants. He's behind in the polls, and his fundraising has been dismal this year. The voters are apparently catching on to what a bad joke he is. Don't kill yourself to save him. He's not worth it."

Huh. He'd assumed Christian would throw himself at him. He didn't know whether to be relieved or disappointed that the guy hadn't.

Stone arched one eyebrow sardonically. "Why don't you tell me how you really feel about your boss?"

A huff of reluctant laughter escaped Christian. "He's your boss too now."

"Don't remind me."

They rode the rest of the way down in silence that was blessedly reasonably comfortable. He had to give Christian credit. The guy had said the one thing that would ease the discomfort between them and make the situation not weird. Pere had the same gift of natural diplomacy. Stone… not so much. But he owed Christian at least a try at civility.

"For what it's worth, I've worked for worse," Stone commented in commiseration as they stepped out into the lobby.

"I find that hard to believe," Christian replied drolly.

"Buy me another Derby sometime, and I'll tell you a few stories that'll curl your toes."

"Deal."

Shocked that he'd been the one to bring up a personal interaction between them, he fell silent. They started across the lobby toward the parrot-infested palm trees.

He spied an incoming figure moving fast and muttered, "Oh joy."

"Gentlemen!" Brittney gushed. "How lucky am I? The two hottest guys in South Beach have graced our hotel with their presence. Call the paramedics—there will be women swooning all over my lobby."

He traded wry glances with Christian over her head.

"Where are you two off to? Can I help you with anything?"

Christian answered smoothly, pitching his voice with a hint of flirtation guaranteed to delight Brittney. Better Christian dealing with her than him. "I'm on my way to show Mr. Jackson the ballroom where the casino night is going to be held."

"Oooh! Let me help." She pushed between their tall bodies, looped an arm through each of theirs, and all but skipped down the yellow brick road toward the bowels of the hotel.

"Are you always this… perky?" Stone asked dryly.

"Oh yes. I was a cheerleader at Florida State, you know. I barely missed being a Miami Dolphins cheerleader at my first tryout last year. Which is really great for a first-timer, by the way. Since then I've gone gluten-free, taken up hot yoga, and gotten crazy limber. I can get into all sorts of uhh-*maze*-ing positions now."

"The mind boggles," Christian commented dryly.

A snort of laughter slipped out of Stone, and he coughed hastily to cover it up.

"I know. Right?" Brittney chirped.

"Totally," Stone replied dryly.

Christian pulled a face at him over the young woman's head.

Brittney unlocked a set of ornate double doors, and he and Christian each pushed one open for her. She stepped inside and spun around dramatically. "Here's the ballroom. It's the most famous feature of the Imperium Hotel. Built in the 1920s, the structure has been refurbished of course, but its original design and architectural details have been preserved. When the hotel was torn down and rebuilt in the 1990s, this part of the building was not touched."

Stone supposed the room was pretty, but he paid little attention to such things. Instead he took note of the many alcove balconies running down both sides of the room, overlooking the main floor. The big orchestra mezzanine across the back of the ballroom. The heavy velvet curtains lining the tall windows that could easily conceal a shooter. The row of french doors opening onto an oceanside terrace, every one of which provided an entrance and exit point. A raised theater stage crossed the far end of the room. Oh, goodie. That meant there would be catwalks and lighting rigs to secure too.

He turned to ask Brittney where the gaming tables and buffet lines would be set up, but she was already on her cell phone. It was in moments like this that he felt a little old. She moved away, talking at light speed, as he strolled the perimeter of the space in silent horror.

He glanced over at Christian pacing along silently beside him. "Gaming tables all over this main floor, I assume. Is there going to be a speech?"

A grimace. "Yes."

"Podium on the stage?" he guessed.

"Correct."

"Do me a favor, Christian. Go up on stage and stand where Senator Lacey will be for his speech, so I can check a few sight lines."

"Sure."

Stone watched appreciatively as Christian jogged up the side steps and took his place center-stage front. The man was absolutely an athlete, body aware and in control of his movements. Stone followed more slowly up the steps, walking around the stage. He looked up. Well, hell. A full, professional theater lighting and rigging setup dangled above him. He moved out to the middle of the stage behind Christian, who tensed.

As aware of him as he was of Christian, huh? Good to know—

He's off-limits now. The job comes first.

Dammit.

He peered over Christian's shoulder, looking at the various spots where a shooter might hide. If he could see the shooter from here, the shooter could see Senator Lacey from his or her hiding spot. He counted approximately twenty possible perches for a sniper. *Twenty.* Holy Christ. How was he supposed to secure all of them simultaneously? This was madness.

He moved into the wings, stage right, to see how blind he would be if the senator insisted on his security team standing offstage while he gave his speech.

Jesus. He couldn't see a thing from back here. He'd be totally blind. Unable to see any threats. He took a few steps forward out of long habit as a bodyguard, scanning the shadows around the edges of the ballroom.

Without warning, a red laser dot blossomed in the center of Christian's chest.

Stone didn't think, just reacted in response to a dozen years of training and exploded forward. He tackled Christian in a flying leap that sent them both to the ground, rolling over and over.

Stone wrapped his arms protectively around Christian and continued the roll, carrying both of them in a tangle behind the curtains, stage left.

Christian stared up at him in shock. "What the hell was *that* for?" He struggled against Stone's weight, and Stone rolled off him, jumping to his feet. He reached down and Christian took his hand. The guy's palm was warm and smooth. Everything his own hand was not. He gave a yank and jerked Christian upright.

With a quick hook of his arm around Christian's waist, he pushed him back and behind his own body. "Stay here," he bit out tersely. "Don't come out from behind the curtains to see what's going on. And if I tell you to run, head for the stage exit and run as fast as your fucking gorgeous legs can go to the front of the hotel and the biggest crowd of people you can find."

"*What* are you talking about?"

"No questions. Just do it." He moved away from Christian, dropping into a crouch as he pulled out his sidearm.

"Whoa," Christian exclaimed behind him.

No time to hold Preppy's hand. Someone had put a fucking laser gunsight on Christian's chest.

Replaying the glimpse of that laser dot in his mind's eye, he took his best guess at the source: the orchestra balcony in the back of the ballroom. Spinning out low from behind the curtain, he knelt in a shooter's stance, pistol braced in both hands for the takedown shot.

"Easy, man," Travis Tucker laughed from the balcony. "I was only testing your reflexes."

Stone stared down the barrel of his weapon at the security man for a stunned moment while his killer brain reluctantly processed that there was no threat.

"Easy there, Double-Oh-Seven," Tucker said in alarm, showing his empty hands well away from his sides, in plain sight.

After a tense, several-second delay, Stone lowered the weapon and stood upright. Swearing under his breath, he registered that his heart rate had accelerated to something like triple its normal speed.

Which was bizarre. Usually, he was ice in the Arctic. In winter. His pulse never spiked. He was the coolest of the cool under pressure. But he'd basically freaked out like a first-timer bodyguard.

Moving with taut precision, he made his weapon safe and replaced it carefully in its holster.

"Tucker," he said in a conversational voice, trusting the room's excellent acoustics to carry his words up to the balcony, "you just came very, very close to dying. Do not pull a shithead stunt like that again unless (a) you have a death wish, or (b) you want me to quit this job on the spot."

The ex-Marine threw both hands over his head in mock surrender, holding in one fist a spotter's scope that was no doubt the source of the laser dot on Christian's chest. Speaking of whom....

Stone looked to his left. Christian was standing in the wings beside the velvet stage curtains, looking more than a little shocked. With his face partially hidden in shadow, his insanely elegant bone structure was sharply highlighted. Class, man. The guy was pure class. Way out of his league.

Stone reluctantly walked over to join him, chagrin coursing through his blood like hot acid.

"Sorry about tackling you. Did I hurt you?"

"I played football at Columbia University. I've taken worse hits."

Thank God. It wasn't every day he randomly tackled his employer's right-hand man and slammed the guy to the floor. "What position? Lemme guess. Wide receiver?"

"Correct. How'd you know?"

"You're too lean for defense or playing around the line. And you don't like being in the spotlight enough to play quarterback. You're tall and have a runner's ass. Which means either a safety or wide receiver. And you're more of a go-getter than the type to block someone else from doing something. Hence, wide receiver."

"God. Even I don't pay that much attention to football."

Embarrassment pumped through Stone. He mumbled, "I watch more soccer these days."

Christian clapped him lightly on the shoulder. "It's all good, man. That was a nice tackle anyway. You ever play football?"

"Nah. No time for it." The truth was, his parents hadn't been able to afford the cost of it when he was little, and in the area he grew up, if you didn't start playing by about age eight, a kid would never be good enough to play in the big high school programs.

"Too busy chasing all the cute boys in high school?" Christian asked lightly.

He snorted. "Yeah. Right."

"When did you come out?"

"Never."

"I beg your pardon?" Christian stopped and turned to stare at him.

"I'd have been killed, like, literally, if I'd done it in high school. Then I went into the Army. Not a great place to announce I was gay either. Then I got to my Ranger battalion, and it never came up there."

"Does anybody but your occasional lover know?"

"My mother has always known, I think."

"Your father? The rest of your family?"

"He's never asked and I've never volunteered it. Doesn't really seem like any of his business who I sleep with."

"Fair." He turned to walk but stopped again. "What if you fall in love with someone? Will you tell him, then?"

His gut clenched with an odd, unfamiliar, and deeply unpleasant sensation. Holy shit. That was fear. For the second time in as many minutes, this man had made him afraid. What the hell was up with that?

"Not a bridge I'm too worried about crossing," he lied.

Christian physically pulled back from him. It was a subtle withdrawal but visible to the observant eye. And he was an observant man. Particularly around this guy he was apparently hyperaware of.

He frowned. What had he said wrong? He wasn't looking for a relationship nor expecting one to come along. He traveled way too much to put down roots and do the whole hearth-and-home gig.

Christian resumed walking, pacing toward the exit and steps that led out onto the main ballroom floor.

For some reason, Stone felt compelled to murmur, "I really am sorry about tackling you."

"It's all good. I'm glad to see you're worth what Lacey's paying for your services. Those are some great reflexes you've got there."

Dammit. Christian's voice was cool and polite. Distant. He'd emotionally pulled back too.

He frowned. "For future reference, if you ever see a laser dot like that again, don't stop to think about it. Don't look around to see where it's coming from. Don't point it out to anyone. Don't ask any questions. Just hit the dirt. Next time it may not be an asshole playing a joke at the other end of that laser beam." He added reluctantly, "I'd take it amiss if someone blew your head off."

Christian's far too intelligent and far too perceptive gaze snapped to his. Stone forced himself not to look away. His adrenaline was still screaming, his reactions still too raw, to bother trying to hide them.

Christian's expression thawed, and the ice in his blue eyes melted into the warm blue of the Caribbean. He nodded slowly and then murmured, "I like you too."

Wait. What?

He hadn't said he—

But apparently, he did.

Sonofagun.

Gobsmacked, he mumbled lamely, "Remember about the dot. If you see one, *move*."

"Got it."

Stone realized in minor shock that his legs felt more than a little weak. Good grief, the effect this man had on him—

Oh, wait. He'd just had a big scare. That wasn't him reacting to Christian declaring that he liked him. It was the aftermath of an adrenaline dump into his bloodstream. Yeah. That was it. Totally about the scare. Nothing to do with him returning any feelings for Christian.

Ahh, the joys of coming down off a hard spike of life-and-death adrenaline. He was going to kick Tucker's ass when he got within arm's length of the guy. Tucker knew better than to mess with a man trained like he was. Truly, his finger had begun the pull-through on the trigger of his gun before Tucker had identified himself. It had been a closer call with disaster than the security man or Christian knew.

Christian asked him low, "You okay? Do you need a drink or something?"

"It's not even 10:00 a.m. yet," he replied dryly.

"It's after noon somewhere."

He grinned reluctantly.

"Come with me. I know exactly what you need."

He looked up sharply at Christian. Hoo baby. What *exactly* did that mean? Did he dare hope?

Nah, don't be an idiot. This guy's too professional to take up where we left off last night.

But he wouldn't say no to it if Christian asked.

Meanwhile, for once in his life, he decided to let someone else look out for him. "Lead on."

CHAPTER THREE

CHRISTIAN WAS frankly startled that Stone followed him out the french doors and toward the beach. The work version of Stone Jackson was wired way, *way* tighter than the man he'd met in the bar last night.

Granted, in Stone's line of work, tight was a good thing. But gone was the relaxed, funny man he'd nearly had sex with....

It wasn't good for anyone to live life always walking the razor's edge. He knew that from personal experience dealing with his mercurial boss. Everyone needed to let go of the reins now and then. God knew, Stone looked ready to kill someone right now.

"Shoes and tie off, Stone," he ordered briskly, kicking off his own leather oxfords and stripping his socks. He untied his necktie and let it dangle around his neck. *Ahh. Better.*

"I'm not cavorting on the beach like some starry-eyed tourist who's never seen the ocean before."

He glared at Stone, eyes narrowed dangerously. "Your shoulders are up around your ears, you can't keep your hands still—they keep reaching for your holster—and I can see the pulse pounding in your temple, so don't tell me your heart's not racing and your blood pressure isn't sky-high. You need to breathe, and you need to burn off a little stress before you hurt someone."

To his credit, Stone seemed to take a moment to self-assess, and then he followed Christian onto the sand without comment. Would wonders never cease?

"How do you know about burning off stress?" Stone asked as the first wave lapped up over their toes, cool and foamy.

"You *have* met my boss."

"Yeah. Giant asshole."

"I often leave work with a burning need to put my fist through a wall."

"And do you?"

"No, numbskull. I go for a run. And if that doesn't work, I hit the gym and beat up a punching bag until my violent urges diminish."

"Should I put you on the list of people who want to take out Jack Lacey?"

"Dude, that list will be huge. We're talking phone-book dimensions."

"Where do you suggest I start narrowing down the list, then?"

"How about we talk about that later? Right now, you're supposed to be relaxing. Catching your breath. Trust me, you'll have a clearer head later if you chill now."

Stone mumbled under his breath low enough Christian didn't think he was supposed to hear, "Damn. Classy *and* smart."

Stone thought that of him? Cool.

Barefoot, he led Stone along the water's edge. The soft, white-sugar sand farther up the beach would already be hot underfoot in the late-morning sun. The hotels and condo associations in this part of South Beach imported truckloads of premium sand every year and actually made it a pretty decent beach. Down here by the water, though, it hardened up enough to be walkable, with only minor cracking of the crusty surface underfoot.

The tangy smell of salt and algae was strong. It reminded him sharply of long summers in Martha's Vineyard spent playing on the beach with his older sister, turning nut-brown and white-haired, carefree and innocent. Before things like sexual orientation and career choice and maintaining a careful facade of respectability became the center of his world.

Stone stopped just far enough into the ocean for waves to wash over his ankles and to begin burying his feet in the sand.

"C'mon," Christian said, taking off down the beach.

"You're seriously taking me for a long walk along the beach?" Stone asked, hurrying to catch up.

He shrugged. "I would have suggested we go for a run if either one of us was dressed for it. You look like you might actually be able to keep up with me for a little while."

A crack of laughter escaped Stone.

Oh yeah? Mr. Macho thought he could keep up with the triathlete? He'd like to see it.

Aloud, he said, "My intent is not a romantic stroll. I'm trying to help you to burn out the adrenaline screaming through you and work off some of the anger that's making you look vaguely homicidal. I need you not to kill someone in the next hour because you're wound so tight that someone accidentally triggers a kill reflex out of you. Particularly since it's most likely to be my boss who does it."

"Why do you care if I kill someone or not?"

"A staff member of Senator Lacey committing homicide would be a PR nightmare. And it would land squarely in my lap to fix. No, thank you."

"Is it up to you to fix everything for everybody, then?"

"Call me Girl Friday," he answered lightly.

Stone did not respond other than to veer out into the surf a little farther.

The tide was out and the ocean was quiet this morning, with lazy, arced sheets of foam creeping up the beach and retreating slowly. Good day for an open-water swim. At this time of year, the ocean was warm enough that he wouldn't even need a wet suit to stave off hypothermia.

Part of why Christian worked out so much was to let off the stress of being around Jack Lacey day in and day out without putting his fist through the bastard's teeth. He could relate to Stone's tension.

He was surprised, however, when Stone paused and turned to take a long look at the hotel. The security guard was still mostly in charge of the man.

Stone shook his head, muttering, "What idiot thought a controversial politician can be safe in there? The joint's completely indefensible."

Christian responded, "I highly doubt the Imperium ballroom was designed with defense of any kind in mind."

"I should bail on this job right now."

"Why haven't you already?"

"I—you—"

Warmth flooded Christian's entire body. Stone was staying because of him? That was kind of spectacular to know. Except—

It was his turn for a mental hitch. They both worked for Jack Lacey. No hint of scandal could touch the senator, who created more than enough scandal of his own already. No way could two of his staffers be seen having a torrid affair in public.

Because it would definitely be torrid if he had anything to say about it.

And he got the distinct impression Stone would not be opposed to torrid either.

Somebody passing by wolf-whistled—whether at him or Stone, Christian couldn't tell.

His entire body clenched. *Ohgodohgodohgod.* Had someone recognized them? Made them as a couple? A denial press release started to scroll through his mind unbidden.

Beside him, Stone jolted violently, his hands coming up in a defensive position Christian recognized from his boxing training.

"Easy there, Rambo. You can come down off the bridge now. No one's trying to kill anyone."

"You don't have to talk me down off any bridges," Stone snapped. "I'm not going to jump."

"Hell, I'm not worried about you jumping. Looks to me like you're up there with an Uzi picking out targets. That's what worries me."

Stone grinned at him reluctantly.

The whistler jogged past, apparently not a paparazzo, not a journalist, not someone who recognized either of them.

Christian sagged in relief.

"Walk with me, Stone. I promise it'll make you feel better."

They continued down the beach, shoes dangling from their fingers and toes tickled by the surf hissing onto the sand. A cool breeze was blowing in off the ocean this morning, making for unseasonably pleasant conditions. Still, the humidity made Stone's dark, collar-length hair wave and curl around his strong features in very European fashion. Usually Christian went for the clean-cut type, but the look was hot on Stone. It softened the harshness of his features. Balanced them.

"Do you have psychology training?" Stone asked him without warning.

"Sort of. I'm a lawyer by education." His profession was as often about head games as it was about the law.

"What kind of law?"

"Criminal. I specialize in overturning prisoner convictions."

A snort. "Is that how you ended up with Lacey? Aiding and abetting his shenanigans?"

He shrugged back. "Actually, I do my best to keep him on the straight and narrow."

And truth be told, it was not an easy job. But between Christian and Lacey's wife, with her iron fist inside that velvet Southern glove of hers, they'd more or less succeeded so far. His secret nightmare was that Lacey would get the bright idea to run a corrupt side gig and tell neither him nor his wife about it.

"Why do you work for him?" Stone challenged.

"He's no worse than other elected officials on Capitol Hill. And with a job as a Senate senior staffer on my résumé, I have a shot at the kind of work I really want."

"Which is?"

"The federal prison reform project over at the Justice Department."

"Although that sounds like massively worthy work, I have to be honest with you. It sounds as dry as dust to me."

Christian grinned at him. "I'll take it over throwing myself on top of people for a living."

A smirk. "It has its perks. You took that tackle surprisingly well. I'd have injured most men."

"I'm not most men."

"No." A pause. "You're not."

Arrested by the undertone in those words, Christian stopped and turned to stare at Stone.

But Stone refused to meet his gaze and kept on walking. Huh. A relationship between them was out of the question. Not only did both of them have demanding careers that took all of their attention, but now they worked for the same man. Ethics alone dictated that they not get involved. Too bad. Stone fascinated him as no man had in a very long time. Maybe ever.

They walked about a mile down the beach before the decent sand ran out. Thankfully, Stone's shoulders had come down from around his ears, and that white line around his lips had mostly disappeared by then.

They turned around to walk back to the hotel at a more leisurely pace than they'd made the outbound leg.

That was more like it. The trained killer had retreated, leaving behind the guy he'd met last night in the bar. The guy he'd almost had gnarly sex with and was still frustrated as hell not to have had sex with. His dick stirred with interest at the mere thought of lying over that sofa, bare-assed and ready to rumble. In fact, he had to grit his teeth against getting any more turned-on in these thin business trousers that would do nothing to contain a hard-on.

Cock still filling and getting heavier by the minute, dammit.

Must. Distract. Self.

"How'd you get into the security business?" he asked. Jeez. Even he could hear the strain in his voice. *Get it together, man.* Christian prided himself on his self-control. He never lost it like this.

A shrug. "Did similar work in the military. It was an easy slide over to the civilian side of the house and a decent paycheck for a change."

"You were a bodyguard in the military?" He was not aware of that being an actual job the military did.

"I trained security teams for foreign heads of state. Taught them how to keep their personal popcorn dictators alive."

Fuck. That was sexy as hell. *Focus on the conversation.* "And how did you learn how to do that?"

"My job for several years before that was to kill foreign heads of state."

Christian jolted to a halt to stare at Stone, who stopped as well. "The US government doesn't kill foreign leaders. Doing so would open our own senior leaders up to assassinations in return. It's one of the few gentlemen's agreements left in the world. You don't kill our guy—we won't kill yours."

"You go right ahead and keep on thinking that, oh, naive one," Stone answered dryly.

"Who? Name me one head of state we've taken out."

"Dude. That kind of stuff is so classified the security-violation fairies would rise up out of the ocean and shoot me dead where I stand if I talked about it."

They resumed walking. "Seriously?" Christian muttered. "We do that kind of stuff?"

"You wouldn't believe some of the stuff we do."

"But why?"

"Threaten the nation, threaten to attack civilians, threaten a high-ranking member of our government—we're coming for you. By responding forcefully to global bad guys, they're on notice not to mess with Uncle Sam."

"I know the logic, thanks. I'm a senior aide to a United States senator. I do, you know, politics?" he said sarcastically.

Stone threw up his hands in surrender. "I wasn't trying to insult your intelligence. I already got the memo that you know your shit."

He subsided and veered toward the hotel, which was drawing near.

Although Lacey wasn't on the Senate Intelligence Committee, certain briefings came across his desk from time to time. Rumors floated around among the Senate staffers. Now and then, the full Senate got a briefing about some activity the military was undertaking. He didn't want to venture a guess at what the CIA might be up to that it didn't brief the Senate on.

"And who exactly is we?" Christian asked. "Who did you work for?"

"Classified."

"I've got a top-secret clearance. Have to if I'm going to handle all of the senator's correspondence. I've heard of some of the types of groups you're talking about."

"I guarantee you haven't heard about the one I ran with."

He got the distinct impression that was all Stone planned to say on the subject. It made sense, though. As fast as one Special Forces group got famous for its exploits, another had to be formed that was a deep, dark secret. Totally off the books. Able to work invisibly in the shadows to do the kind of stuff Stone was hinting at.

"What's Senator Lacey up to this morning?" Stone asked as they slogged up the beach to the hotel. "All his itinerary said was executive time."

"That would be staff-speak for sleeping in late and eating brunch in his suite before heading down to the spa for a massage and mani-pedi," Christian answered wryly.

"He gets mani-pedis?"

"Real men are allowed to have decent grooming, you know."

"Yeah, but pedicures?"

"He likes the kind where the fish eat the dead skin off his feet."

"That's gross. It sounds like something the Romans would have done when their decadence ran amok."

Christian shrugged. "The perks of power."

"Why that tone of voice?"

Give Stone Jackson points for hearing the sarcasm. "Lacey comes from the school of letting his staff members do all the grunt work while he… indulges himself. We brief him on the highlights, and he skips the real work. But of course, he takes all the credit."

"Similar thing happened in the military sometimes. We put our necks on the line, and some asshole drinking coffee in the Pentagon snagged all the glory."

Christian sincerely hoped the generals running the military didn't have Jack Lacey's vices. He changed subjects and veered for safer waters. "I have a briefing scheduled with Jack after lunch to go over his votes on a couple of major bills coming up in the Senate in the next few weeks."

"Shouldn't he know how he's going to vote on a bill if he's the guy doing the voting?"

"One would think."

"Jeez, Christian. Is there anything redeeming about your boss?"

"His wife rocks. She does a ton of charity work and outreach to Texas constituents."

"How did an asshole like him land a woman like her?"

"I chalk it up to her being young and in love when they met in college. And the ladies seem to think Jack's hell on wheels in the sack."

"Ladies plural?" Stone echoed. "Just how hard does this dude sleep around?"

"Well, he's had a long-term mistress for the past fifteen years or so. Her name's Valerie. Valerie Micklethwaite."

"Aren't the Micklethwaites big in real estate or something?"

"Yes. That's them," he answered ruefully. "They own a decent amount of New York City and northern New Jersey. Makes for some interesting staff work trying to keep Jack and Valerie out of the news. She's quite the socialite in her own right."

"Does Jill suspect anything?"

"I wouldn't be surprised if she doesn't send cards and flowers on Valerie's birthday. Jill has no interest in sleeping with Jack these days. She's delighted to pass that task off to someone else."

"Umm. Okay."

Christian realized what he'd just said and added hastily, "I'll deny having ever said any of that. You can't repeat a word of that. Not even a whisper—"

Stone cut him off gently. "Christian. I never reveal anything I see, hear, or learn about my clients. Relax. I've got your back."

And suddenly, an image of Stone standing behind him, memory of Stone lubing up his ass and stepping between his legs flashed through his mind. If only Stone had his back in that way too.

Stone cleared his throat as if something had abruptly stuck there… perhaps memory of nearly having literally had his back last night?

In a frantic attempt to distract them both, he mumbled, "You have your classified secrets. Senate staffers have theirs."

"I need you not to keep secrets from me if I'm going to keep your boss alive. I'm beginning to believe that will be a harder task than any of us anticipated."

The hotel loomed in front of them.

"Promise me you won't die, Stone."

"I can't promise that. I will put my body between Jack Lacey and death if it becomes necessary."

God, he hated the sound of that. They stopped outside the french doors and their stares met, Stone's stark.

"Thanks for the walk, Christian. It did clear my head. I may let your chief of security live now."

"Please do. You have no idea how hard it is to find a good man for the job who will put up with Lacey's antics."

Stone shook his head. "If the threat against your boss is as real as Tucker says it is, Lacey may not survive too much longer anyway. His security is completely inadequate to face a real threat from a determined assassin."

Christian sighed. "I was afraid you'd say that. Just do your best. But I meant what I said before. Don't die to save him."

"No matter how epic a jerk he is, my reputation in the security business would be ruined if I let a client die on my watch. I've got no choice but to do my best to protect him."

Christian didn't actually wish ill upon his boss, and certainly not death. But it didn't seem fair that a decent, upright, competent bodyguard should be put in this impossible position. He sighed. "Is there anything I can do to help you?"

"Make sure the senator follows our instructions if Tucker or I tell him to do something. I'm going to take advantage of the senator's spa date to have a little conversation with Mr. Tucker."

"Don't be too hard on him. The staff jokes around a lot in an effort to stay sane. He actually likes you or he wouldn't have pulled a prank on you."

"Noted, and thanks for letting me know. But I don't have time for any more hijinks. As far as I can tell, the threat to Lacey is real. Which means Tucker and I need to get down to business and figure out exactly how we're going to keep the senator alive, with or without his cooperation."

"Yeah. Good luck with that," Christian replied dryly. "Jack's more likely to do the opposite of what you say just to show that he doesn't have to follow your orders."

"Also noted."

"Will I see you at the five o'clock press conference the senator has scheduled?" Christian asked.

"I'll be at every public appearance the man makes from now on. You're going to get sick of my face."

Christian highly doubted that. Stone Jackson had the kind of face he could look at a long damned time without the slightest hint of sickness. Even if he did bear a more than passing resemblance to Jack. "The senator will go straight from the press conference to the cocktail party afterward."

"Talk to me about that party. Who'll be there? What will happen?"

"A bunch of rich political donors will go to rub shoulders with celebrities who've been quietly paid to show up. Jack will shake a lot of hands, slap a lot of shoulders, and kiss a lot of asses. There'll be plenty of drugs, underpriced alcohol, and overpriced hookers."

"I'm familiar with that type of event. It'll be crowded, and no one will have been properly vetted, searched, or checked off a guest list."

Christian nodded. "You would not be wrong."

Stone sighed and muttered, "Fucking security nightmare."

"Also not wrong."

"Will Jack partake of the drugs, booze, and women?"

"He'd better not. He doesn't do drugs, knows not to drink in public. He gets way too talkative when he's drunk."

Stone straightened his spine. "And after the party? Then what?"

"He'll likely leave there and retire early. Probably not alone."

"I thought the wife was in Texas."

"She is."

"And the mistress?"

"Not in Miami."

"Ahh. Well, at least sleeping around isn't technically a crime. As vices go, it could be worse."

They traded knowing looks. Christian expected that in Stone's line of work, he'd seen it all. Men cheating on their wives was probably kid stuff to him.

"So, where is the mistress? Valerie, you said her name was?"

"She's in Washington." He added reluctantly, "At least I think she is. Jack doesn't let us keep tabs on her."

Stone opened the door leading back to the lobby for him, and Christian stepped through it. As he passed close to Stone, he said, "Let me know how your talk with Tucker goes. I'll do my best to run interference for you if he's not on board with what you want to do."

"I can fight my own fights."

He got the feeling Stone's words were habitual, more knee-jerk than thought-out response. "I'm sure you can," he answered evenly. "But in Washington politics, it's not a bad thing to have a few friends in your corner who can back you up. Trust me. You're going to need that one of these days."

An eloquent eye roll was Stone's only response.

He'd done his best. He'd tried to warn Stone exactly what he was up against in trying to keep Jack Lacey alive.

Frankly, he hoped the would-be killer was an amateur lunatic without the wherewithal to plan and execute a decent attack. But something deep in his gut warned him that this time, the senator might not be so lucky. Which, in turn, made him worry for the dark and dangerous man walking away from him with a grim set to his jaw.

Chapter Four

STONE STOOD beyond the bright lights, scanning the crowd of reporters and cameramen. As press conferences went, this one reminded him of an awkward seventh-grade dance where everyone fidgeted around the edges of the gym and nobody actually wanted to be there.

Was it because the press didn't like Lacey, or was this a symptom of something darker hanging over the senator?

Was it possible that Jack Lacey's political real estate was in more trouble than the analysts at Wild Cards had realized?

Why, if that was true, was the man rumored to be considering a run for president? Either Jack had access to some nearly bottomless well of money Wild Cards hadn't discovered, or he had dirt on people. Lots of people. Powerful ones.

The good news was today's event hadn't been advertised to the public and only a few civilians had shown up. They'd been easy enough to photograph and run fast facial recognition on. Nobody popped any red flags in law enforcement databases. Everyone else in the room was displaying press credentials and was bored out of their minds.

Not that Stone was complaining about the bored crowd of journalists. He'd been able to carefully assess the body language of every single person in the room and determine that no one was showing the signs of stress associated with someone about to kill another one.

Truth be told, he was more fascinated by the dynamic between Christian and his boss than with any of the reporters. About twenty minutes prior to the start of the press conference, Christian had delivered a sheaf of papers that contained every question any of the reporters would be asking the senator today, along with a prepared answer, presumably written by Christian.

While a pretty young woman did his makeup and hair, Lacey read through the papers and familiarized himself with the contents.

Stone had sidled up to Christian at one point and murmured, "Aren't the journalists allowed to ask whatever they want to?"

"Not with Jack. He insists on them submitting question lists in advance, which he edits and approves or disapproves, question by question."

"I thought the free press was a thing in America."

Christian rolled his eyes. "It's one of the pillars of the Constitution."

"How does Lacey get away with it?"

"He pulls big ratings, and all the news shows want coverage of him. He shuts reporters out of his press conferences if they don't play by his rules."

"Can he do that during an election cycle?"

"He's got about one more month before he officially kicks off his reelection campaign. After that, he'll have to put on his big boy pants and deal with the press like anyone else."

Which meant a journalist was probably not the source of the death threats. In a few weeks the press could declare open season on Jack Lacey with their pens. A sword to the guy's neck wasn't necessary now.

When the press conference got rolling, Christian had stationed himself in the front row of reporters, in plain sight of Lacey. Each time someone asked the senator a question, Christian subtly held up his fingers to indicate a number. It took about three questions for Stone to realize that Christian was signaling to his boss which page in his notes held the answer to the question.

His opinion of Jack Lacey shifted from "what a douche" to "holy crap, put that asshole out of his misery."

The press conference went on for an anemic twenty minutes. But then a journalist apparently went off script and asked, "There are rumors that you've been getting death threats, Senator. Do you take them seriously, in light of the fact that you've got a new member on your security team?"

Jack's gaze lifted from the notes. Stone frowned as the senator actually looked... gleeful. Lacey leaned in to the mic. "In my experience those who do the hard work in need of doing in this country often get threats. I take it as a badge of honor that I'm making big enough changes in Washington that I've earned the privilege of receiving death threats."

Badge of honor? That was a weird way of looking at it.

Christian rushed forward and cut off any more off-script questions as the journalists abruptly started shouting all kinds of questions at his boss. "Thanks, ladies and gentlemen. The senator has another meeting and has to wrap this up now."

The camera lights went off and the reporters packed up. Stone spied a half-dozen civilians approaching the senator and dutifully moved in beside his client.

"Great job as usual, Senator," one of them boomed. "Keep performing like that and you'll be front and center in presidential debates in no time!"

Christ. Could the man stick his head any farther up Lacey's ass? Lacey didn't act like he could spell his own name without Christian's cheat sheets. Stone doubted he could take those on stage with him in a debate, and he got the distinct impression the guy would be shit outta luck without them.

"Do you need a lift over to the party, Jack?" Booming Voice asked.

Stone interrupted politely. "We'll be taking care of the senator's transportation."

Boomer slapped Stone's shoulder jovially, which made him grit his teeth behind a stiff smile. *Don't touch the armed man who already thinks you're a waste of oxygen.*

"Gonna be a hell of a bash. Plenty of whatever you could want."

Was the loudmouth actually suggesting that the bodyguards would stop doing their jobs long enough to catch a little action on the side? Just what kind of incompetent yahoo did this jerk think he and Wild Cards, Inc. were?

A familiar voice muttered in his ear, "Ignore him. He has the social skills of a spoon. He's no threat to Jack."

Holy cannoli, Christian was good at reading him. It was actually starting to be a little uncanny. He'd no sooner felt the irritation at the loud buffoon than Christian said exactly the right thing to defuse his annoyance and refocus his attention on his work.

The reporters dispersed to cull through their footage for sound bites to put on the late local news, and he and Tucker herded Lacey out to the armored SUV waiting at the Imperium Hotel's loading dock.

The drive into Coral Gables was interminable. Saturday night in Miami apparently involved every single resident going out cruising in vintage convertibles or clogging the sidewalks on foot and tying up crosswalks. But eventually they pulled into the circular drive in front of an obscenely opulent Spanish-style mansion. He'd seen some obnoxious places in his work as a bodyguard to the rich and famous, and this place was right up there.

Stone held the car door for Lacey and was surprised when Tucker didn't fall in behind his boss. Stone started to follow the senator, and Christian touched his sleeve. He turned, frowning.

"He won't want you sticking too close to him."

"Then how in the hell am I supposed to do my job?" he demanded.

Christian shrugged. "Watch him from a distance."

"And do what? Call him on his cell phone to tell him to duck?"

Christian winced.

"Look. I shouldn't bite your head off. I know you're only the messenger. But your boss is making it impossible for me to do my job."

"I know." Christian sighed. "Just do what you can."

"In my line of work, that won't be enough. I want to go on record right now as having told you I will not be able to prevent an attack on the senator under these working conditions."

"So noted."

He couldn't tell if Christian was irritated with him, with Lacey, or with the whole situation in general.

They stepped into the grand foyer, and Stone stared around at the crowd, which was standing room only. Even if he spotted an assassin, no way in hell he could get over to Lacey's side in this crush to protect the guy.

His gaze roved across the room, and he easily spotted Christian's chestnut hair and chiseled features. No surprise, a hot Latina was already flirting with him.

Something unpleasant twisted at his gut. *Oh puh-lease.* He did not get jealous. And certainly not of women who stood no chance with his lover. Of course jealousy presupposed actual relationships, and he did not do those. For that matter, he and Christian were not lovers.

He continued scanning the room, looking for the telltale signs of individuals with murder on their minds. There had to be five hundred people crowded into this house, and more were coming in the front door every minute. He'd worked in nightclubs and rock concerts with crowds a lot bigger and a lot wilder than this one before. But he'd never had to work in one halfway across the damned room from the client. Hell. He was having trouble even keeping Jack Lacey in sight.

Following the senator, Stone shoved his way across the foyer toward what he presumed was the back of the house. Oh Christ. The crowd extended to the backyard and spilled around and into a huge swimming pool. There had to be at least two hundred more people out here. Of course, the swimmers were exclusively young bikini-clad women.

He took a hard look at the men outside. Most were focused on the women in the pool, drinking and speculating on which ones they could end up having sex with before the night was over. At a party like this, there would be a number of call girls who expected compensation for their efforts, sprinkled in among the groupies who'd fuck a politician for free in hopes of living a perceived high life, or perhaps a little lucrative blackmail. Yup, sweet little barracudas and politicians. A match made in heaven.

Jack Lacey was right in there with the other males trawling the edges of the pool, scoping out the local talent. The bastard moved around the pool with a connoisseur's concentration. Hard to believe the guy had a wife, and apparently a formidable one at that.

The ladies wasted no time hitting on Stone. They rubbed up against him like cats in heat, brazenly groping his junk and purring at what they found. He pasted on a polite smile and mumbled what he hoped was an inoffensive apology about being at work while he brushed their hands away.

Stone happened to be passing by Christian—well, not just passing by—when a particularly aggressive brunet threw herself at poor Christian. She seemed determined to get into his pants, and Christian looked like he'd passed beyond panic into mildly homicidal. The young woman reeked of alcohol, and Stone unobtrusively grabbed her by the elbow, half lifted her off her unsteady feet, and bodily hauled her off Christian.

It was a move he'd perfected over years of protection work. He kept his grip hidden between their bodies so nobody would notice the disturbance, and then he walked her away from Christian quickly and powerfully enough that the woman had no choice but to move with him or fall down.

"Hey!" she protested.

As if anyone would hear her over the din of dance music and drunken shouting.

"Trust me, darling," he shouted in her ear in his best British accent, "you're not that guy's type." For some reason, British accents tended to disarm Americans, as if their owners were automatically classy and polite or something.

Sure enough, she cooed and turned toward him, looping her arms around his neck. He twisted his body so she ran right up against the gun under his left arm.

She started. A vaguely alarmed look passed over her face, and her arms fell away from his neck.

Free.

He spun away from her vodka-and-vomit breath and scanned the crowd, trying to reacquire Jack.

A voice murmured in his ear, "Thanks. I owe you one." Warmth flowed through him. *Christian.*

"My pleasure. Any idea where the boss is?"

"I think I saw him head inside. This way. Follow me."

Also with pleasure. Although, he didn't allow himself the luxury of scoping out Christian's backside. His priority was to find Jack.

Alcohol flowed, couples disappeared upstairs, and inhibitions evaporated around them.

They headed into a huge room decked out as a disco, complete with colored lights and mirrored balls. It made for a lurid and damned-hard-to-see-in environment. Easily a hundred dancing people were moshing in a pseudo-orgy.

Christian stopped abruptly in front of him, and Stone all but plowed into him from behind. Which was why he heard Christian swear sharply.

"What?" he demanded over Christian's shoulder, following Christian's glare.

"What the hell is *she* doing here?" Christian demanded.

"She who?"

"Valerie."

"The mistress?"

"Yes. Dammit."

Christian tried to plow through the crowd but made little headway. Stone touched his elbow and slid past, murmuring, "Allow me."

Whereas Christian had tried to be polite, Stone had no such compunction. Using his body as a battering ram, he shoved through the crowd mercilessly, pushing and lifting drunks out of his way like so many sacks of sawdust. He crossed the room in a matter of seconds.

Christian touched his elbow and he paused, letting Christian move in front of him again. He stopped in front of a highly curved, highly coiffed, highly made-up woman with black hair that couldn't possibly be natural in color. She was attractive but older than he would have expected of Jack Lacey. The senator struck him as the type to go for young models or aspiring actresses. Beautiful, empty-headed arm fluff.

"Valerie," Christian said with what Stone now knew to be fake pleasantry. "What brings you here?"

"Where's Jack?" she shouted over the noise.

"No idea. He left a while ago. I can have him call you when I see him. Where are you staying in town?"

"Don't give me that political double-speak crap. I want to talk to Jack. Now. I just saw Tucker. I know Jack's here somewhere."

Her thick New Jersey accent had an edge that set off warning bells in his head. She was royally pissed off about something to do with Jack and trying to hide it. In Stone's experience with VIPs, pissed-off mistresses could be both violent and irrational.

He stepped forward. "I'm sorry, ma'am, but I'm going to have to ask you to go through regular channels to contact Senator Lacey. If you'd like to talk with him, I'd suggest you call him during business hours. I'm sure Mr. Chatsworth-Brandeis can arrange for the senator to take your call—"

"Who's the new boy, Chris? He with you? He's pretty."

There was something about her... something that reminded him vaguely of the mafia. As if she was used to intimidating and threatening underlings to get her way. She hadn't said or done anything specific to warrant the impression, but it clung to her, nonetheless.

He asked evenly, "Ma'am, are you carrying a weapon on your person?"

"Maybe I am, maybe I'm not. It's none of your business."

"Actually, it is my business. I'm part of the senator's security team."

"Since when?" she exclaimed.

He ignored her question. "Here's the deal, Ms. Micklethwaite," he said calmly. Her eyebrows shot up when he used her last name. "This is a private event. Unless you can produce an invitation right now, you're going to have to leave. Immediately."

"Do you have any idea who I am?" The arrogance became more evident all of a sudden.

"I don't need to know who you are, ma'am. This remains an invitation-only event."

"Most of the people here don't have invitations, you moron."

"Most of them aren't being aggressive and threatening toward my client," he said coolly. He stepped forward, crowding close to and forcing her to take a step back if she wanted to keep glaring up at him.

She teetered on ridiculous platformed stilettos that added a good six inches to her height but still barely came to his shoulder. "Don't get all up in my business. I'll have Jack fire your ass so fast your head flies off."

Whatever. He'd be delighted to get out of this gig. "Be my guest to complain to the senator if and when you speak with him."

She seemed surprised that he didn't seem to care if he lost this job.

"Chrissy-poo, go find Jack and tell him I'm here, will you? Be a good boy."

Stone had to bite back a smile when he spotted the muscles literally rippling along Christian's jaw. To his credit, the man said nothing. He merely turned smartly on his heel and went looking for Jack.

For his part, Stone stayed with Valerie. No way was she leaving his sight until either she or Jack left this venue.

"What brings you to Miami, Ms. Micklethwaite?" he asked conversationally.

"Obviously, Jack."

"Do you have business with him?"

She snorted. "You might call it that. He made a promise to me, and I'm here to see to it he ponies up."

"Oh? And what did he promise you?"

"That's *totally* none of your business."

Christian was actually gone long enough that Stone was considering calling his cell phone to find out what the holdup was. But then he spied the familiar face swimming upstream against the crowd to reach them.

He drew near to Stone and leaned in close to put his lips on Stone's ear. "Jack's gone."

"Roger that."

Christian turned to Valerie. "As I said before, the senator left the party some time ago. If you'd like to give me a message for him, I'll be happy to pass it along when I see him."

Valerie screeched. Literally screeched. No words, just a howl of rage that brought everyone within about a fifteen-foot radius to a staring halt.

One of the bouncer types hired by the homeowner for the night came over and zeroed in on Stone. "Everything okay?"

"This woman was about to leave. Would you mind showing her out?"

"Not at all, sir," the bouncer said, smirking.

He reached for Valerie, who threw off his hand, shouting, "Don't you put your paws on me! Jack will hear about this! My daddy will hear about this!"

At this rate, half of Miami was hearing about it this very second.

Another bouncer joined the first one, and they quickly escorted the woman out of the room and, presumably, out of the house.

"Who's her daddy?" he asked Christian. "Should I be worried?"

"Maybe. He's reputed to be one of the biggest traditional Italian-style mobsters left on the East Coast."

"She's a mafia princess? What's Jack thinking?"

Christian shrugged. "He's thinking her old man can do him favors, funnel him cash, and do the occasional dirty deed to advance his political career."

"Christ," Stone muttered. "Take me to Jack. I've had quite enough of this damned circus."

"I wasn't kidding. Jack has left the party."

"He headed back to the hotel with Tucker? We might want to contact the front desk and make sure they know not to reveal that Jack is a guest to anyone who asks about—"

"No, Stone," Christian interrupted. "Jack didn't leave with him. Tucker is still out front with the SUV."

Stone stared. What the actual fuck?

Christian did that uncanny mind-reading thing of his again and shouted, "Come with me. There's a quieter place where we can talk."

He followed Christian to the kitchen, which was bustling with caterers and waiters but still quieter than the room with the DJ and blaring speakers.

"Did he leave the house?" Stone asked tersely.

"I don't know. But he's nowhere to be found."

"Where's the homeowner? A place this size has to have a security room where all the cameras feed to."

"This way."

Christian led him to a billiards room and a silver-haired man who was more drunk than not. But the guy readily took them to a small room at the back of the house where, indeed, a man was sitting in front of a bank of cameras.

Stone didn't waste any time. "I need the last footage you've got of Jack Lacey. Where did he go?"

"The senator? Last I saw of him, he was headed upstairs. If you know what I mean." The guard waggled his eyebrows. "Hey, is it true that he's got himself a stalker? Someone out to kill him?"

"Where'd you hear that?" Stone demanded.

"Saw a thing in the news about it. Quoted the senator, himself."

Christian replied dryly, "Not all quotes are real, and don't believe everything you read in the news."

"Was he alone?" Stone jumped in.

"No, sir. And I'm afraid there aren't any cameras in the bedrooms."

"How many bedrooms in the house?" Stone demanded.

"Six on the second floor, four on the third."

"Got it." Stone whirled for the door.

"You can't go barging into them, though!" the guard called at his back. "There are people in them!"

Stone 100 percent didn't care. He was finding Jack Lacey and quitting this damned job.

Christian rushed after him, half running to keep up. "The guard's right. You can't bust in on everybody in those bedrooms."

"Watch me."

"Give me a chance to at least ask around for which room he might be in, okay?"

Stone shrugged, irritated as fuck and not in the mood to make nice with anyone.

"Stay right here," Christian said, parking him at the foot of the sweeping staircase. Christian disappeared into the billiards room once more and came out in under a minute. He said merely, "Come with me."

They jogged up the stairs side by side, and Christian strode down a long hall, then paused before a pair of double doors. "Master suite," he muttered.

Of course, Jack would fuck in his host's own bed. Class in a glass. Stone bit out, "I'll go first." He reached for the door handles. Locked. Shaking his head, he pulled out his pocket knife and jimmied the childishly simple interior lock. "Anybody with a goddamned coin could open this door," he muttered direly.

"Don't kill him," Christian warned. "You're supposed to keep him alive."

Stone's glare narrowed even more. "Don't remind me."

They stepped into the suite, and Jack Lacey was sprawled out on the bed, naked as the day he'd been born, with a blond straddling him, wearing cowboy boots, a cowboy hat, and not another stitch of clothing. And she had possibly the largest breasts of any woman Stone had ever seen.

Christian stepped forward and said politely, "Sorry to interrupt, ma—" He broke off. "Oh! Hello, Ms. Hills. Like I was saying, sorry to, umm, interrupt. But something's come up and the senator needs to go now."

Jack drawled, "Something's come up, all right, and this li'l filly knows just what to do with it."

"Sir. There really is a problem. I need you to get dressed and come with us."

"Have the Russkies nuked America?"

"No, sir."

"China?"

"No, sir. No nuclear weapons have been fired."

"Then get the hell out of here, boy!"

Stone stepped forward, picking up discarded clothes as he went. "Ma'am. If you could please put on your clothes."

The blond pouted but took her clothes and crawled off the bed.

Swearing up a blue storm, Jack swung his feet to the floor. "Well, hell. Hey! Tell ya what. Darlin', come on back to the hotel with me and we'll pick up where we left off before these yahoos busted in."

"Sure, sugar pie," the blond cooed.

Christian glanced over at him. "Any objections?"

"I gather you know her?"

"Uhh, yes. Her name's Chesty Hills. Adult-film star. She was in California the few months back when we were there for a series of interviews and fundraising events. She, umm, spent some time with the senator."

Stone shrugged. "If you can vouch for her, she's as good a choice as any other woman here. Might as well be her we take back."

Chesty gave a suggestive wiggle as she tugged her mini dress down her thighs. She smiled up at him winningly. "Honey pie, I've got some business to discuss with Jack. If y'all aren't going to let us finish this discussion here and now, I'm gonna have to go with y'all." Her Southern twang was as pronounced as Valerie's New Jersey accent had been.

Stone sighed. "What's your real name, ma'am? I need it for security purposes."

"Chesty. Chesty Hills."

"Jesus." He looked over at Christian in time to catch the momentary grin that disappeared as quickly as it came. "Did you change your name or did your parents have an inkling of how you'd turn out?"

She laughed, and it was actually an infectious sound. If a guy could lift his gaze from her bodacious endowments, she was actually quite pretty.

Christian helped Jack into his suit coat and held out a comb for the senator to run through his rumpled hair. He even tied the man's tie efficiently. God. How did Christian stand having to do that kind of work for his boss?

"We good to go?" Stone asked from over by the door.

Christian nodded.

Stone radioed to Tucker, "Can you bring the SUV around back by the kitchen? We'll meet you there."

"You got it," Travis replied.

Except the minute they hit the ground floor of the crowded mansion, Jack veered away and started greeting people and shaking hands.

Swearing, Stone circled back to grab the senator by the scruff of the neck and haul him the hell out.

"Stop, Stone," Christian murmured. "You won't win this fight. Let him do his thing. I'll take Chesty out to the SUV to wait, and you can play bodyguard until he's ready to leave."

Scowling until his face hurt, he followed Jack around as best he could.

Whether Jack Lacey was eliciting pledges of funds or blackmailing every person in the goddamned room was anybody's guess. Stone couldn't get close enough to the man to hear anything he talked about with anyone. The one time he did venture close enough to hear, Jack turned and snarled at him to get back.

To get back, for fuck's sake! Who did that to their own freaking bodyguard? It was an ongoing struggle in Stone's gut whether or not to just go get a beer and let the bastard rot.

The longer this travesty of a protection detail dragged on, the more furious he grew. Finally, he couldn't take it any longer, and he pulled out his cell phone. Time to talk to his own boss.

It was early morning in London. Very early morning. But Peregrine Cardiffe, one of the two founders and CEO of Wild Cards, Inc. was used to middle-of-the-night phone calls.

"Go ahead," the familiar British voice said after one ring.

"Up early or still awake?" Stone asked, amused.

"Both. No rest for the weary, my dear Stone. What prompts this call?"

"The client refuses to cooperate with me or with his own security man. There's no way the Wild Cards can or should take responsibility for keeping this jerk alive."

"The jerk is paying us a substantial sum of money."

"I'm not kidding, Pere. I've worked with some assholes in my day, but this guy's in a class all his own. I'm at an unsecured party right now with close to a thousand unnamed, unvetted, unsearched partygoers, at least one quarter of whom are consuming controlled substances and another quarter of whom are paid prostitutes. And I'm under strict orders to stay away from the client. *Away from the client*, Pere."

"How far away?"

"He snapped at me the one time I ventured within thirty feet of him. Stormed over and told me to lurk somewhere else, entirely out of his sight."

A long silence. "Does the senator have a death wish? Maybe get an adrenaline rush from flirting with disaster?"

Stone bit back his knee-jerk response to objectively consider the questions. "It's my professional opinion that the client does not take the threat seriously. At all."

"But he called us."

"His chief of security called us. Poor dude was probably as frustrated as I am and hoping that writing a fat check might get Lacey's attention."

"What do you suggest I do? Send the senator a letter refusing to accept responsibility for his untimely demise should it occur?"

"I don't want the company's reputation to suffer if something bad happens. Without at least a modicum of cooperation from Lacey, there's no way to protect him. Not in the venues he's scheduled to appear in. You've got to believe me."

"Stone. You're one of my best men. How do the Yanks say it? This is not your first rodeo. If you think this client is unprotectable, I trust your judgment. I'll contact Senator Lacey and tell him we don't think we will be able to provide the service he's contracting us for. I'll pull you out of there first thing in the morning your time."

"Thank you, Pere. I'm sorry."

"No need for you to apologize. If the man doesn't want protection, he doesn't want protection."

Stone disconnected the call, feeling dejected. Failure was not a thing he was accustomed to. In fact, in his line of work, the failure rate was zero or a guy got out of the business.

"What's wrong?" Christian asked, materializing beside him.

"How in the hell do you do that?"

"Do what?"

"It's like you're psychic. You know exactly when I'm bugged by something."

"Although I'd be happy to take credit for having superpowers, your scowl is visible at twenty paces, Stone. Even the call girls are steering clear of you."

Now that Christian mentioned it, the women hadn't been hitting on him much for the past half hour or so. "Is there something you need from me?" Stone asked in resignation.

"I came to tell you the principal is going to be ready to leave soon."

"In other words, he has extracted all the money he can from working the room and now he wants to go home and screw Chesty?"

Christian grinned. "Exactly."

Stone shook his head in disgust.

They made their way toward the kitchen and outside to the valet parking area, where Tucker stood beside the SUV, arguing with the valets about how to move other vehicles to let them out. The car shuffle was just finishing up when Jack Lacey came staggering out of the kitchen with a pair of giggling girls draped all over him.

Christian swore under his breath while Tucker chuckled.

"What am I missing?" Stone asked.

"I made a bet with Tucker over whether or not he would hit on the twin Playboy bunnies."

"But what about Chesty? She's in the damned vehicle!"

"I know," Christian sighed. "But I'm still out a hundred bucks to Travis."

Jack kissed each of the bunnies farewell—with tongue, lots of tongue—and then climbed into the SUV.

Christian opened the front passenger door. "Front seat or back bench seat?"

"In other words, view or no view of the sex Olympics?" Stone asked dryly.

"Bingo."

"Front seat."

"Bastard," Christian breathed.

"You asked."

"Damn my good manners, anyway."

Stone watched in appreciation as Christian started to lever his long body into the far back of the SUV.

"Sit up front," Jack mumbled with Chesty's tongue planted in his mouth.

Aww, hell.

Stone slid across the bench seat to the hump in the middle, his knees parked practically under his chin. Christian climbed in deliciously, uncomfortably close to him and murmured across him to Tucker, "The package is secure."

Stone looked back and forth between Tucker and Christian. "You do know that real security details don't use that kind of language, right? That shit's only on television."

The two men laughed. Christian remarked, "We wondered how long it would take you to complain."

"Your boss's smartassery is rubbing off on you."

Christian threw him a horrified look. "Perish the thought."

Tucker raised the privacy panel behind them as moans began to emanate from the back seat.

The drive to the hotel took nearly a half hour in the still-atrocious midnight traffic. Stone abstained from the new bet between Tucker and Christian of whether or not Lacey would have had full carnal knowledge of his companion before they got to the hotel.

Whether the pair had sex or not, Chesty was more or less clothed and her hair and makeup reasonably intact when Tucker opened the SUV door beside the hotel's loading dock.

Interestingly enough, Lacey asked cautiously from inside the vehicle, "Can anyone see us? Are there cameras out here?"

Now the guy showed caution? Stone scanned the immediate area. Not a single camera was visible to his trained eye. He gave a thumbs-up to Tucker, who said, "We're clear, sir."

For just an instant, Jack looked more disappointed than relieved.

Weird.

He *wanted* to be spotted with Chesty? Surely not.

They moved inside to where Christian was already holding open a service elevator that was otherwise empty. The others stepped into the conveyance, and Stone moved to the front of the lift, using his body as a living wall. This was territory he knew. They arrived on the twenty-third floor, and he stepped out, clearing the hall. It was deserted.

Tucker hustled the senator and his giggling girlfriend down the hall to the luxury suite. They disappeared inside, leaving Christian and Stone standing alone in the silent hall.

"You got a minute?" Stone asked quietly. "I need to tell you something."

"Yeah, sure. The children are tucked in bed. I've got all night." His gaze snapped to Stone's as he realized what he'd said, and suddenly electricity leaped between them.

Turned-on and dreading what he had to tell Christian, Stone headed for his own suite at the far end of the long hallway. He stepped into the soothing elegance of his room, turned, and caught Christian exhaling a long, hard breath of what looked like relief.

"I know why I'm relieved to be away from your boss. But why are you?"

Christian flopped down on one end of the sofa and rubbed his eyes with his right hand. "He's a nightmare. If only he weren't the leading proponent in the country for prison reform and didn't promise to write me a personal recommendation for the prison reform project, I would so be out of here."

"How does he stay in office?" Stone asked.

"He's so charismatic he could talk a tiger into donating its stripes to him."

"And yet, shenanigans like tonight's ought to tank his career. How does he get away with that?"

"Because he's careful only to act like that among other people already acting like that, and I'm that good at covering his tracks."

"Then why don't you let him crash and burn?"

"Same reason you'll take a bullet for him. It's my job. My reputation is based on how well I take care of my employer. And I have other goals beyond him."

"Get that other job now."

"Easier said than done in the work I want to pursue. The reform project is wildly political and threatens to overturn some long-held sacred cows. I'll have to go into it with a strong reputation behind me."

Stone shrugged. "You won't know if you're at that point until you try."

Christian answered starkly, "I can't fail. I refuse to go home in disgrace."

Ahh. Now they were getting to the heart of the matter. "Someone back home told you that you'd never make it in the big city?"

"Something like that."

Stone sank down on the other end of the couch, half-turned to face Christian. Their knees were only inches apart. "Where's home for you?"

"Rhode Island. Tiny, rich enclave outside of Providence."

"Tiny, rich, and conservative?" he asked.

"Yup."

That lone cynical syllable held a wealth of meaning. Antigay community. Fake acceptance that masked condescension. Sniggers behind his back. Stereotyping. Oh yes. He knew it well. "Hey. You could have grown up in the South like I did, where they didn't bother to hide their contempt. When I got bigger than the bullies, stronger and meaner, they just attacked me in gangs."

They sat in silence for a while, contemplating the difficult roads that had brought both of them to this place in their lives. Both successes by the standards of the outside world but still fighting their private internal wars.

At length Christian spoke heavily. "You said you needed to tell me something."

"Right. I talked to Peregrine Cardiffe earlier. Wild Cards, Inc. is withdrawing from this job. The senator's money will be refunded in full. But we cannot take responsibility for Jack Lacey's life under the circumstances he's forcing us to work in."

Real pain crossed Christian's face. But whether it was a personal sense of loss or simply misery at having to manage yet another fuckup by his boss, Stone couldn't tell. He wasn't a Zen master at reading people like Christian was.

As the silence drew out, he finally muttered, "Talk to me."

"I don't know what to say. I understand your company's position. But I wish you would stay."

"Why?" he asked bluntly. "I can't do anything for Lacey. He won't let me."

"Not for him. For me."

And there it was again, that intense attraction. The irresistible pull between them. Unlike the last time, when it had been all about lust and sizzle, tonight it was more. Deeper. They had a tiny patch of common ground now. Shared experiences in their past. Hell, he *liked* Christian.

"Look, Christian. I'd be remiss if I didn't warn you that I suck at relationships."

"Yeah. I got that memo. But God help me, I don't care. There's something about you...."

He knew the wordless frustration Christian felt. He couldn't explain it either. Something about the big, clean-cut man beside him called to something deep in his gut. They... fit.

He sighed in genuine regret. "I'm out of here tomorrow. I have to let Tucker know that Wild Cards is pulling out of the job, and I have to get a new assignment from the company. But then I'll hit the road."

"Do you have to go?" Christian asked quietly.

"Afraid so. If there's no work for me here, I'll move on to the next assignment." He hesitated and then added quietly, "I'm sorry I have to go. I… like you too."

"Then I guess we don't have much time to waste."

They stood at the same time and ended up bumping chests and laughing at each other. Christian reached for Stone's tie while Stone reached for the remote that controlled the room's various electronics. He turned off the lights, and darkness embraced them.

"But I like looking at you," Christian protested.

"I like looking at you too. But you scare the hell out of me."

"What? Why? You're the big bad bodyguard."

"You're the savvy, classy, put-together congressional aide."

"Ahh." A pause. A low chuckle. "I think I like scaring the big bad bodyguard."

"Come here, you."

Christian plunged his hands into Stone's hair, drawing him forward into a hot, openmouthed kiss that actually made Stone groan aloud. Rare was the lover who could match his strength and force of personality. It was sexy as hell.

While Christian plundered his mouth, Stone reached for the buttons of that perfectly pressed and tailored dress shirt for the muscular torso he knew lay beneath. Ties slithered free and went flying. Buttons popped loose. They stood, never breaking the lock of their mouths, their tongues sparring as they tried to inhale each other. Belts slipped free and thudded to the carpet. Zippers buzzed down in the dark. Slacks and briefs peeled away.

And then nothing impeded his hands from roaming over Christian's chiseled physique. His fingers painted a picture in his mind of planes and bulges, filling in details of musculature, prominent veins, cut muscles that had to have taken years to develop.

"You're built like an Olympic athlete," he muttered against Christian's mouth.

"Says the pot to the kettle."

"I'm a scarred-up old warrior."

"Stone, you are not old. And your scars are hot. Tell me how you got each one."

"That would take all night."

"Lucky for you, I happen to have all night." Christian backed him up slowly, taking his time edging them both across the living room, into the bedroom, and over to the big, king-sized bed.

It felt so damned good to be on equal footing with this man. They were physically well matched, but they were mentally even better matched. Christian was no lightweight to be pushed around, and yet he was willing to share the whole alpha-male gig. And shockingly, for this man, so was he. For this man, he could let go of at least one of the reins of control.

The covers went flying, and a tangle of sheets bound them together as they stretched out side by side, exploring each other's bodies in the dark. Christian was beautiful in the way of a Greek god. He was masculine as hell, but his perfection of form made Stone's soul ache. Christian rose onto an elbow beside him, a bright shadow in the darkness of his world.

He traced the thin scar along Stone's shoulder with one finger. "What's this?"

"Shoulder surgery to repair a torn rotator cuff I got dragging a drug lord clear of a meth-lab explosion."

"Why did you save him? Were you his bodyguard?"

Stone laughed. "No. I was his arresting officer."

"Where is he now?"

"Rotting in the basement of a federal prison for life plus about a million years."

"Nice." Christian's finger traveled down his chest. A short, thick scar about two inches long got stroked lightly next.

Stone didn't wait for the question. "Knife wound. Kandahar, Afghanistan. Details are classified. But we couldn't use guns because of the noise and ended up in hand-to-hand combat. And yes, we got our guy."

They'd actually gotten a half-dozen guys that night. Couriers for a high-level group of terrorists who'd been attacking US military bases all over the country. It had been a good bust. A dirty knife had punctured his lung and put him out of action for weeks, though, as medics pumped antibiotics into him to counter the infection he'd picked up. It had been one of his closer calls with death.

One by one, he cataloged his other scars for Christian, who grew steadily quieter. Enough so that Stone started to get worried. He asked, "Am I freaking you out?"

"No. A more accurate description would be humbled."

"Why? Because I have a compulsion to prove how manly I am that borders on a death wish?"

A chuckle floated out of the dark. "Some shrink tell you that?"

"Uncle Sam's finest."

"The shrink obviously wasn't gay."

"Why do you say that?"

"Because I can think of a lot better way for you to prove how manly you are."

"Oh yeah? I'm all ears."

Christian chuckled quietly. "God, I hope not. I don't want to make love to a bunch of ears."

Make love. Not fuck. Not have sex with. Make love. Something cracked open painfully in his chest.

"You want to be a real man? Make love to me, Stone Jackson."

All of a sudden, at the age of thirty-five, with all the life experience and sexual experience he'd accumulated, he didn't have the slightest idea what to do next. He confessed reluctantly, "I'm not sure I know how."

"Listen to your gut and go with the flow."

That he could do. His belly muscles contracted as Christian traced a path with his mouth down his chest, across the acreage of his stomach, and lower. Oh God. Lower.

One advantage of a guy making love to another guy was that they knew exactly what felt the best. Christian knew when to squeeze hard and when to back off a little, when to lick suggestively and when to suck a golf ball through a garden hose. The man played his body like a musical instrument, making him groan, then shout, and then nearly sob with pleasure.

And all the while, that crack in his chest opened wider and wider, breaking apart everything he'd thought he was, shattering his illusions of strength, of control. Of self. In this man's arms, he was so much more than he'd ever known he could be.

An urge to return the favor, to break down the walls of Christian's self-control, rushed over him. And hey, the guy had said to listen to his gut and go with the flow. With a bunching of muscles, he rolled

Christian onto his back and returned the favor, exploring Christian's perfect physique with his mouth, finding his ticklish spots, aka the weaknesses in his armor, inciting a riot, and reveling in the cries he wrung from Christian. He was merciless, spurred on by his own raw vulnerability to lay open his lover emotionally until they were both this exposed.

Back and forth they went, one driving the other ever closer to the edge and then surging up to return the favor. They were both fit, with stamina to spare.

It was Christian who finally muttered, "Easy, Stone. There's no rush. We can take our time and enjoy ourselves. Savor the experience."

"Oh. Right. Sorry. I'm used to grabbing a quickie in between duty periods or on a short leave. I never get more than a day off at a time."

"Dude. And you call me a workaholic?" Christian retorted.

"I'm not working now. My boss should be contacting your boss first thing this morning to inform him that Wild Cards is withdrawing from this detail."

"Like I said," Christian murmured, soothing his tongue up and down Stone's quivering erection. "We've got all the time in the world."

Well, not technically. But Christian had a point. They didn't have to be in a huge hurry. The tension of earlier in the evening gradually fell away under the leisurely onslaught of Christian's mouth. The guy had an insanely talented tongue and teased responses out of Stone he didn't know he was capable of. A rolling groan from the back of his throat startled him as he arched into the heat and wet and sweet suction of Christian's mouth.

He planted a hand on the back of Christian's head and urged him deeper, being careful not to force the guy to gag.

But damned if Christian didn't jam his mouth down on Stone's cock, swallowing him deeper and deeper until he had to be partway down the man's throat. It was tight and hot, and Christian's throat muscles worked convulsively around his cock.

Stone's eyes drifted toward the back of his head as waves of pleasure threatened to consume him.

Christian retreated at the last possible second before Stone came. Acute disappointment... and relief that there would be more of that... swept over him.

He licked the thick vein along the underside of Christian's cock and relished the groan it wrung from his lover. He did it again. Christian's hips pushed forward a little, and he took more of Christian's cock into his mouth. His asshole flexed in anticipation at the idea of taking all of Christian.

He'd never been to bed with another man who seemed accustomed to being in charge most of the time, and it was an interesting give-and-take as they each experimented with relinquishing control, and then wresting it back. It wasn't a dominance fight, per se, but it did turn competitive from time to time.

Who could make the other come closest to an orgasm without exploding? Who could make the other one cry uncle on tickling or on a blow job that became too intense? Who could exhaust the other physically, first?

The upshot of it was that they were as well matched physically as two human beings could be.

They ended up settling into shared, mutual blow jobs, lying on their sides facing each other, head-to-foot. They matched rhythms, sucking off each other together, fucking each other's mouths hard, arching their pelvises into each other's faces simultaneously, groaning as one.

They even came at the same time.

It was sexy as hell, shouting around Christian's cock as Christian spurted into his mouth, and he returned the favor.

Afterward, they shared shots of whiskey that Christian rolled out of bed and poured for them. As for Stone, he was too sated and exhausted to move. They lay in bed in the dark, breathing heavily together.

The salty taste of cum and the smoky taste of the whiskey blended into an intoxicating effervescence that relaxed him and threatened to knock him out.

He probably ought to think about how Jack was going to react to Pere's call and prepare a few noncommittal responses that would extract him from an uncomfortable conversation the most quickly. But he was too damned relaxed to think about such things. Tomorrow morning would be soon enough to resume real life.

For tonight, he just wanted to go to sleep with Christian's taste and scent on him. To wake up for once and not be alone.

He gratefully settled into a state of mental emptiness that was utter and complete. And he'd never felt so emotionally full before. His body felt drained, his soul shredded, his mind blown.

He was wrecked.

And he was a new man.

CHAPTER FIVE

CHRISTIAN WOKE up slowly, groggy as hell. Which was odd. He hadn't had much to drink last night, but he felt hungover. Maybe not odd. He'd gotten drunk as hell on Stone Jackson. For the first time in his entire life, he felt well and truly understood—body, heart, and mind. He and Stone were simpatico unlike anything he'd ever experienced before. In some ways, they were so much alike it was eerie. But in others, they were different enough to create a fascinating tension between them.

The man had a gift for stripping away the layers of his mental self-defenses, laying him bare, and then devouring him whole. And yet he felt as if Stone had given himself back in return. A fair trade. A soul for a soul.

The sex hadn't been that adventurous, truth be told. But Christ, it had been intense.

No wonder he felt so exhausted this morning, like he'd run a couple of Iron Man triathlons last night. It felt so damned good to just lie here, utterly relaxed, the cool air-conditioning blowing across his naked skin, his limbs tangled with Stone's until he wasn't sure where he ended and Stone began.

A cell phone rang, and Stone jolted awake.

"Relax. It's mine," Christian murmured. He rolled across Stone's chest, pinning him down and enjoying the feel of chest hair against his stomach as he reached for the far nightstand. Stone was rousing slowly. Last night knocked him out too, huh? Awesome.

He put the device to his ear. "What's up, Travis?"

The security man was as frantic as he'd ever heard him. "He's gone."

Christian lurched and turned to sit on the edge of the bed, and Stone stared up at him in gathering alarm. "What do you mean, gone?"

That brought Stone bolt upright beside him.

Tucker talked in a rush. "Gone. No sign of Jack or Chesty. Suite's empty. Poof. Disappeared."

Stone must have heard the ex-Marine, for he snatched Christian's phone out of his hand. "Don't touch anything. Don't move. We'll be there in sixty seconds."

Stone tossed the phone at him, snatched up his own cell phone, and dialed with one hand as he yanked on underwear, khaki slacks, and a black polo shirt.

Horror, hot and pure, poured over and into Christian, filling his eyes and clogging his throat. He'd taken one lousy night off the job and disaster had struck. He'd dared to steal a moment for himself, and fate was punishing him for it now. Son of a bitch.

"Martin, it's Stone. Senator Lacey has disappeared. Did he talk with Peregrine? Did my quitting trigger this? If so, I've got to help find the guy. Did he give Pere any idea where he might have gone? Or are we looking at a kidnapping?"

Sweet baby Jesus. Kidnapping? Christian's mind hadn't even gone there until Stone said it. Had Jack fallen prey to foul play? God knew, he had plenty of enemies. Or was this the work of whoever'd been threatening him?

Christian's mind spun off into all sorts of hideous scenarios while he yanked on his own clothes. How in the hell was he going to explain this to the public? Or should he cover it up until Jack was found? The wrong handling of this crisis could completely tank his career—

Not that his career was the priority, of course. The first order of business was to locate Jack. Rescue him if necessary, and make sure the man was returned safe and sound.

He glanced up in dismay at Stone. God, this could wreck Stone's career too. This was what the guy had been talking about when he said bodyguards had one failure in their entire career. Lose one principal on your watch, and you were finished.

He got it now. He and Stone were both *done* if they didn't fix this mess fast.

Which was the cherry on top of this sundae of suck.

"Talk to me about Chesty," Stone snapped at him as they threw on shoes and socks.

"Porn star. Been around the biz for a while. Professional on the set. Smarter than she looks. A sweet girl from all accounts. Apparently can deep throat a twelve-inch dick. Hence the career success."

"Not what I was going for, but okay. Is she the type to blackmail Jack? Participate in kidnapping him? Capable of violence?"

"As far as I know, no to all three." He stood up grimly. "But everybody's got their breaking points, don't they?"

Stone's gaze snapped up to his, dark and guilty. "Correct."

Apparently this was their breaking point. Both of them were castigating themselves for leaving Jack to his own devices last night.

Swearing under his breath, Christian raced for the door. The phone conversation with Martin—likely Martin Wylde, cofounder of Wild Cards—wound down.

Stone was on his heels. "My boss says Lacey was shockingly *un*concerned at this morning's cancellation of the security contract. Bad news is he said nothing about leaving Miami. Good news is the Wild Cards, Inc. computer guys have picked up no chatter to indicate that a kidnapper might have taken him."

"You have people who would find something like that?"

"Oh hell, yes. We put a close watch on every client. Regular web, deep web, and dark web."

"What's the dark web?"

"The places the really bad actors hang out and not the wannabe posers."

"I'm sorry about this—" he started.

"Save it, Christian. Not your fault the bastard disappeared. I'm the one who quit the job and left the man underprotected."

"Jack doesn't let Tucker stay in his suite when he's got a girl with him. He surely wouldn't have let you stay with them last night."

"If we'd had any idea that a kidnapping was on the table, Travis and I could have stood guard outside the door."

"Jack wouldn't have allowed it. I guarantee it."

"You can't know that."

"I know my boss."

They raced down the long hall to Lacey's suite, and Christian let them in with his key. Stone stopped just inside, presumably to prevent the disturbance of any evidence. Tucker was standing still in the doorway to the senator's bedroom and didn't move when they came in. Oh, right.

Stone had told him to stay still. The man could by God follow an order. Christian squeezed in behind Stone and closed the door.

"What have you got?" Stone asked Tucker from his position.

"They had sex in the bed. His cell phone and wallet are gone. Toothbrush and razor still in the bathroom. No clothes missing. Nothing out of place. No sign whatsoever of a struggle."

"His laptop?" Christian asked.

Tucker glanced over his shoulder into the bedroom. "Don't see it."

"May I look around the living room for it if I don't touch anything?" Christian asked Stone.

"Yeah. You can move now, Tucker. And touch whatever you want. There won't be any fingerprints or hairs lying around. If he was in fact kidnapped, pros did it."

"How can you tell?" Christian asked as he moved into the large room, lifting newspapers and stacks of briefing papers, hunting for any sign of the senator's thin, brushed-aluminum laptop.

"No struggle. Tucker knows his shit. If nothing's out of place, then nothing's out of place. Lacey either walked out of here or was carried out carefully by a pro."

Christian spotted the computer under a briefing about an upcoming vote in the Senate Commerce Committee pertaining to imports of Cuban sugar. "He didn't take his laptop with him. Either he wasn't planning on working, or whoever took him didn't care about his personal files." He looked over at Tucker. "Have you called Jill yet?"

"And told her what? Her husband and his porn-star girlfriend have gone missing?"

Christian winced. He really liked Jill. He and Tucker both did their best to shield her from the worst of her husband's excesses. This was a freaking nightmare. The moment he told Jill he'd lost her husband, she was going to fire his ass. And he would completely deserve it. Heart heavy, he pulled out his cell phone.

STONE WATCHED resignation settle on Christian's features. He had to give the man credit. He was willing to man up and face the consequences of what he believed to be his mistake.

"Not so fast," he murmured, putting a hand over Christian's phone. "Give Travis and me a little while to find out what we can." He knew from bitter military experience that the more information you could give a loved one about how their family member had disappeared or met their demise, the better it went. Questions and unknowns ate at a person's soul like nothing else.

Christian nodded reluctantly.

"Does hotel security have anything on his departure?" Stone asked Tucker.

"Nope," the security man replied. "They were the first people I called. The Imperium's surveillance is so porous that he slipped right through it."

Hell, Lacey had been sitting in this very room, listening, when he'd complained to Tucker about how easy it would be to slip unseen out of the hotel by the stairwells. He didn't think the senator had been listening to his comments, but maybe he had been, after all.

"Have you tracked the GPS in his cell phone?" he asked next.

Tucker shook his head. "Not yet. I haven't called the police to ask them to locate his phone."

Stone snorted. "It doesn't take the police to track a phone if you have the right contacts."

He made a quick call to a friend who owed him a favor. After a short pause, the guy announced that Lacey's phone was turned off. Of course, it was. Either the kidnappers knew not to make such a rookie mistake, or else Jack didn't want to be found.

Frankly, he favored the theory that the bastard had taken off with his porn star and was getting a kick out of fucking with his staff.

"Thanks, man," Stone muttered to the contact. He reported to Tucker and Christian, "No joy on the cell phone's location. It's turned off and its locator function is deactivated." He thought for a minute. "Did any of the emails or letters Lacey's received threaten a kidnapping?"

Tucker answered, "Negative. They were all death threats."

The Wild Cards analysts had already combed through the letters at the start of this job and the threats had mostly revolved around shooting Lacey. Which was a specific threat and specifically not kidnapping. A stalker could always change their end goal, but it would be unusual.

Stone had been briefed to be ready for a direct assault—shooters were likely to barge into a public space, guns blazing, and try to make a big, public statement. A sophisticated and unseen kidnapping was not the letter writer's likely MO.

Frowning, he widened the net of possibilities they had to consider. "The girlfriend, Chesty," he said abruptly. "Anyone got a real name, address, or cell phone number on her?"

Tucker shook his head. "She legally changed her name. I have no idea what her birth name was."

Stone made another call. "Martin, it's me again. I need an original birth name, address, phone number, anything you can get me on a porn star who goes by the name Chesty Hills." A pause. Then dryly, "No, I'm not going over to the straight side of the force. I have to find her ASAP. We think Jack Lacey may be with her."

Christian smiled faintly, but the expression disappeared so fast Stone wasn't sure he'd seen it.

On top of his acute anxiety over his boss's disappearance, the guy was clearly experiencing severe morning-after regret. He knew the feeling. His life was all about keeping moving, staying in motion, never letting anything bad catch up with him.

Last night had been an anomaly. He'd actually slowed down. Physically and emotionally, he'd come to rest in Christian's arms. He'd been so damned tired of the rat race, and it had felt so good just to stop. To be in one place, one headspace for a few hours. And not to be alone.

He yanked his attention back to the crisis at hand. If Jack had taken off for shits and grins without telling Travis where he'd gone, Stone was going to break him in half, client or not. Christian and Travis worked their asses off for Jack Lacey. He owed them both better.

A voice in his ear announced, "I found your porn star. And may I say she's, umm, improbable? Are those things real?"

"I have no idea," Stone snapped.

"Hey, if you're gonna go straight, I say go big, mate. You ready to copy some information?"

Stone picked up a pen and yanked a piece of hotel stationery out of a drawer. As Martin gave a name, address, and phone number, he scribbled it all down. "Got it. And I'm not dating her. The client is, fuck you very much."

"The married senator? What a naughty, naughty boy."

Huh. That was one way to describe it.

Stone disconnected and punched Chesty's phone number into his cell. "Service provider says the device is not turned on."

Christian blurted, "So she got grabbed too?"

"We'll have to swing by her place to be sure she and Jack aren't just drunk or passed out there before I definitively declare this a missing person scenario."

"Don't the police want someone to be missing for a couple of days before they'll take any official action?" Christian asked nervously.

"There are ways around that. Particularly for a VIP," Stone answered. They made eye contact, and he tried to send a silent message of reassurance to Christian. They would figure this out. And if Jack was still alive, they would get him back in one piece.

Tucker headed for the door. "I'll drive," he declared.

The three men raced to the parking garage and piled into the SUV. Tucker drove west through Miami to the Doral address where Chesty lived under her birth name, Chelsea Jenkins.

The address belonged to a modest, newly built cottage that was about as far from porn star as Stone could have imagined. He would bet a million bucks the neighbors didn't know how Miss Jenkins made her living.

A quick walk around the house to bang on all the doors and peer in all the windows made it abundantly clear that Chesty and Jack Lacey were not in residence.

The trio climbed back into the SUV, and Tucker spoke grimly. "I've got no training in kidnapping recovery. This is out of my league. Now what? Call the FBI?"

Stone shrugged. "I'm not technically on this assignment anymore. Wild Cards, Inc. pulled its contract early this morning and refunded Lacey's money."

"When did that happen?" Tucker demanded.

"Last night after Jack disappeared at the party, I called my boss. He agreed to terminate our services for the senator."

"Why?"

Stone threw a withering look at Travis and didn't bother to answer.

"Yeah, I know," Tucker grumbled. "He's an asshole. But my kid is one semester from done with college, and then I won't need this lousy paycheck. I can tell Jack Lacey to fuck off, and I can retire."

Stone replied, "I've worked for plenty of assholes. But Lacey's complete unwillingness to listen to any advice from me or follow any instructions whatsoever is what caused the Wild Cards to pull the contract. The man didn't give a damn that someone was threatening his life. You know as well as I do that he's a sitting duck if there really is someone out there with serious intent to kill him."

"More like a dead duck," Christian corrected from the back seat.

"It's time to call the police," Stone said grimly.

Tucker glanced at Christian in the rearview mirror. "You're the slick talker. You call the police."

"I think we'd better call Mrs. Lacey first. If this thing goes public, I don't want her blindsided."

Stone nodded. "Good idea. I'd rather have her on our side than trying to crucify us."

Christian looked reluctant as he placed the call to the senator's wife and put her on speakerphone. "Good morning, Mrs. Lacey. How's Texas?"

"Do you know why there's no sinning in Texas during the summer, Christian?"

"Why, ma'am?"

"Because Satan himself would rather stay in hell than come to Texas at this time of year." Stone smiled as the woman asked, "What can I do for you this morning, Christian? It's a little early in the day for Jack to have messed up already."

Stone's eyebrows rose. The lady knew her husband well.

"I'm afraid you're being optimistic, ma'am. You haven't by any chance heard from him in the past twelve hours or so, have you?"

"No. Why?" The keen intelligence Christian had mentioned before had obviously kicked in, and her voice was sharp with concern, or maybe suspicion. He didn't know her well enough to read that tone. Either way, she was definitely not happy.

Christian winced, obviously taking her tone personally. Had the two of them been alone in the vehicle, Stone would have been inclined to give the guy a supportive smile.

Christian said heavily, "Jack has disappeared from his hotel room, ma'am. There's no sign of a struggle and no ransom demand to indicate there was any foul play. However, we also can't rule it out."

"What about that fancy security firm he hired? How did they lose him? Does this have anything to do with those death threats he's been getting?"

"I'm sure Jack is fine. But, the security firm terminated the contract, effective late last night. Jack was... singularly uncooperative... with them, and they felt they couldn't guarantee his safety. Ethically they felt obliged to pull themselves off his security detail."

Stone noted that Christian neatly dodged the question of whether or not Jack had been kidnapped or worse.

Jill swore rather more saltily than one would expect of a genteel Southern woman, and Stone grinned reluctantly.

She asked tartly, "Has the Wild Cards' man left Miami yet?"

"No, ma'am. He's here with me now."

"Hire him to work for me. I need him to find Jack and keep me from killing him."

Christian looked over at Stone questioningly, but he wasn't prepared to answer Christian's silent question until he spoke with his boss again. Stone held out his hand and rocked it back and forth, indicating that maybe he would take the job and maybe not.

Jill Lacey was speaking again. Her tone of voice was leaning sharply toward anger now. "For God's sake, Christian. You have to keep this whole thing from turning into a media circus. The election is in just under a year. He can't afford any scandals between now and then."

Stone stared down at the phone and up at Christian, silently asking, *Are you going to tell her?*

Christian sighed.

"Speaking of which, ma'am...." Christian trailed off, obviously unsure of how to tell her delicately about Chesty.

"Jiminy H. Christmas. There's a woman involved, isn't there?" she asked baldly.

Give the woman full marks for knowing her husband.

Christian visibly winced. "Uhh, there might be, ma'am."

"Don't pussyfoot around with me, Christian Chatsworth-Brandeis. I know my husband. How bad is it this time?"

This time? Okay. Jill Lacey really had her spouse's number.

"She's a porn star, ma'am. Famous enough that the media would run with it. I'm afraid they'll have a field day with the story."

"Tell your man from Wild Cards to prepare a quiet plan to dispose of Jack's body, just in case."

He couldn't tell if she was being sarcastic or not. He was willing to cross a lot of lines in the performance of his job, but hiding a body was not one of them. Alarm sluiced through him.

She continued, "And tell your fancy security man he'd better find Jack before I do. Because I am going to pull his scrotum over his head and feed his balls to him one by one before I choke him to death."

"Got it, ma'am. Scrotum. Balls. Choking. Check."

Christian's dry comment made her laugh enough to break the tension a little.

"We'll find him for you. Don't you worry, Mrs. Lacey."

"I trust you completely to handle this with speed and discretion, Christian. It goes without saying that there will be no police or FBI. Cops gossip like old women, and we can't afford a leak to the media. If Jack doesn't get the infusion of cash he's supposed to be paid for this Florida publicity junket, he's going to have to suspend his campaign."

Stone was startled. He'd had no idea the senator's campaign was in such dire financial straits. No wonder Christian was stressed-out.

"What about his scheduled appearances specifically over the next several days, ma'am?" Christian was asking.

"We can't cancel them. Find Jack and make him by golly appear. Make it clear to him that he has *got* to go to every scheduled appearance. Each one represents a *large* and *vital* campaign donation."

"But, ma'am." A pause. "He's not here. I can't make him materialize out of thin air."

"You'll figure out something, Christian. You always do."

Right. Because Christian could fix anything apparently. Stone did not envy the guy this particular toxic-waste cleanup. This mess might be too big even for him to manage. He glanced into the back seat at Christian, who looked nonplussed. What the hell did Jill expect the guy to do anyway?

Christian replied blankly, "I'll do my best, ma'am."

Brave man.

Christian disconnected the call and stared off into space, either thinking hard or just completely in shock. An urge to crawl into the back seat, gather Christian in his arms, and hug it out until the guy relaxed and breathed a little, came over Stone. Unfortunately, they both needed to be on their A game at the moment and not miss some crucial detail in figuring out what the hell had happened to Lacey.

At length Christian roused himself in the back seat to ask, "So. Stone. Any chance I can interest you and your employer in a new client with a missing husband she needs found very, very quietly?"

CHAPTER SIX

STONE HAD no idea if Wild Cards, Inc. even took missing persons cases. "Let me call my bosses. I think this one will take both Martin's and Pere's sign-off."

He called the cofounders of the firm, got them on a conference line, and filled them in briefly.

"What's your gut telling you about this one?" Pere asked him grimly. "Did this guy take a runner with his porn star?"

"That's my belief, sir. He has hooked up with her before apparently. I don't think she's a one-night stand gone wrong."

"Can you find him?"

"He's not that smart. I can find him." He added grimly, "But it's a hell of a risk for you to take with your company's reputation."

"We are aware of that, thank you," Martin replied wryly. "Pass the phone to the senator's aide, Mr. Chatsworth-Brandeis."

It took a while, off speakerphone, for Christian to talk the owners of Wild Cards into taking the job. They weren't happy at the prospect of having to deal with Jack Lacey in any capacity. Eventually, for an exorbitant fee, Stone was back on the job, this time working for Jill Lacey.

"Thank God," Christian muttered as he disconnected the overseas call. He looked grimly at Stone. "You're up, slugger. Find my boss."

"Here's the thing. If this is an actual abduction, we've got nothing, and the kidnappers have a nearly insurmountable head start. We would have to sit tight and wait for a ransom demand."

Christian frowned.

"So," Stone continued, "we're going to operate for now on the assumption that Jack was not kidnapped and that he and Chesty took off of their own free will and are tucked away somewhere private, having a good old time."

He pulled his pistol out of its holster and reversed it in his hand, holding it out butt first to Christian.

"What are you doing?" Christian asked sharply.

"Handing you my weapon."

"I don't want it!"

"If I pull a B and E in Chesty's house while armed, it's a third-degree felony. If I'm not armed when I do it, it's only a second-degree misdemeanor. Take the gun."

"Whoa. Wait. As in breaking and entering? You're going to break into her house?"

"As in taking a look around inside for any leads and not disturbing anything?" Stone replied. "That would be correct."

Christian winced. "Technically, I can't let you do this."

"Take a nap and don't watch. This is what Mrs. Lacey is paying all that money for."

Christian subsided but he looked unhappy. It was sexy as all get-out the way he glared at Stone, promising hell to pay later. Not that Stone anticipated having a minute alone with him until the senator was located. Dammit.

But he would love to see how Christian punished him for being bad. The idea sent a ripple of delight up his spine and a tremor of trepidation down it. For a pretty man, Christian could still pull quite the grim scowl.

Stone said to Christian, "If it makes you feel better, I don't like having to do stuff like this either. It's why both my bosses and I are so reluctant to work this job."

He hopped out of the SUV, ignoring the partial erection filling his slacks, and jogged around to the back of the quaint house.

As break-ins went, this one was as straightforward as they came. Chesty's backdoor lock was ridiculously inadequate. He could've opened it with a paper clip. Literally.

He checked the sink: no dirty dishes. He opened the refrigerator: no milk. No fruit or fresh vegetables either. Nothing that would spoil quickly. Either Chesty didn't cook at all, or she was an extremely neat person who ate no healthy food, or she'd been planning to be out of town for a while.

A quick look around the house revealed that all the laundry was done and key toiletries missing from the bathroom. She'd definitely buttoned up her house to go out of town. But when? And why?

A blinking light on her answering machine shed more light on the situation. "Chelsea, it's Bob. Pick up the damned phone. You missed *another* audition yesterday. You've got to quit doing this. You're going to get a reputation for being a flake, and you can forget getting decent-paying roles once that happens. There are a hundred girls hotter than you, younger than you, and kinkier than you just waiting to take your place in the adult-film industry. So get off your ass and call me, or I swear, I'll dump you as a client."

Stone guessed that ruled out Chesty being gone on location at a film set. And she'd been up to something yesterday during the day that had been important enough to miss an audition over.

There was no more to see in the house. He headed back outside, locking the door behind himself. He strolled back to the car. Running people drew attention, but walking people who looked unconcerned and acted as if they belonged in a place rarely drew any.

He climbed back in the vehicle and reported his findings to the other men.

Christian frowned. "So if she was planning to be out of town for a while already, did she kidnap Jack?"

An interesting theory. He replied, "She would be a rocket scientist among porn stars to plan a kidnapping in advance, manage to catch Jack's eye at that party among all the other professional talent working the joint, and then to successfully disappear with him."

Tucker added, "Not to mention Jack left the hotel without a fight. If she was, in fact, abducting him, she tricked him into walking out under his own power."

Stone replied, "You're assuming she didn't drug him and call in an associate to carry him out."

"As in she had an accomplice?" Tucker exclaimed.

"I have no reason to suspect that, but neither do I have a reason to rule it out."

Tucker swore as he drove. "Why didn't she kidnap him back in California, then? They actually went back to her hotel for most of their assignations. Why not snatch him then?"

Stone shrugged. "Maybe it was a test run to see if she could lure him out. Or just a preliminary interaction to see if she could make contact with him."

Tucker observed, "That makes it sound like spies grabbed him."

Stone replied, "I'm not ruling anything or anyone out at this point."

They drove in silence back toward South Beach.

He asked, "You two know your boss better than I do. Is he gullible enough to be trapped by a woman and/or ruled by his dick?"

Both men snorted.

"Oh, hell yes," Christian answered.

Okay, then. Jack Lacey was stupid enough to be hoodwinked, and he was addicted enough to sex to let it ruin his life. Part of him wanted to let this jerk go down in flames and not get found in time to avoid a scandal.

But one look at Christian's stricken, pale face and Stone cursed under his breath. Fine. He'd find the damned senator. If not for Jack's wife, then for his own lover.

"Where to now?" Tucker asked.

They had to find a trail. No matter how faint or how cold. They needed a starting place from which to move forward. He answered, "Back to the hotel. If they snuck out, they probably didn't walk to their final destination. Let's check out the taxis that worked the hotel last night."

The next several hours were tedious and frustrating as they combed through hotel security camera footage. Eventually Christian pointed at the video monitor. "There. That's him."

Stone leaned down over his shoulder to peer at the grainy image. "The guy in the baseball cap?"

"I'd know his walk anywhere."

Stone watched a nondescript sedan pull up at the curb in front of the senator. Chesty stepped into the camera frame briefly before sliding into the back seat of the car. Baseball Cap followed her, never showing his face to the camera. But the height and build were right for Lacey.

"That looks like a private car, not a taxi," Christian commented. "Unless it's a rideshare vehicle."

"Possible. Or, it could be Chesty's accomplice driving."

Christian swore quietly.

Stone commented, "That's the first time I've seen Jack and Chesty together when she hasn't been crawling all over him. If anything, their body language is somewhat formal. What's up with that?"

Christian shrugged. "Your guess is as good as mine."

He said encouragingly, "The good news is Jack and Chesty weren't being herded into the vehicle at gunpoint. I think we can safely say Jack entered that vehicle voluntarily. Either we're not looking at a kidnapping, or he hadn't figured out what was happening yet."

"What the hell was he thinking?" Christian burst out.

Stone grunted. "Did you get a good look at her? I don't think thought has much to do with it."

They made brief eye contact, and Christian looked away guiltily. Yeah. Neither one of them was in a position to cast stones at Jack Lacey for thinking with his dick last night.

It took a bit of calling around to figure out that the owner of the vehicle registered to the license plate in the video did, indeed, drive part-time for a ride-sharing service.

After that, it took only a quick call to the Wild Cards, Inc. operation center to yield the destination to which the Uber driver had delivered the senator and Chesty. Stone had no idea how the guys at the company obtained the information, and he didn't ask. He reported the destination tersely to Christian. "They were taken to the South Miami Marina."

"Oh God. What do you want to bet he's gotten on a party boat with a bunch of women and booze?" Christian groaned. "The press will get ahold of this for sure. How soon can you get him back here, Stone?"

"Depends on where he is. If they're fucking their way through the Florida Keys, pretty fast. A quick call to the Coast Guard, and they'll have him on a helicopter back to Miami in a few hours."

"And if they're not in the Keys?"

Stone shrugged. "If he's gone outside of US jurisdiction, it could take longer."

"How much longer?"

"Days or weeks. Depends on how willing he is to come back to America."

Christian groaned. "He's got a major appearance at a Latin American Chamber of Commerce event the day after tomorrow. Massive campaign donations will come from it. You've got to get him back in time for it!"

"I'll do my best. Let's head down to the marina and find out what boat he's on and where it's headed."

It turned out not to be that easy, however. Stone had to more or less threaten the marina manager's life before the name of the yacht—the *Wrastle Castle*—was forthcoming. As for its intended destination, the beleaguered manager disappeared into a back office to get the navigation plan.

"Do you always bully people into giving you what you want?" Christian muttered.

"Do you want to find your boss or not?" Stone muttered back. "Mrs. Lacey didn't hire me to be nice. She hired me to get results."

"Yes, but your tactics are making enemies for my employer."

"Do you care?"

"In this case, not particularly. Jack created this mess. He can deal with the fallout. But in general, I don't approve of such tactics." Christian tilted his head, considering him. "You don't stick around long enough after a job to face the consequences of your actions, though, do you?"

"What the hell is that supposed to mean?"

"You cause havoc and then split. You move on and leave behind a mess for other people to clean up."

"Is this about you and me?" Stone demanded under his breath, glancing cautiously at Tucker, who was across the room, staring out a big window at the marina.

"No." A pause. "Yes." Another pause. "Maybe."

"Take pot shots at me later," Stone bit out. "Right now, we need to find Jack."

"That wasn't a—"

The marina manager stepped out of his office.

"*Later.*"

CHRISTIAN WINCED. Stone had a point. The first priority was to find Jack Lacey. Not to mention that he wasn't in the habit of dragging personal crap into the office either. His ambitious family had taught him that lesson at an early age—long before they realized their golden-haired scion was gay and the family name irrevocably disgraced.

The marina manager held out several sheets of paper, looking none too happy about it.

Christian said soothingly, "Thank you so much for your help. I can't tell you how much we appreciate it."

The guy seemed to thaw a little, at least until the man glanced over at Stone and his gaze hardened once more.

Sigh. He'd tried to do damage control. But like Jack, Stone would have to stew in his own mess, he supposed. In some ways, the two men were a lot alike. Both stubborn and too damned good-looking for their own good.

Thankfully, that was where the similarities ended. Stone had a moral compass that Jack had no concept of.

"Oh, for the love of God. Check out your boss's destination," Stone blurted.

Christian took the float plan with grave trepidation and glanced through it. "Barbados?" he squawked. *Crap, crap, crap.* Totally not under US jurisdiction. "How long will it take them to sail down there?"

The marina manager supplied helpfully, "On the *Wrastle Castle*? Four or five days."

"Four. Or five," Christian repeated blankly.

"You okay?" Stone asked.

"Hell to the no, I'm not okay," he burst out. "Jack Lacey has to make a campaign appearance in two days. Hell, the casino night is in five days! He'll barely make it back in time if we're lucky!"

Stone commented gently, "You're assuming that they'll go directly to Barbados and won't stop at any other ports of call along the way. Or sail in circles for the hell of it."

"I'm dead," Christian announced, throwing up his hands. "Finished."

"C'mon. It can't be that bad," Stone said sympathetically. "Let's go back to the hotel. We'll figure something out."

"There's nothing to figure out. Jack has finally managed to destroy his career, and he's going to take me and a bunch of other people down with him."

He was literally sick to his stomach. He knew Jack was a jerk, but he'd never realized how selfish a jerk the guy ultimately was.

He'd been let down by so many people in his life. This one felt special, though, in a bad way. He wasn't so much worried for himself as he was all the other people who depended on Jack. He had a law degree to fall back on, if push came to shove, and he had to give up his hopes for a job at the Department of Justice. He would land on his feet, but what about the other aides and staffers? Jack's wife? Heck, his constituents?

A sense of having personally failed them all landed on him, weighing him down until he could hardly walk.

Stone and Tucker headed back to the SUV while Christian followed behind. He ought to be furious, but all he felt was numb. Jack had really gone and done it this time. Not only could he kiss reelection goodbye, but the bastard was going to end up in front of the Senate Ethics Committee over this stunt. His wife was going to be forced to divorce him. And the aide who let him slip so badly off the leash would be persona non grata in extremis in Washington, DC.

A plan. He had to come up with a plan. There had to be a way out of this crisis. But for the life of him, he didn't see it. "Can we still send the Coast Guard after him? In a ship or something?"

"By now, the *Wrastle Castle* is in international waters. The US Coast Guard has no jurisdiction."

"What about the Navy?"

"It's not their job to scrape senators off party boats. And it would go public for sure. Naval vessels have big crews and Wi-Fi."

He said softly, "Fuck."

Stone stopped just outside the SUV and turned to stare at him with concern plain on his face. "Can you cancel the Chamber of Commerce thing?"

"You have no idea how hard I had to work to schedule the appearance in the first place. After last year's vote on immigration, Jack's been in the doghouse with every pro-immigration group in this hemisphere. He's giving a speech day after tomorrow to announce his support for the newest round of immigration reform."

"He's flip-flopping on the issue?" Stone asked in surprise.

"Not exactly. It's more like he's moving ninety degrees. I finally convinced him he's on the wrong side of the polling numbers and he has to move off his personal beliefs if he wants to get reelected."

"It doesn't look to me like the guy has much interest in keeping his job."

He sighed. "Jill gets as much or more good work done than he does. She's pushed him to run for reelection so she can keep doing her charity work."

"Can't she do that as the wife of a retired senator?"

"It's all about power in Washington. She's got power if Jack's in office. She's an afterthought once he loses."

"Too bad he's hosing her over too, with this little adventure of his," Stone commented.

Christian slammed both palms down on the side of the vehicle. A satisfying sting exploded in his hands. "There has to be something I can do!"

"Mind if I offer a little advice?" Stone asked more gently than Christian would have expected out of a hardened soldier.

"I'm open to any suggestions."

"It's going to sound stupid, but breathe for a minute. Don't think about anything else. Concentrate on your breath. In and out. Long and slow. Clears the mind."

He took Stone's advice, inhaling and exhaling in big, ultimately calming, breaths.

He nodded at Stone to indicate that he was better. More in control, if not thinking more clearly.

They climbed in the back of the SUV, and Tucker headed back to the hotel.

Stone murmured, "We'll figure it out. There's a solution to this mess."

"But what?" Christian ground out.

"We'll know it when we think of it. We just haven't thought of it yet."

He smiled a little at that logic. Stone reached across the back seat and surprised him by squeezing his hand. "You're not alone, and this mess isn't your fault. Keep repeating that until you believe it, okay?"

He nodded and gave a grateful squeeze back.

Oddly, it was the warmth and strength of Stone's callused hand clasping his that steadied him more than anything. The man was smart, competent, and in his corner. That had to count for something.

Tucker parked the SUV in the hotel garage and they exited the vehicle.

Stone commented, "Short of coming up with a doppelgänger for Jack, the outcome of this episode is inevitable. Wild Cards, Inc. will do what it can to help you and Mrs. Lacey with damage control. You have my word on that."

"Thanks."

They entered the elevator in heavy silence. "Hell, I might even consider hiring a body double for the bastard if I could find—" He broke off, staring at Stone.

"What?"

He looked up at the camera mounted in the corner of the elevator and muttered without moving his lips, "In the room."

Obviously aware of the sudden cloak-and-dagger turn of conversation, Stone did his full security he-man sweep of the hallway before he would let Christian or Tucker out. Which was actually kind of sweet. It was nice for a change to feel like someone else was looking out for him.

The three men hustled down the hallway to Lacey's suite, and Stone spun to face him the minute the door closed. "What's up?"

"I need a body double for Jack Lacey, and you bear a more than passing resemblance to him."

"Emphasis on passing," Stone blurted in alarm. "I didn't sign up to impersonate your boss."

"But you said it yourself. You'll do whatever it takes to get the job done."

"My *job* is to find Jack Lacey and get his ass back here quietly."

"I'm desperate, Stone."

"There's another solution—get him back."

"And if we don't? Surely you, of all people, understand my need to have a contingency plan in my back pocket."

Stone huffed. "Yes. I do. But I couldn't possibly—"

He cut Stone off before the guy could talk him out of the notion of impersonating Jack. "You owe me," he blurted in desperation. He lowered his voice so Tucker, in the second bedroom, couldn't hear him. "If we hadn't been busy making love all night, we could've stopped Jack from taking off."

"Doubtful. No way would he have let us stay in his suite while he screwed Chesty, and he was clear on the first day I arrived that he didn't want a guard stationed outside his front door."

"*Please* do this. For me. Because you give a damn about me." The words were out of his mouth before Christian could stop them. He knew—he *knew*—that his night with Stone had been a onetime deal. He had *no* business invoking personal feelings between them and certainly not in the name of professional arm twisting.

Stone stared at him. The silence that stretched out between them was painful, damning him for going to that taboo and forbidden place of feelings.

But then Stone shocked him by mumbling, "I wouldn't have the slightest idea what to do. I'm not an actor."

Hope flared like an arc welder in his chest. "I can teach you. Hell, I tell the man what to say all the time anyway. His clothes are here. I'm sure they'd fit you. Maybe a little alteration to make room for your biceps...." He continued in a rush, "For the love of God, say yes. I know I have no right to ask this of you. But you'd be saving my life and the jobs of everyone who works for Jack."

Stone said low, "I would do this for you and nobody else."

"Say you'll do it for me. Everything I've worked for. My career. My reputation—" He broke off. His respectability. Proving to his family that he wasn't a failure. He wasn't exaggerating. *Everything* about his life hung in the balance.

He met Stone's doubtful gaze. In the play of their expressions, an entire silent conversation took place rapidly. Awareness of what was on the line. His desperation. Stone's awareness that this was going to take their relationship to a new and more personal level. His acceptance of everything that entailed. The fact that they were entering into a dangerous game together with only each other to rely on. A flare of attraction between them at the idea of being a team against the world.

Stone let out a long, unhappy sigh. "Look. I'm happy to do a favor—even this favor—for you. But I have a bad feeling about this."

Christian threw his arms around Stone and laid a big, grateful kiss on his surprised mouth. Realizing belatedly what he'd done, he stumbled back abruptly. "Jesus. I'm sorry. That was out of line."

"I dunno. I'm thinking you're going to owe me some serious sexual favors for this."

Christian stared. Stone said it straight-faced. He still was interested in a physical relationship? Really? Well, son of a bitch. "Sexual favors later. Right now we've got work to do."

CHAPTER SEVEN

STONE LOOKED into the mirror in shock. His longish hair had been shorn off and trimmed into a short, conservative side part to match Jack Lacey's. The barber who'd come up to the suite had close shaved him with a straight razor as well. Stone fingered his smooth cheeks, familiarizing himself with their foreign texture as the guy packed up and left.

He commented to Christian, who looked on, grinning, "I look younger than him."

"I've got a stage makeup artist coming up in a few minutes. She'll fix that."

"Makeup?" Stone echoed in dismay.

Christian patted his cheek, crooning, "There, there, Stone. Your macho mojo will still be in place even if you have to wear a few cosmetics."

Stone muttered *sotto voce*, "Payback's a bitch."

Christian grinned and let a sexy dare glint in his gaze for a moment. And answering heat flashed through Stone's gut.

Christian commented, "I'm sure I'll cause you enough headaches in the next two days to give you a few extra worry lines. Besides, everyone knows that television ages a person. People will be able to comment on how young and healthy you look in the flesh. Or you can tell them Miami has been good to you."

"It was. Until you came up with this cockamamie idea."

"Cockamamie? Wow. You really did grow up on a farm, didn't you?"

"Screw you, preppie boy."

"Anytime, cow pie."

"Oh, you did not just go there—" Stone started, rising out of the chair threateningly.

Grinning, Christian interrupted. "Let's go pick out a few suits for you." He led the way to the senator's bedroom to raid the closet.

"This feels weird," Stone announced. "Like I'm stealing his life."

"You're not getting cold feet on me, are you, Mr. Big Bad Soldier? Do I have to double dog dare you to do this?"

His natural urge to accept a dare surged forward. The brilliant bastard was playing him, and they both knew it. He scowled back at Christian's triumphant grin.

"Try this one." Christian held out a conservative, charcoal summer-wool suit. "It's one of the suits Jack wears when Tucker insists on a Kevlar vest."

"Jack has to wear bulletproof vests? Are death threats that frequent for him? Is that why he wouldn't take this one seriously?"

"To take your questions in order, Tucker orders them as a standard precaution when we're touring high-crime areas. Death threats are common enough for high-profile politicians but not usually as persistent and psychotic as this one has been. And last, I have no idea why Jack refused to believe Tucker or you when you tried to tell him his life was in real danger."

Stone stripped off his own shirt and dropped his pants, aware of Christian staring appreciatively at him. "Fantasizing about doing the senator?" he quipped.

"You do realize that's twisted as fuck, right?"

Stone shrugged. "Who knows if you have daddy issues or something weird?"

"I'm sure I do have some daddy issues. My father doesn't approve of my life choices," he said, adding air quotes with his fingers, "but I emphatically don't want to sleep with him."

Stone threw up his hands in surrender. "I was making a joke. In a lame attempt to change the subject, let me ask you this. Do you find older men attractive?"

"I don't know. How old are you?"

A laugh burst out of his chest. "Ouch. I'm thirty-five. Damn. You're ready for the retirement home, old man."

"How old are you? Law school plus a bit would make you, what? Thirty?"

"Thirty-one."

Stone shrugged into a crisply starched white shirt and tucked it in. He gave the pants, which were rather too loose on his lean hips, an upward tug. "Do I look hot in this monkey suit?" he quipped.

"Do you seriously think I'm shallow enough to like a guy solely because of how he looks?" Christian retorted.

"I dunno." He finished tying on one of Jack's expensive silk ties. "Do I look like Jack?"

"Don't be an asshole. Wild horses couldn't drag me to Jack's bed, assuming he even swung that way."

"You really don't like him, do you?"

"That's an understatement."

"Do all his staffers feel that way about him?"

"Pretty much everyone who knows him hates him."

"Except for Chesty, of course."

Christian snorted. "Give her a week on that boat with him. She'll be out to kill him too."

Stone belted in the trousers to his hard, flat waist. "Not a terrible fit."

Christian held the suit jacket for him, and Stone slipped his arms into it. Christian's hands rested briefly on his broad shoulders and then fell away. But in that second of contact, heat had permeated the fabric and permeated his gut. His entire body felt hyperalert to the man standing behind him. Yeah, he was aware of Christian that way all the time too.

He flexed his arms and reached across his body. "A little tight across the shoulders."

"The tailor should be able to let that out some. Jack's suits are custom tailored, which means they have plenty of fabric left over in the seams for alterations."

"Is it necessary to mess up the guy's suits?"

"Do you want to be able to move your arms?"

Stone scowled. "What if the tailor and barber and makeup artist or whoever else you hire to pull off this makeover tell someone I'm not the senator?"

"It's a chance we're going to have to take."

As if on cue, a knock at the door turned out to be the tailor. Stone spent the next hour being poked, prodded, felt up, and otherwise groped as the tailor marked several suits and a half-dozen dress shirts for tailoring. The shoulders and sleeves needed letting out to accommodate his more athletic build.

"While you're at it," Stone commented to the tailor, "I need you to let out the left side seams of the jackets to accommodate a sidearm in a shoulder holster."

"You can't wear a gun as a senator!" Christian exclaimed.

"Watch me."

"I'm serious."

"So am I," Stone retorted. To the tailor he said tersely, "Do it."

The tailor looked back and forth between the glaring combatants, grabbed the suit coats, and fled the suite.

The door closed solidly, and Stone stalked over to where Christian leaned against the bedroom wall. "In case you'd forgotten, someone is trying to kill Jack Lacey." He planted a hand on the wall beside Christian's head and leaned in aggressively. "And thanks to your ingenious evil plan, *I'm* about to be Jack Lacey."

One side of Christian's mouth lifted in amusement. "Your usual intimidation tactics won't work on me, you know."

Stone stared. What intimidation—oh. He shoved away from the wall but didn't go so far as to step back. He was still close enough to smell Christian's expensive aftershave. He felt his resolve weakening in the face of the man's general gorgeousness and close proximity.

He sighed. "I need a weapon. And Jack's from Texas, for crying out loud. Nobody will think twice if the guy's packing a piece."

"That's why you've got Tucker."

He did the protecting. He wasn't the protected. He wouldn't even begin to know how to let someone else be responsible for his safety. The mere idea was giving him mental hives.

He resorted to asking, "Speaking of Travis, have you told him about this whackadoodle plan of yours?"

"Not yet. I thought I might test out the finished product on him and see how close a match you are."

He rolled his eyes. This was arguably the dumbest stunt he'd ever pulled. He had a sinking feeling that when this all went to hell—and it surely would—his ass was going to be grass right along with Jack's and Christian's.

He spun away from Christian and all that smoking-hot temptation. How was he supposed to focus on becoming Jack Lacey when all he wanted to do was take the senator's aide to bed?

Strong, soothing hands touched his waist. Slid around to the front, where his abdominal muscles contracted, and his dick expanded. A warm body pressed against his back as Christian leaned in. He felt Christian's cheek come to rest against his neck.

He let the comfort and commiseration the man was silently offering soak into his bones. It steadied him. Centered him.

In the bubble of calm that built around them, he was able to think clearly for a moment. Yes, this was a crazy plan. But it could work. Even if it didn't work, they could claim it was a protective measure to safeguard the senator, who was being threatened. He didn't know a damned thing about politics, but Christian was super smart. He would figure out a way to spin the whole thing to Jack's advantage.

It would be okay. With Christian supporting him, he could pull this off.

He laid his hands over Christian's in silent thanks for the man's reassurance. They stood like that for a minute, and he soaked up the unfamiliar and wholly lovely intimacy. This moment wasn't about raw sex. It was about more. About shared stress, about working together, facing down the world as a team. This would be what it felt like if they were in a real relationship with each other.

And he loved it.

Stunned, he went stock-still and absorbed that revelation.

Huh.

A relationship—at least a relationship with Christian—might not be that bad a thing after all. In fact, it might be kind of spectacular.

A knock on the door made them both jump apart guiltily.

He didn't like the sensation of feeling guilty and secretive about Christian. A completely unfamiliar urge to go public, to tell the world about the amazing man he'd found, came over him.

Whoa.

It was the makeup artist at the door. She was young and cool and seemed to think it was a great joke to make him up to look like Jack Lacey. She studied the eight-by-eleven glossy headshot of the senator that Christian handed her and then compared it to Stone's face for long enough that he started to feel squirmy.

Finally she announced, "I can do it. I can transform him"—she pointed at Stone—"into him." She waved the picture of Jack. "And I don't even think I'm going to need any prosthetics."

Thank God. He really didn't need bits of latex glued all over his face. This was going to be hard enough without trying to keep those from falling off at an inconvenient moment.

"Get comfy, big guy. This is going to take a while." She went to work with a triangular sponge, dabbing something all over his face.

"Mind you," she added, "I'll get faster at this the more times I apply the makeup."

"How long—" he started.

"Don't talk," she ordered absently, already engrossed in her work.

Christian piped up, "But you can listen to me. I need to bring you up to speed on all the stuff Jack would know."

Mentally he groaned.

Christian launched into a mind-numbing briefing on who was going to be at this Chamber of Commerce shindig tomorrow evening. He sounded as if he needed the distraction of work as much as Stone did. Had that embrace in the bedroom gotten to him too?

"You'll need to practice Jack's speech, of course. I'll go over it with you and show you how Jack pauses and breathes."

A speech? In front of people?

Aww, hell.

He could stand up to a hail of bullets and face down armed hostiles without even a hint of fear. But a crowd of people, all staring at him? Listening to him talk? Judging him? Bored to tears by him? Oh, God.

"Don't tell me," Christian said abruptly. "You don't like public speaking."

He broke the makeup artist's command for silence long enough to mutter, "Hate it."

Christian laughed. The bastard actually *laughed.* "Well, the good news is no one scheduled to attend this speech has ever met Jack in person. If you blow it completely, they'll be none the wiser that Jack is actually a damned fine speaker."

Great. He got to humiliate himself in public in addition to running around wearing makeup and another man's clothes.

True to his word, the tailor had the first suit back up to the suite in about an hour. Which was about when the makeup artist finished with her masterpiece. He hadn't been allowed to watch in a mirror as she did her transformation, but he could only imagine he looked like a clown.

How on earth one human being could wear so much makeup all at once, he had no idea.

Stone donned the newly tailored suit and stomped into a pair of Jack's cowboy boots, which, fortunately, fit him with only a little pinching in the toes. He jammed a cowboy hat on his head and scowled as Christian stepped back to observe the effect.

A slow smile spread on his lover's face. The kind of smile that needed to be kissed away and then put back for entirely different reasons—*focus, dammit!*

"Dude. You're a dead ringer for him," Christian declared.

The makeup artist stood beside Christian, smiling and nodding in agreement. She and Christian traded fist bumps.

"You have no idea how unhappy that makes me," Stone grunted back.

Christian grinned unrepentantly. "Hey, he's a handsome man. He performs very well among the middle-aged female demographic."

"He uses *sex appeal* to get votes?"

"Whatever works. Jack will do just about anything to get a vote, scruples be damned. He would flat-out buy votes if he thought he wouldn't get caught."

"My impression of him was that he would rob a bank if he thought he wouldn't get caught," Stone snorted.

"He can be a wee bit… ethically challenged," Christian allowed.

"Is the pope a wee bit Catholic?" Stone snorted. "You're giving me a scary education into the inner workings of our political system."

"Some people think it's rotten to the core. As for me, I'm optimistic that the ship can be righted from the inside. Hence my goal to work at the Justice Department on its prison reform team."

He hadn't pegged Christian for such an idealist. It was a character flaw he'd also been accused of during his military career. It got in the way of success there too, from time to time.

He got it. Sometimes a guy had to do what a guy had to do. Orders came down for pragmatic reasons, and soldiers like him had to suck it up and do the job, no questions asked. Except he'd asked questions more often than not. He'd argued with superiors and pushed back against the orders that couldn't be justified ethically. It was why he'd left before he'd put in his twenty years to earn a full retirement. And it was also why he got along great with his bosses now. They knew not to ask him to do anything he couldn't approve of.

But this. Taking over another human being's life—a famous person's life, no less—this was pushing his boundaries.

He looked up sharply as the suite door flew open and Tucker barged in. "Hey, Christian. What did you need me—" Tucker broke off. "Senator Lacey! When did you get back?"

"Told you it would work," Christian crowed.

Tucker advanced farther into the suite. "What's going on—"

He drew within spitting distance of Stone and finally discovered the ruse. Tucker's jaw dropped.

"No way."

"Wild transformation, isn't it?" Christian asked archly.

"Okay, that's freaky," Tucker replied. He walked a three-sixty around Stone. "Day-umm. You look exactly like him. And why are we playing Impersonate the Boss?"

Stone's stare narrowed a little. He frankly didn't like reminding everyone in sight of a giant asshole. "This was Christian's lame idea. As you know, the senator will be out of pocket at least four or five days. Mrs. Lacey told Christian to find a way to make all of Jack's appearances happen, and this was the only thing he could come up with."

"Crazy, man."

Stone scowled. "Batshit crazy, if you ask me."

The other men laughed.

"All I have to say is it's a damned good thing Jill Lacey is paying Wild Cards a freaking fortune to help you out. Otherwise, I'd be out of this clown suit so fast your head would spin."

"It might work," Tucker said thoughtfully. "I know the guy like I know my own mother, and I had to practically be in your shorts to realize you weren't Senator Lacey."

Tucker was emphatically not the person Stone wanted in his shorts. That person was currently smirking in satisfaction at the success of the ploy.

"Then you'll help us with the ruse, Travis?" Christian asked. "Even if it gets discovered straightaway, we can still use Stone as bait to draw out whoever's trying to kill Jack." Christian explained, "I'm trimming the itinerary to cancel the events where close personal friends of the senator's are supposed to attend, of course."

Tucker grinned at Stone. "Talk about dedication to duty. You're willing to become the guy to protect him."

"That's me. I'm the job. We'll need you to act as my bodyguard tomorrow."

Tucker nodded. "Sure thing. Could you send me the day's itinerary, Christian?"

"Will do. We'll be staying in more and not exposing Stone to anyone until we have to, particularly anyone who's met Jack before. The senator has the Latin American Chamber of Commerce event tomorrow night. I've got a crap-ton of briefings to get through if Stone's going to convince them he's Jack."

"I assume you're moving into this suite, then?" Tucker asked.

Stone started. He hadn't given it any thought.

"Yes, he is," Christian answered smoothly. "And I'll be remaining in the second bedroom to keep working on teaching him how to be Jack."

Tucker grinned. "Good luck with that. Just don't turn him into a giant jerk, okay?"

Christian grinned broadly. "I promise. Jack 2.0 will be significantly nicer and easier to work with than the original, even if I have to beat it into him."

Hah. He'd like to see the guy try. His gaze and Christian's met, and challenge glinted between them.

Travis headed for the door. "I'll let you two get to it, then. G'night."

Stone shoved a hand through his newly short hair. He'd love nothing more than to get to it with Christian.

"Walk across the room," Christian ordered.

"What? Why?"

"To see if you walk like him."

"No one's going to watch how I walk. As long as I look like him and say what you tell me to, they'll buy the act."

"We can't be too careful. You need to walk like him, talk like him, have the same mannerisms—"

"Let's not get too carried away, bro. I'm not an actor."

"No, but you do have to save both our careers."

Gee. No pressure there. Frowning, Stone walked across the spacious living room.

"No, no, no. That's all wrong. You march. Jack strolls. You have to roll from your bootheel to the ball of your foot. It's a cross between a ramble and a swagger."

"What the hell are you talking about? What does a ramble look like?"

"It's how Jack walks. Try again."

He didn't take three steps before Christian stopped him, saying, "Watch me."

Stone stared appreciatively at Christian's muscular thighs and tight ass as the man strode away from him. "Do it like that."

"Like what?" Stone echoed.

"Concentrate!"

"I am. On your ass."

Christian whirled, glaring.

Stone grinned broadly. "I'm just saying. Those jeans fit you like a glove, and you have a great caboose. I can tell you do a shitload of squats to get it. A guy's allowed to appreciate hard work, isn't he?"

"Don't you try to butter me up, Stone."

"Butter, huh? I usually go for a nice water-soluble lube—"

"Stop it," Christian snapped, grinning reluctantly.

Stone threw up his hands in mock surrender. "All right, already. Show me this walk thing one more time...."

CHRISTIAN WORKED Stone hard all evening long, having him practice Jack's fake Texas drawl and the even more fake cowboy saunter. He did it as much to distract himself from wanting to jump Stone's bones as he did it out of necessity.

Honestly, it was a little weird wanting to fuck the man who looked exactly like his much-hated boss. It messed with his head.

Thankfully, Stone's playful mood passed, and he quit tempting Christian almost beyond endurance. Christian had to admit he secretly enjoyed the flirting that flared up between him and Stone from time to time. His life had never been structured to enable or encourage anyone to actively seduce him or vice versa.

Stone might not be an actor, but he was a hella quick study. In just a few hours of coaching, he had impersonating Jack Lacey down to a fine science.

Moreover, Stone could flip in and out of Jack mode at will. It was mind-bending being hot to trot whenever he dropped the act to be himself and then repelled by the guy when he went full Jack.

As the evening aged and they continued interacting in close proximity to each other, the attraction between them became more and more difficult to ignore.

Stone was feeling it too. Any time he stopped being Jack, his eyes practically lit on fire with desire. It was flattering as hell and too sexy to resist. More than once, Christian leaned in for a kiss, only to pull back hard when Stone drawled something in Jack's Texas twang.

Weird, weird, weird.

He had to find some other way to keep their minds off the hot sex they both craved. Worse, Tucker came and went, stopping by as if to assure himself that Stone really could pull off the impersonation or maybe that he wasn't imagining the resemblance between Stone and Jack.

Like it or not, he and Stone were back to being coworkers, and no hint of impropriety whatsoever must mar Christian's sterling reputation if he was ever going to work at the Justice Department. His work life must remain entirely separate from his private life, which was, well, private. But Lord, that man was tempting.

God help them all if the two of them got caught making out while Stone was in Jack mode. The scandal—it didn't even bear imagining.

Satisfied that Stone had mastered all the physical aspects of being Jack Lacey, it was time to move on to the mental aspects. And that meant bringing Stone up to speed on Washington politics in all its messy glory. And fast.

He reached for a file of position papers he'd printed out earlier and pulled the top one off the stack. "I can stop reporters from asking you any questions off script, but I can't necessarily stop big donors from quizzing you. You're going to have to learn at least enough about Jack's politics to fake saying the right thing."

Within about a half hour of starting to brief him, Stone complained, "Can't you just step in if someone tries to ask me anything and claim I've got another engagement to go to or something?"

"People at a certain level of influence won't stand for me deflecting them like that."

"How do you stand being this asshole's flunky? You're too smart to be stuck in a job like this."

"From your mouth to God's ear," he replied dryly.

"I mean it. You don't value yourself highly enough."

What was he supposed to say to that? He resorted to a noncommittal shrug.

"If I'm stuck being Jack anyway, is there something I can do as him to help you get another gig? Some job that'll advance your career but without having to sell your soul to Satan?"

"As tempting as that is, it wouldn't be ethical."

"Ethical, smethical. I can tell part of you is dying a slow death in this job. I want to help you leave."

He managed a smile of gratitude, but he felt more like crying at the idea of being done with Jack Lacey at long last. The degree of relief he felt at the idea of quitting this job was shocking.

"You okay?" Stone asked quietly in Stone voice.

"Not really."

"I didn't mean to upset you. I just want you to be happy."

Happy. Now there was a concept. Had he ever been truly happy in his life? To date, his entire modus operandi had been always to look forward to the next goal, to the next brick in the house of life he was trying to build for himself.

But Stone brought up a good point. When was he going to stop and enjoy what he'd already built?

He'd give anything to step off this never-ending treadmill. But not yet. First, they had to get through this crisis Jack had precipitated for all of them.

"Let's get back to work," he said heavily.

Stone nodded grimly.

It was a nightmare trying to cram years' worth of position papers and political platforms into Stone. But the man did an admirable job of absorbing the information being shot at him out of a virtual water cannon.

The good news was that Jack rarely absorbed all the details and nuances of Christian's position papers, so any holes in Stone's knowledge wouldn't come across as strange. Stone was, indeed, as sharp as he'd seemed in the hotel bar when they'd bantered over proper whiskey consumption. And hoo baby, were all those smarts *hot*.

"Whoa, whoa, whoa," Stone blurted, staring down at yet another position paper.

Christian looked up sharply.

"Lacey's opposed to an equal rights amendment that includes the LGBT community?" Stone demanded.

"Correct."

"So you knowingly work for the devil."

"Oh, he's a racist and misogynist too, in addition to being a bigot."

"What the hell?" Implied in Stone's tone of voice was huge disappointment in Christian for selling out his beliefs and his identity.

Christian sighed. "Thousands of brilliant, bright-eyed wannabes graduate from law schools every year and flock to DC, convinced they're the next great thing to hit that town. At best, a couple hundred of them will get entry-level coffee-pourer jobs on Capitol Hill. I landed a job as a senior staffer to a senator who does happen to support a position I do hold very dear, which is that prisons in this country desperately need immediate reform."

"Still. Satan."

"Newsflash—most of them are both good and bad. Jack's not the worst of the worst."

Stone shrugged. "Fair enough. I'm sorry for jumping you about working for him. I get it. A job is a job, man. Sometimes, you've got to do a little you hate to do a little you love." He added, "Like impersonating a client."

"Touché."

They traded smiles of commiseration.

It was nice to know he wasn't alone in disliking the moral compromises his work demanded. Who'd have guessed a man like Stone, so different from him, could make him feel so much better about himself?

Never would he have pegged a guy like Stone to be his perfect partner—

Umm. What?

"Something wrong?" Stone, ever perceptive, asked.

He blatantly dodged the question and countered with "Can I order us some room service? I'm famished, and you've been working as hard as I have." Plus, he really needed something to distract him from all that understanding and sympathy radiating from Stone. It was possibly the sexiest thing about the man to date.

While he ordered up cold sandwiches, Stone ran both hands over his scalp, standing his newly short hair up on end. It reminded Christian sharply of sex between the two of them, and his groin tightened.

Practical reality intruded into his fantasies, however. It was one thing to imagine a relationship with a man like Stone, but it was another thing altogether to actually live it.

Stone Jackson was the kind of man who would derail Christian's carefully ordered life. The guy would jet off to his next assignment and resume his nomadic lifestyle while he'd be left behind to wait and worry.

Oh, it would be a wild ride while it lasted, full of thrills and chills, but at the end of the day, it would be a train wreck. And he couldn't afford that. He couldn't afford anything that would make true all of the dreadful things his family thought and said about him.

He really ought to give up trying to impress them. But crap on a cracker, that was easier said than done. They'd sunk their hooks of judgment into him when he was young and impressionable, and as long as they continued to yank at those strings, he continued to dance on them.

"Earth to Christian, come in."

He looked up, startled. "Oh. Sorry."

"Was it a good fantasy?"

He screwed up his face. "Not even remotely."

"Damn."

Christian smiled apologetically. "Have you got any questions about Jack's position on global warming?"

"Nope. Global warming doesn't exist and it's a left-wing conspiracy." Stone rolled his eyes. "All I have to do is say pretty much the opposite of what I think, and I've got this guy nailed."

"His foreign-policy positions are generally sensible," Christian responded.

"Yeah, and I'll bet you wrote every one of them, didn't you?"

"Well, maybe."

Stone grinned and started for the door as a knock announced the arrival of their late snack.

"Sit," Christian ordered firmly. "You're the senator. Other people do the menial chores for you."

Stone muttered under his breath, "Prima donnas… think they're better than all the rest of us regular folks… oughta take 'em all out back and shoot 'em… or give them a shovel and a big pile of shit to move…."

Amused, he commented, "You must be fun in a foxhole with a mouth like that."

"You have no idea," Stone drawled, sticking his tongue in his cheek.

Christian rolled his eyes at the crude gesture. "Crawl back up onto the curb, dude."

"Hey, you're the one who said it."

And that was how eating egg-salad sandwiches turned into a metaphor for their relationship. Stone grinned unrepentantly and charged ahead while Christian glared disapprovingly and held back.

After the snack, Christian asked, "Do you need me to go down to your suite and get any of your stuff for you since you'll be staying here for the foreseeable future?"

"Actually, my gear needs to come up here where I can keep an eye on it."

Glad for an excuse to escape Stone's magnetic appeal, he headed for Stone's room. The metal trunk in the corner was surprisingly heavy. He hoisted it and hauled it down the hallway. When he stepped into the suite, Stone jumped forward to help with it.

"What's in this thing, anyway?" Christian asked.

"Weapons. Spare ammo. Bullet-resistant vests. Surveillance gear. The usual."

Right. Usual. "You live in a strange, strange world, Mr. Jackson."

"And gettin' stranger by the second, y'all," he drawled in Jack's accent.

Christian went back to Stone's room to fetch underwear, razor, and toothbrush. Impersonating Jack Lacey could only be carried so far, after all.

It felt weird to be handling Stone's personal stuff. Which was disconcerting, given that they'd crawled all over each other's bodies already. How much did he really know about Stone?

He'd been so gobsmacked by all that sizzling sexuality that he hadn't really stopped to know the man himself. And he couldn't very well start asking Stone a lot of personal questions now. He needed the guy to immerse himself in being Jack Lacey, not dredging up childhood memories and digging into what made Stone Jackson tick. He sighed.

He found a sports duffel and stuffed in Stone's undies and toothbrush. He was careful to leave the room looking lived-in, in case a maid from the hotel were to say something to the wrong person.

Which was probably a little more paranoia than the situation called for. But he was more nervous about them all pulling off the impersonation ruse than he cared to admit.

It might be Stone's job to anticipate everything that could go wrong, which meant it would be Christian's job to focus on everything that could go well. Stone needed a cheerleader right now, not a naysayer. The man was already skeptical enough about this project without him adding his own doubts and fears to the equation.

As always, he repressed what he was really feeling and painted on a positive face as he stepped back into the senator's suite.

"Thanks, man," Stone said warmly as he took the bag from Christian and peered inside it. "That was thoughtful of you."

"That's me. Always thinking."

"Yeah. I noticed. Do you ever let your hair down and go off the clock? You know, just relax?"

"I met you in a bar. Drinking. I was relaxing."

"That's unwinding, not relaxing. Doesn't count."

He'd been more relaxed than he had been in years when he'd woken up in Stone's bed. But he wasn't about to hand over all the power that sharing such a detail would give Stone.

Instead he opted to go on the offensive. "You're pretty tightly wound yourself, Stone. What do you do to relax?"

"I run. Or go to a firing range."

"You shoot guns to wind down? Holy hell. I'd hate to see what you do to rev yourself up!"

"I listen to god-awful rap music. Puts me in a foul mood in ten seconds flat."

"Duly noted," he commented drolly.

Stone stepped close to him and said quietly, in a charged voice, "I can think of one more thing I do to relax…."

Christian gulped. In light of the current crisis, they shouldn't. Really, really shouldn't. But damned if he wasn't going to go there. Just one more time.

And then he'd swear off of this man before he became an irrevocable addiction.

CHAPTER EIGHT

STONE HAD done some crazy shit in his life, but impersonating Jack Lacey was right up there. A crowd of close to a thousand people crammed into the auditorium of a local community college while he stood in the wings at stage right, sweating all over the printed copy of the speech Christian had written for Jack.

"You've got this," Christian muttered encouragingly. "Just remember the Texas accent."

"Got it. Twang."

"And flirt." A pause, and then Christian added hastily, "With the women."

That drew a bark of laughter from him. "Check. Chicks."

"This is no laughing matter—"

"Relax, babe. I've got this."

Christian sputtered and turned an interesting shade of crimson as the introduction concluded.

"Here goes nothing," he muttered.

"I believe in you," Christian whispered.

God bless him. That was probably the one thing Stone could hear right now that calmed him the fuck down enough to follow through with this.

Stone stepped out from behind the curtain and fell into Jack's I'm-the-Shit swagger. He threw in his best jaunty salute too. And then he reached the podium and turned to face the crowd. And every last one of the people out there was looking back at him.

Mind. Blank.

Cold sweat. Pulse pounding. Hyperventilating.

So, stage fright was a thing.

Surely, they saw him for the fraud he was. Jesus, he felt naked up here. *C'mon, man. Pull it together. You're a highly trained operative and can overcome any challenge.* Including a bunch of harmless civilians and reporters.

He stared down at the blurry sheaf of notes, and the words swam into focus. *Breathe. Think of Christian.* He could do this for Christian.

"Howdy, y'all!"

Bah-dum-bum. No reaction *at all* from the crowd. Oh, great. A hostile audience. Frowning in determination, he plowed into the speech.

The pauses—applause breaks, Christian had called them—got a tepid response at first. But as the speech progressed and he outlined the new and more lenient immigration policy that Jack was now supporting, the applause grew.

By the end he had the crowd in the palm of his hand. And it was heady as hell. Sheesh. No wonder politicians got addicted to this stuff.

The speech ended to thunderous applause and cheers. The front two rows, mostly reporters, rushed the stage and started shouting questions at him. God bless Christian and his position papers last night. One of the voices rose above the others, and the crowd of journalists quieted to let the most aggressive one have the floor.

"*¿Qué piensa usted de que español se convierta en la segunda idioma oficial de los Estados Unidos?*"

He actually felt Christian's gasp offstage. Apparently, Captain America hadn't anticipated someone throwing a question at him in Spanish. Did Jack speak Spanish or not? Stone did, but he had no idea about the senator.

He dared not glance offstage for support, or Jack would look weak. Unprepared.

What the hell. Jack spoke Spanish now.

He said rapidly, "*Creo que es importante que cada persona los Estados Unidos aprenda inglés. Sin embargo, muchas personas los Estados Unidos hablan español como su primera idioma. Si queremos que todo el mundo aquí hable inglés, entonces el gobierno debe pagar y proporcionar educación en la forma de hablar a todos los que viven aquí.*"

The crowd went crazy. Not only because he was advocating that the government fund and provide bilingual education for everyone, but because his own Spanish was fluent and effortless.

Leery of being thrown any more curveballs, he dared not let the moment turn into a mini press conference. Instead, he walked directly off the stage and up the main aisle of the auditorium to a crowd line that had been set up outside. He'd gone off plan by exiting through the crowd, but he had to make a snap decision and avoid those reporters.

Well, damn. He thought back to all those times he'd been exasperated at clients for going off script and offered up a mental apology to them.

It was hot as hell outside, the height of the midafternoon heat, and now he got to shake a few hundred sweaty palms. Awesome sauce. Moist, clammy, awesome sauce.

He was a strong man with an iron grip, but after a hundred or so people did their damnedest to crush his fingers in the name of machismo, he was close to crying uncle. Cripes. How did politicians do this day in and day out? No wonder they opted for kissing babies. Tiny rug rats didn't try to break their metacarpals.

He'd almost reached the end of the line and Tucker, waiting at the door of the SUV, when a fast-moving body came flying out of the crowd at him. He caught the movement out of his peripheral vision, and his bodyguard instinct took over.

He whirled and absorbed the hit, grabbing what turned out to be a young man. He used the kid's momentum to carry them both to the ground, roll, and pin the kid under him all in one fast move.

He stared down into glazed eyes that showed no awareness of place or self as the young man muttered in an incoherent babble. Drugs or a psychotic break. Stone knew the signs cold.

Tucker shoved Stone aside—or at least tried to. But he shielded the kid from his security man until he could bite out, "He's no threat, Tuck. Stand down."

Tucker stopped. "You sure?"

"Look at his eyes."

A brief pause. "Got it."

Together they helped the young man to his feet. A woman stepped out of the crowd, wailing in panic. Stone muttered, "And there would be the mom. A hundred bucks says the kid went off his meds."

"Not taking that bet," Tucker replied.

The very fact that the young man stood passively between them now, mumbling to himself as if barely aware of them, confirmed Stone's suspicion. Screams and shouts erupted around him, but Stone was only vaguely aware of the noise. He was wholly focused on the target and safely suppressing any additional outbursts.

A pair of policemen rushed up aggressively, Tasers drawn.

Dammit. This could get ugly fast.

Stone physically stepped in front of the youth to protect him from the cops.

"Stop," he bit out sharply. "This young man is not dangerous and is likely mentally ill."

The police stared over his shoulder at the youth suspiciously.

It took a few tense moments to get them to focus on him and stand down enough to register what he was saying. But eventually they lowered their stun devices.

By the time he got through to Miami's finest, the mother was beside the young man, hysterically explaining the same thing and begging the police not to kill her baby.

Man, he hated drama. And he sucked at drama from women. Especially mothers. The last thing he—Jack—needed was to freak out some poor woman in public.

Stone put his arm around the distraught woman's shoulders and guided both her and her son away from the police.

Christian rushed forward, and Stone pushed the pair at him, murmuring, "Get them inside and away from the police before the kid does something stupid to trigger a violent response."

Nodding and looking massively relieved, Christian hurried mother and son away, and for the first time since the kid came charging out of the crowd, Stone looked up. Abruptly, he became aware of all the people staring and pointing their cell phones at him.

Aww, hell.

To take matters from bad to worse, a reporter stepped forward and jammed a microphone under his nose. "What happened, Senator? Will you press charges?"

He didn't hesitate. He said scornfully, "Of course I won't press charges. The way we treat those with mental health issues in this country is deplorable. We could all use a little more compassion and a whole lot more funding for treatment and care of people like that young man. They're human beings, for cryin' out loud."

He spun, muttering over his shoulder at Tucker, "Get me out of here."

The reporter yelled after him, "Is it true someone's threatening to kill you?"

Dammit. That rumor seemed to be gaining more traction day by day. More than a few assassins had killed for the fame, and he was hoping to keep the story out of the press in case Jack's would-be killer was one of those publicity hounds.

The ex-Marine hustled him into the waiting SUV. This one was set up like a limousine with only one bench seat in the rear, set way back from the side doors. He stretched out his legs all the way and rolled his head, trying and failing to release the tension from the appearance.

After a short delay, Christian slipped in the back beside Stone and reached over low, out of sight of Tucker and the rearview mirror to squeeze Stone's hand.

It was as if Christian's touch released all the stress he'd been forcing down. He let out the rattling breath that it felt as if he'd been holding for the past two days.

"When I saw that kid rush you—" Christian started raggedly.

"It's all good. I handled it."

"Speaking of which, that would not be your job. You've got to let Tucker take care of stuff like that."

Unfortunately, Christian was right. He was supposed to be a senator, not a trained security operative. "Christ, I'm sorry. I blew it, didn't I?"

"Don't beat yourself up. I get that you've got hard-wired reflexes to a situation like that."

"You would not be wrong. I don't know if I can break my habits. I've spent a long time carving them into my brain."

Christian was silent. He looked as if he was still absorbing the relief of the attack having been nothing dangerous. Still. It had obviously been a hell of a scare for him.

To distract him, Stone asked, "Does Jack even speak Spanish? And then that kid. And his mother. Poor woman was convinced we were gonna kill him. Not that I blame her—"

"Stone."

"—And the cops. I wasn't sure they'd listen to me and not tase him—"

"Stone." Christian spoke a little more forcefully this time.

Jeez. He was babbling.

He never *babbled*.

"You did fine," Christian said gently. "Better than fine."

"I panicked when that reporter threw that question at me. And then I figured, what the hell. Go for it. I figured the crowd would like it."

Christian smiled a little. "They loved it. And to answer your question, Jack speaks enough Spanish to proposition a whore, but that's about it."

"Crap. I'm sorry. I had to make a call on the fly...."

"Your call probably just got Jack an extra several million in campaign contributions. I've been telling him forever to support bilingual education, and he's refused to listen to me. You've put him on the right side of the polls on the issue whether he wants to be there or not. And besides, now I can force him to learn some more Spanish, or at least to pretend to know more."

"Hah! That's what he gets for taking off with Señorita Chesty."

Christian grinned.

"You know, we could rewrite a bunch of his positions while he's gone," Stone suggested.

A snort of humor escaped Christian. "You have no idea how tempting that is."

"Then do it. He left you holding the bag. He can't very well complain about what you do with the bag."

"If he flip-flops on too much, he'll lose his voter base."

"I dunno. You have to admit it's an appealing idea."

"Don't encourage me," Christian laughed.

Their gazes met, and there it was, that intense sexual attraction that hung between them any time they let down their guards for even a second. They both looked away hastily, and Stone stared out the window at nothing.

Every time they connected emotionally for even a second, it proved yet again that their smoking-hot chemistry wasn't only in his imagination. That the sex between them was as hot and intoxicating as he remembered it. More so.

Not to mention the more they got to know each other, the more they knew how to evoke each other's emotional and erogenous hot buttons.

Take Christian, for example. On the outside, he was all about control. But Stone was secretly convinced that he wanted more than anything to give up control. He was certainly willing to do so in bed, given the opportunity. How to get him to relax a little about the rest of his life, though?

He leaned forward. "Hey, Tucker, how long till the hotel?"

"In this traffic, at least an hour. Sorry."

Perfect. "No problem. Take your time and be safe."

"You got it."

Stone sat back and ran up the privacy panel between the front and back seats. "Is this thing soundproof?" he asked casually.

"More or less. Tucker could hear if someone screamed."

Christian was frowning slightly, not seeing where this was going. Excellent. It was high time the man was ambushed and surprised out of all that self-discipline.

He reached for Christian's fly and unzipped it all the way in one smooth, quick move.

"Hey! What are you doing?"

He didn't bother answering. Rather, he leaned over and freed Christian's cock from his briefs.

"What the—" Christian squawked.

But when Stone leaned down and closed his mouth around the abrupt spring of a fast hard-on, Christian broke off on a gasp. His hips surged up against Stone's face.

Yeah. As he'd thought. All that control was a thin veneer at best.

He circled the bold head of Christian's cock with his tongue and then stroked the length of it, drawing his tongue along the underside and back up in a delicious slurp. Sucking gently, he drew it into his mouth while he dipped his hand lower, cupped Christian's balls, and pressed his fingertips into the sensitive spot behind them. A tug with his hand in time with the sucking action of his mouth, and Christian's anus, balls, and dick all clenched in unison.

"Jesus, Stone. Not here."

He lifted his mouth away long enough to mutter, "Wrong answer. Sing for me, Christian."

"Huh?"

He closed his mouth around Christian's now rock-hard, heavy cock. The man was impressively endowed. Stone took enough of it into his mouth that the head bumped against the back of his throat. Forcing his throat muscles to relax, he sucked his way up the shaft and then rammed his mouth back down on it, hard and deep.

Christian's hips bucked again, and his breath hissed in and out.

That was more like it. Stone grasped the base of Christian's cock with his left hand while he continued squeezing and tugging rhythmically at Christian's balls with his right hand. And then he set up a merciless rhythm with his mouth, up and down, slow then fast. Shallow and ever deeper with each downstroke. And each time he retreated, he swirled his tongue around the straining head of Christian's penis.

Christian started making strangled sounds of pleasure that were so tortured and sexy they nearly drove him to come in his own pants. The moans became a steady stream of cursing from behind Christian's clenched teeth.

He kept up the sliding movement of his lips and swirling tongue, steadily, inexorably, stripping away the layers of Christian's self-control. It was intoxicating, exposing his lover like this.

Christian plunged his hand into the short hair at the back of Stone's head and tried to pull his head faster and harder against his lap, but Stone resisted.

Oh no. They were doing this on his terms, and Christian was going to lose his mind before this was over.

"Fuckfuckfuckfuckfuck," Christian chanted in a breathy whisper.

His dick strained against Stone's throat, rising eagerly to meet each down thrust of his mouth.

Christian's breath became ragged and then devolved into hoarse pants.

Soon now. Smiling around the base of Christian's dick, Stone squeezed everything a little tighter, sucked a little harder, drove a little deeper down his throat.

Christian was large enough that a true deep throat wasn't feasible, but with a combination of fist and mouth, he was able to envelop the guy's cock in a tight, wet, hot glove of relentlessly pumping stimulation.

He felt Christian's balls tighten in his hand. Beneath him, Christian's entire body tensed. Out of the corner of his eye, he saw Christian yank up his tie, shove a length of it between his teeth, and bite down on it as his entire body exploded. He surged up off the bench seat into Stone's face, his cock pulsing and pulsing as he emptied himself in a massive ejaculation.

Christian collapsed, limp against the seat, a drop of perspiration rolling down his temple and tracing the line of his square jaw. "What the... hell was... that for?"

"That was about you giving up control."

Christian's right eyebrow arched skeptically. "Looks to me like you're riding a hell of an adrenaline rush after that kid jumped you. Or did you like hearing that crowd cheer for you a little more than you're letting on? Are you sure you're not the one who needs to let go of the reins a little after the head rush of power?"

Stone stared at him. Damned if the man wasn't spot-on. It was getting a little freaky how Christian seemed to know him better than he knew himself sometimes. He mumbled, "What do you suggest?"

"What do you need?"

Such a simple question. And yet packed with so much significance. Recognition that he was wired tighter than a spring. Willingness to help. An offer of his body to fulfill Stone's needs.

Lord, the generosity of it. Did he dare accept the gift? His knees went weak at the prospect. And yet….

Fear trembled low in his belly. He was starting to need this man a hell of a lot more than he wanted to need anyone. He was a lone wolf, dammit. But a lone wolf who wanted Christian, body and soul.

Christian rolled off the seat to the carpeted open space in front of the single bench seat and onto his knees. He pulled his trousers down and planted his elbows on the bench seat. Looking over his shoulder, he said soberly, "You know you want to. And I know you need to. Take me. *Do* what you want to me. I trust you."

Christian trusted him?

A wave of warmth rolled through him, so emotional he wasn't sure he could handle it. This man. It was shocking how perfect he was.

Christian's rear end stuck out impudently. The man really did have great glutes. They were round and firm, with white, smooth skin sandwiched between dark tan lines on his hips and thighs. Reluctantly, Stone trailed his fingertips down the deep indentation of Christian's spine from his waist to the crack between those muscular cheeks.

Christian shuddered a little, and Stone's entire body clenched with desire.

This way lay madness. But damned if he could do a thing to stop himself from racing down the road to hell. It was *Christian*. Handsome, classy, brilliant Christian. Strong, graceful, elegant Christian. Kind, generous, caring Christian.

He unzipped his own fly, then leaned forward and spread Christian's cheeks wide with both hands. He ran his tongue around the puckered rose there, amused at how Christian's muscles clenched and released convulsively.

Apparently we are, in fact, going to do this. His erection practically doubled in mass, density, and hardness in the length of time it took him to have the thought.

Capitulation complete and damnation assured, he surged up, covering Christian's body with his. He reached around Christian's hips and was not surprised to find his cock already hardening again. The guy was in great shape—and he needed the stress relief nearly as badly as Stone did.

He took Christian's cock in his grip and stroked it into a brand-new throbbing mass of hungry lust. Christian's hips rocked faster and faster against his fist as he pumped him toward another huge orgasm.

When Christian was moaning incoherently, Stone positioned his cock at Christian's opening and murmured, "Last chance to say no. Are you sure about this?"

"Yes. Oh God. Yes," he groaned.

After taking a moment to tear open a lubricated condom packet and roll it over his throbbing cock, Stone pushed forward triumphantly. He felt like a fucking conquering Roman general. Barely hanging on to his control, he paused, the tip of his cock lodged in Christian's tight heat. He nearly came right there.

He felt a fractional relaxation of the muscles gripping him and pressed forward. Christian gasped, and Stone froze.

"Keep going," Christian ground out.

Stone pressed forward carefully. It took maybe ten seconds total to seat himself all the way to the hilt. But it was the most incredible eternity of his life. This self-disciplined, high-powered, blue-blooded intellectual had just given all of himself to him. The triumph was so heady it almost made him faint.

It was, in a word, glorious.

Christian took all of him, grasping every inch of him so tightly with his internal muscles that it was his turn to bite back a groan. He withdrew fractionally and then pressed forward carefully again.

Ever so slowly, he worked Christian's body, coaxing the muscles to relax enough for him to move safely. Gradually, gradually, Christian's tension eased. His body relaxed beneath Stone's.

He checked in quickly. "You okay?"

"Uh-huh," Christian panted. The sound was laced with a big fat helping of lust. Exactly how Stone liked his lovers. He grasped Christian's cock and stroked it in time with his pumps in and out of his body. It was, bar none, the sexiest feeling he'd ever experienced.

Cars whizzed by on the freeway, oblivious to the epic sex going on behind the blacked-out windows of the SUV. It was erotic and forbidden, and he took Christian in front of them all.

He pumped faster and faster, and Christian's hips rocked back and forth in a matching frenzy that drove him out of his mind. Who was the one being taken here? He was methodically being torn out of his body, his whole being focusing on where their bodies joined, his emotional defenses shredded.

Christian began chanting again, whimpering more and more urgently that he felt a second orgasm coming. Every syllable devastated Stone. He'd never felt anything like this—not physically, not mentally, and definitely not emotionally.

His own orgasm began to build, and everything disappeared except the pounding lust, the irresistible pull of Christian's body, the need to mark this man as his and only his, and…. *Oh… my… God….*

The explosion, when it came, all but tore him apart. His entire being emptied itself in a massive eruption of hot, convulsing pleasure. This time Christian shouted into the crook of his elbow and shuddered uncontrollably around Stone as their bodies continued pulsing in aftershocks.

Carefully, Stone pulled out of Christian, relieved to see no blood. He genuinely didn't want to cause him any pain. Only pleasure. Loads of mind-blowing pleasure. After disposing of the condom, he turned, half fell onto the seat, and weakly started putting his clothes to rights.

He was both amused and gratified that Christian didn't move right away. He had to absorb what had happened for a minute, huh? Good.

Slowly, a little gingerly, Christian pulled up his pants and sat down beside him. Eventually he zipped his fly and fussed with his tie where he'd bit down on it before, trying to smooth the teeth marks out of the silk.

Stone said quietly, "Thank you for giving me that. It was... spectacular."

Christian responded, his voice resolute, "And it can't ever happen again."

CHAPTER NINE

STILL IN a state of minor shock, Christian stepped into the suite behind Stone, who insisted on playing bodyguard for him from the elevator down the hall to the hotel room. Old habits die hard, apparently.

Although, hell's bells, his careful habit of keeping his private life far, far away from his professional life had kicked the bucket spectacularly tonight. He needed a long, hot shower. He was sore and messy, but damned if he wasn't so exhilarated he could hardly see straight.

Which was exactly why they could never do that again. For the first time in his life, he was tempted, genuinely tempted, to walk away from the career—from the identity—he'd constructed so carefully over so many years. He was ready to throw in the towel and give it all up for Stone if the man would have him.

Which, of course, would never happen. Stone was so busy staying in perpetual motion, running from whatever demons dogged his heels, that he couldn't, or wouldn't, slow down long enough to have a real relationship, let alone a permanent one.

Christian might be a fool for love, as it turned out, but he was no dummy when it came to reading people. And he was not wrong in his assessment of Stone Jackson.

The message light on the phone was blinking, and Christian rushed over to it, hoping against hope it was Jack calling to tell them he'd be back shortly. Or at least to check in and let them know he was *alive*. The bastard.

"Good evening, Mr. Chatsworth-Brandeis. This is the *Miami Morning Crowd* calling. We were wondering if there's time in your senator's schedule for a live, on-camera interview tomorrow morning."

He advanced the machine to the next message.

"This is the *Miami Enquirer*. We'd like a quote from the senator on this evening's incident. He's being touted as a hero for protecting his attacker."

And the next.

"This is the *Tampa Examiner*. Does Senator Lacey have a comment on the attack against him earlier?"

The next half-dozen messages were more of the same. Nothing from Jack, though.

Damn him, anyway. Part of him hoped the bastard never came back. That the whole train went off a cliff, and he would be forced to completely reinvent his life. With or without Stone in it.

He watched through the open bedroom door as Stone stripped off the senator's suit, article by article of clothing. The jerk was doing that on purpose to tantalize him. And it was working.

He picked up the TV remote and pointed it at the television without taking his gaze off Stone, who was kicking off Jack's boots and peeling out of the pants at the moment. Damn, that man was built like a rock. He wasn't thick, but he was hard. Everywhere. His name fit him to a T.

"—visiting senator and possible presidential hopeful defends himself against an attack and then protects his assailant from police in this dramatic footage from tonight's Latin American Chamber of Commerce event...."

Oh, shit. He'd really, really hoped the media wouldn't pick up on the incident, but he knew better. A senator protecting his assailant from the police was sound-bite gold.

"Hey! That's me on the news," Stone exclaimed from the doorway. "Cool!"

Christian actually felt the blood draining from his face as he prayed that the footage would be of poor quality and not show Stone's face too clearly. "People who know Jack are going to see this."

His prayer wasn't answered. As clear as day, Stone took down that kid and then protected him from the police.

Stone murmured, "Dude, you don't look so good. Maybe you should sit down."

Christian made his way over to the sofa. Numb, he switched channels. Of course, all the local news outlets had picked up the story. He said weakly, "Please, God, let the national outlets not have picked it up."

"Let's see." Stone flopped onto the sofa beside him, lifted the remote out of his paralyzed fingers, and turned to one of the all-news channels.

They watched in silence for long enough to be certain they'd dodged that bullet. For now, at least. Oh Lord. This was a disaster.

"The footage isn't *that* high quality, Christian. And I really do look like Jack."

"Problem is Jack would never, ever defend himself in the first place or turn around and show compassion for his attacker in the second place."

"Who else but his immediate staff knows that, though?"

"His wife. Maybe a few hunting buddies. Fortunately, he's got too big of an ego to maintain sincere friendships."

"Well, he defends himself from attacks and shows compassion to his attackers now. Let the media make of it what they will."

"Do you have any idea how dangerous it is to let the media form its own opinions?" Christian mumbled, thinking a mile a minute.

It went without saying that they would have to turn down the interview requests. No way could Stone pass as Jack in a close-up television setting. But they would have to spin the refusals in such a way that the press didn't take offense and go for Jack/Stone's jugular. As long as this thing stayed local, it shouldn't be that hard to contain.

As if on cue, the phone rang. Christian picked it up warily. It was a major television affiliate this time. Crap. The story was going national. He got off the phone with a noncommittal comment about the senator being shaken by the incident, heavily booked, and promised to get back to the production assistant in the morning with a statement from Jack.

He'd no sooner set the receiver down than the phone rang again. He glared across the room at Stone. "What the hell am I supposed to do about this?"

"Draft a press release saying that the senator does not wish to benefit politically from a young man's mental health issues. I'm declining all interview requests regarding the incident at the Chamber of Commerce event out of respect for the privacy of the family of the victim."

"But you're the victim."

"Say it the way I did. The public won't miss the message. And thank the Miami police for their professionalism and restraint. Might as well give those guys some good press for a change. Poor bastards don't get much love, and they've got a rough job."

It wasn't a bad way to spin it. Christian nodded slowly. "That could work." He added, "You've got a charity fundraiser tomorrow night. The press is going to climb all over you. I'll call the event organizers in the morning and warn them to have extra security in place. Tucker can figure out how to sneak you in the back entrance. We'll have to keep your exposure minimal and dodge the press to the best of our ability."

"I have faith in you. It'll work out."

Christian was too wired to sit any longer and moved over to the desk. "Let me print out your remarks for tomorrow so you can practice them. I'll make sure the press knows you're not taking questions tomorrow, and you're not talking about today's incident—"

A hand touched his shoulder, and he spun, startled.

Stone murmured, "Go take a shower. Relax. You've got tomorrow covered, and I know what to do. Today was a big day. Recover from it tonight, and worry about tomorrow in the morning."

His brain heard the sense in Stone's advice; however, his panic was such that he doubted any relaxation was possible.

Stone herded him into the bathroom and shut the door firmly behind him. And it was nice being herded into a few minutes' worth of self-care.

He was the one who took care of everyone else, not the other way around. But this was nice. He stripped and stood under a hot shower for a long time, his brain flatly refusing to function. For once, he allowed himself to just zone out. Eventually, when he was a ton more relaxed, he got out, wrapped a towel around his hips, and padded into the living room.

Stone looked up from a copy of tomorrow's speech and smirked. "Terry cloth is a good look on you."

He vogued until the towel began to slip and he snatched at it to hold it up.

"Tease," Stone complained. "Go to bed before I can't restrain myself any longer."

He frowned, his playful mood abruptly evaporating. He hadn't been kidding when he said sex couldn't happen again between them. He was only so strong, and he couldn't risk an addiction to Stone that derailed his entire life.

Still. Stone unable to keep his hands to himself? He rather liked the sound of that. After all, he knew the feeling. He almost reversed his personal edict to himself that there would be no more hanky-panky between them.

No! Be strong!

Swearing at his stupidly overdeveloped sense of responsibility, he beat a tactical retreat from the living room, away from temptation.

Stone might accuse him of being the great people reader, but the guy wasn't doing a half-bad job himself tonight. He *was* beat after today's wild emotional swings. A press release could actually wait until first thing in the morning. Media outlets wouldn't expect one until then anyway.

By the time he reached his bed in the suite's second bedroom, he was all but stumbling with exhaustion. Everything from the past few days—hell, the past few decades—seemed to be catching up with him all at once. He fell into bed and passed out, asleep practically before he got horizontal.

Sometime in the thick darkness of the wee hours, he woke up enough to feel the mattress shift. Warm arms enveloped him, and he drifted toward sleep again, safe in their embrace.

Very faintly in the back of his mind, a little voice suggested that something was wrong with how right those arms felt, but he was too unconscious to sort it out. Relaxed and comfortable, he went back to sleep.

He woke abruptly, panicked for no apparent reason. And then it dawned on him that he was not alone in his bed. Crap! He'd promised himself he would swear off Stone after yesterday's erotic encounter in the SUV. He leaped out of bed like the pillows were on fire.

"What's wrong?" Stone bit out tersely, sitting up sharply.

"Nothing. Go back to sleep. I've got to put out a quick press release."

Stone frowned but did lie back down. Thank God. Christian didn't have the energy to spare for a fight just yet. First, he had a few crises to manage. Then maybe there could be fighting.

Four more days. He had to get through today's charity benefit, tomorrow's golf tournament, and the big casino night on Saturday. And then Jack Lacey could spend the next month floating around the damned Caribbean, screwing his girlfriend, and no one would be the wiser. Please, God, let Jack's paranoia about paparazzi protect him from discovery in the meantime.

Christian drafted the press release quickly and sent it out, and then he headed for the shower. By the time he emerged, he'd developed a long to-do list for himself.

Stone observed him with hawklike intensity but seemed content to leave him alone this morning to work. Or to at least pretend to work, as it turned out.

It was impossible to concentrate with those intelligent eyes registering his every tiny movement. He felt like an antelope squarely in the sights of a hunting tiger.

He managed to scroll down through Jack's email, answered the easy requests, scheduled a few meetings for when they got back to Washington and added them to Jack's calendar, and stored the other messages in a file to deal with later.

And then he opened an innocuous-looking message titled simply, "For Senator Jack Lacey—Urgent."

> *Your time is coming very soon, you worthless piece of shit. Settle your affairs and say goodbye because I'm coming to send you to hell where you belong.*

It wasn't signed. The "From" line said simply "unnamed sender." The email address itself was a random-looking string of numbers and letters. Not helpful.

He snatched up the phone and dialed Tucker. "Where are you, Travis?"

"At the venue for tonight's gala. This place is a nightmare—"

"I need you to get back here right now," he interrupted.

"What's wrong?" Tucker's voice already was jumping, as if the man was running while talking.

"Stone's safe. But Jack just got another death threat. And this one said specifically that he's going to be attacked soon."

"Keep Stone in the room, and I'll be there in thirty minutes."

"Got it." He hung up the phone anxiously.

From the sofa across the suite, Stone said grimly, "And you didn't think to tell me first that there's another death threat? Given that I'm the expert security consultant *and* effectively the target?"

"You heard at the same time I told Tucker."

"That's not my point. You see something alarming, something that has to cause you significant stress, and you don't tell me first?"

"I followed protocol," he said defensively. "Secure the principal and tell the bodyguard immediately."

Christian braced himself for an explosion out of Stone but instead got only a terse, "Give me everything you've got on tonight's benefit. I need the full list of attendees."

Christian handed over the hard copy of the guest list and went to work downloading and printing out the schedule of events, timeline, and correspondence from the event organizers. Stone turned his attention to the paperwork, but anger rolled off his muscular shoulders in palpable waves. What the hell did Stone want him to say?

His mind was blown by what had transpired between them yesterday, and he needed some time to process it. And now was not the moment to have a huge fight with Stone over the fact that he'd meant it when he said they were over last night.

The silent standoff grew more and more uncomfortable as Stone appeared to grow steadily angrier. Christian was by turns defensive and irritable himself.

The first priority was Stone's safety, and that meant telling his chief of security immediately about any incoming threats. He'd done the right thing by calling Tucker first, dammit.

At least they'd established that the two of them could have a knock-down-drag-out fight without ever uttering a single word aloud to each other. It was a first for him with any man and actually a rather impressive feat.

Gradually, Stone's focus shifted to the papers he had spread out all over a table. He was poring over some sort of tourist map of downtown Miami when Tucker burst into the suite and into the middle of their silent battle of wills.

Christian had never been so relieved to see the man. "What's the plan, Tucker?" He felt a bigger, better wave of irritation surge off the couch at him for asking Tucker and not Stone for a plan of action.

"Lemme see the email," Tucker replied.

While Christian pulled it up and turned his laptop for Tucker to see the short message, Stone reported tersely, "The tech experts at Wild Cards have had no success tracing the sender of the email. It was likely sent from a location outside the United States and bounced off a bunch of servers to anonymize it."

Tucker nodded as he glanced through the short message. "What else did your analysts have to say?"

"As for the message's content, there's nothing new except the addition of the attack coming soon. The Wild Cards' profiler says the assassin is hinting at having a concrete timetable. You and I could have figured that out for ourselves, though. Talk to me about the venue."

"You're not going to go through with the appearance, are you?" Tucker demanded, sounding startled.

"We might as well catch ourselves a psychopath while we wait for Jack to get tired of Chesty."

Christian's mouth opened and a protest danced on the tip of his tongue. Why in the name of God didn't Stone value his life more than this? Why was he so damned willing to throw himself in front of a madman and roll the dice with death?

At least Tucker was also staring in what looked like shock.

Stone muttered, "Talk to me, Tuck."

The security chief moved over to the venue map on the coffee table in front of Stone and started jabbing at intersections and buildings, giving a rapid-fire description of the area around the large plaza where the evening charity auction and ball would be held under the stars.

"The whole plaza will be blocked off for the night with police barricades here, here, here, and here. They'll be manned by cops but should be considered porous."

Stone made a noise of disgust.

Tucker continued, "At least ten high-rises are close, with a half dozen well within five hundred yards."

Stone grimaced and Christian asked, "What's significant about five hundred yards?"

"Any half-decent sniper with a half-decent weapon can kill a man at that distance," Stone replied.

"Are we worried that the stalker is going to make a hit tonight? I thought you guys decided the casino night was the event the attacker would target because of how high profile it will be."

"Given the latest communication, I think we have to consider every appearance that I—Jack—makes to be at high risk."

"And yet you're going through with it. Look. Jack bailed out on all of us. If he ruins his ability to collect any campaign donations and blows his chances for reelection, it's no skin off my nose at this point. Although you may be prepared to sacrifice your life at the drop of a hat, Stone, I am not willing to throw you to the wolves. I'm pulling the plug on this thing right now. I'll write up a press release that Jack has had to leave town unexpectedly and is bowing out—"

"And what happens when this would-be killer shows up at your DC office and shoots the entire staff, including you? Or he shows up at Jack's home and murders his wife… and the dog too, just to make his point?"

Jeez. The bald violence Stone was hinting at stopped him in his mental tracks.

Stone continued grimly, "Hiding from nutjobs gives them a sense of control. They're successfully manipulating their target. If we can draw this person out into the open without Jack around to screw up our plans, as only he can, it would be a win for everyone."

Christian reluctantly saw the logic. But he didn't like it. Not one bit.

Nope, and his dislike of this plan to proceed on schedule had *nothing* to do with his feelings for Stone Jackson.

And he had a bridge in Brooklyn to sell.

God. Damn. It.

STONE WASN'T fond of bulletproof vests. In the first place, they weren't actually proof against a high-caliber round, and there was always a head shot to consider. Even if the Wild Cards guys didn't believe this attacker was a pro, a shooter could still get lucky and nail the target in an unprotected part of the body.

Bullet-resistant vests tended to give their wearers a dangerous and potentially life-threatening sense of invincibility. Furthermore, they were hot and bulky, and they made his—well, Jack's—suits lie funny, no matter how good the tailor might be.

But Tucker was having no part of him going out in public without one.

Christian had opted to sit in the front seat of the SUV with Tucker en route to the gala tonight, and Stone didn't know whether to be insulted, hurt, or amused. He settled on being a little of all three.

At least he had the satisfaction of knowing he'd really shaken up Christian yesterday. Poor guy didn't know what to do with himself when all that careful control he wore like armor was stripped away from him.

He didn't for a minute think Christian was serious about the two of them never making love again. He'd just overwhelmed the guy a little. Or maybe a lot.

Good. Christian had been badly in need of a shock. He was stuck in the mother of all ruts and was too awesome a human being to languish in the bottom of it forever.

His mind drifted to the insane pleasure they'd shared, and his fly started to bulge alarmingly. Swearing, he pulled out the dry-as-dust speech and practiced reading it aloud in Jack's Texas accent.

Thankfully, it did the trick of killing his erection, and he would be able to walk upright when they arrived at the venue.

The SUV pulled to a stop, and the privacy panel slid down. "All right, then, sir. Good luck," Tucker announced.

Stone responded, "Christian, I want you to stay away from me at the gala tonight."

Christian's eyes registered hurt, but he quickly masked the expression.

"It's nothing personal," he explained quickly. "We just need Jack to play the flirt with the ladies. He wouldn't do that in front of his senior aide who knows his wife well, would he?"

"Not so much," Christian responded thoughtfully. He added, "But you don't have to throw yourself at women in the name of impersonating Jack—" Christian started.

"It's okay. I knew what I was signing up for when I agreed to play this role. Also, I happen to know Jack has a history of making his security staff stay away from him."

Tucker snorted from the driver's seat.

"More importantly, though," Stone continued grimly, "I don't want you hit by a stray bullet in case our stalker chooses tonight to find out how lousy a shot he is."

"Oh." The single syllable from Christian thudded like lead between them.

Christian swore quietly and got out of the SUV without waiting for Jack. Remorsefully, Stone watched him walk away.

Jesus, his job sucked sometimes.

And then it was time for him to climb out of the SUV, get mobbed by sycophants, and play United States senator for the next hour. Suddenly, being a plain old bodyguard who only risked death for a living didn't seem quite so bad.

Maybe he was just feeling antisocial tonight, but the aggressive interest of a huge crowd of people all eager to steal a minute of his time went against every minute of training he'd ever had at covert operations, avoiding detection, and above all, not being noticed.

And the women. *Oy.*

Apparently, this event had been declared some sort of open season on the politicians in attendance. At least every two minutes, some beautiful woman came sashaying his way, inviting him silently to look down her dress or feel up her thigh.

Truth be told, it was more than a little creepy. There was something desperate and needy in the seductive invitations these women threw at him. He didn't for a minute think any of them were genuinely attracted to him personally. How in the hell did Jack Lacey mistake any of this for real desire? Or maybe the guy was so desperate and needy himself that he couldn't see the calculation lurking in the women's cold eyes.

Stone painted on a fake smile and politely rebuffed them all, doing his damnedest not to show his revulsion at the unspoken traditions they represented.

A number of people asked about the previous day's attack, but he steadfastly refused to be drawn into conversation about it. People seemed taken aback that he would decline to make political hay from the incident. Was the real Jack that morally bankrupt, then?

A man approached, greeting him loudly. "Jack, old buddy. How the hell are you? I can see that Florida agrees with you. You look great. How've you been since the hunting trip?"

Fuck. Someone who knew Jack. This wasn't supposed to happen. He had no idea who the dude was, and worse, he'd sent Christian away. He leaned over to murmur to Tucker, "Get Christian ASAP."

"Right, sir."

Stone turned to face the backslapper. "I'm great. How the hell are you?"

He resorted to asking about the guy's latest hunting exploits, and when that topic petered out, he shifted to asking about how the job was going. Apparently, the guy was the CEO of some sort of paper manufacturing company. Unbelievably, the man didn't seem to realize he wasn't the real Jack Lacey. Obviously, the loudmouth knew Jack a great deal less well than he was pretending to. Thank God.

Christian strolled up, a smile on his face but his eyes were grim. He said smoothly, "Henry Spencer! What a nice surprise."

God bless him. He'd diagnosed correctly that Stone had no idea who this man was and that there was a grave risk of their ruse being exposed.

Christian continued pleasantly, "I didn't realize you were on the guest list. How's Millie? I haven't seen her tonight."

Lord, that man was smooth at this social stuff. Stone was mesmerized by Christian's effortless charm. Apparently, Jack had it to some degree as well. But Stone was completely at sea with all this small talk and name-dropping. Spencer spied someone in the crowd and declared that Jack had to meet him.

The man moved off to fetch the must-meet, and Stone muttered to Christian, "I retract my previous order to stay away. I can't do this without you."

Christian's eyes registered surprise. And then a slow smile spread across his face. "Stick with me, kid. You're on my turf now."

"And for the love of God, please run interference with some of the female sharks cruising this event."

"Not a chance. You're on your own in that department."

However, a fair share of the women did veer toward Christian, particularly after Stone politely ignored their come-hither antics. It was gratifying not being the only man in the joint uncomfortably pasting on a fake smile and pretending to be complimented by the come-ons.

The chicken was, indeed, rubber, and the emotional prostitution real as people vied for a piece of him in return for cold, hard cash. Thankfully, Christian handled most of the delicate negotiation of pimping out Jack's soul in return for campaign contributions.

During a momentary break from the sleeve-tugging and ass-kissing, Stone murmured to Christian, "How do you stand doing this for a living? Don't you feel like a flesh peddler?"

"I keep my eyes on the prize. Someday I'll be free of this rat race. And in the meantime, I'll know this world as an insider. It can't help but give me a better perspective on how to nail these bastards when they stray into corruption."

Stone's jaw tightened. There had to be a way to break Christian loose from the prison he'd locked himself in.

"Excuse me, Senator Lacey. The charity auction is about to begin, and we've had a wonderful idea. We'd like to auction off drinks and a dance with you."

Alarm sluiced through him, and he glanced over at Christian in panic. But the big jerk smiled broadly and replied for him, "The senator would love to auction off his body for the cause."

The woman moved off, chirping happily as Stone glared at Christian. "What the fuck?"

"You're here to play nice and make them money for their hospital." He added under his breath, "And girls don't actually have cooties."

He told Christian what he thought of that in no uncertain terms, and Christian merely laughed.

The auction ensued, and the bidding commenced for a date with Senator Lacey. He was hauled up on stage and paraded across it like a piece of meat. Of course, the real Jack would have eaten this up, so he was forced to flash a come-hither smile and flirt outrageously with the crowd in general. It was horrifying.

He felt like a prize bull.

A number of well-maintained divorcees battled against a bevy of bodacious twentysomethings for him. Based on the shouted comments flying across the crowd, everyone seemed to think they were buying more than drinks and a dance. Apparently, Jack's reputation preceded him.

The price climbed quickly to five thousand dollars, then started to slow. He called out, "C'mon, ladies. I'm prepared to give my all for the new children's wing of the hospital. Surely you are too."

He seemed to have signaled that sex was, indeed, the actual item for sale, and the bidding leaped past ten thousand dollars in the blink of an eye. He moved to the side of the stage where Christian stood and muttered, "Jeez. I had no idea Jack was such a stud."

"It's the power. It's an aphrodisiac."

"If you say so. I'll take a great mind, a sense of humor, and a heaping helping of class any day of the week and twice on Sunday."

Christian's gaze snapped to his, and Stone let the truth of his words shine naked in his gaze. Christian looked away hastily, but a hint of color climbed his cheeks.

Rattled himself, Stone moved back out to the center of the stage. "Who wants this hunk o' burning love? I promise you a dance you'll never forget."

A new voice called out from a dark corner near the front of the room. "Twenty thousand dollars."

A hush fell across the crowd. Stone looked out over the turned heads and was stunned to see an elderly woman with snow-white hair holding her hand up.

Christian gasped.

Stone looked back and forth between the woman and Christian, who were staring at each other fixedly. What was he missing here?

The auctioneer quickly dropped the gavel, and Stone jogged down the stage steps toward the winner. He couldn't wait to find out who she was and why she'd made Christian go pale.

He arrived at the table and bowed gallantly over the woman's hand, kissing it. "Shall we dance?" he asked.

"I'd rather go for a walk."

"Your wish is my command. You have me at a disadvantage, though. I don't know your name, darlin'." He helped her up from her seat and offered her his arm.

She took it, chuckling a little. "Oh, you're good. I'm Marielle Chatsworth."

"Chatsworth? As in Christian Chatsworth-Brandeis?" he blurted.

"He's my grandson."

"Then it's doubly a pleasure to meet you. He's an extraordinary man. Tremendous at his job."

"Indeed. It's a pleasure to meet you as well... Jack."

His gaze locked on hers. Definite humor laced her voice when she said his name. He led her away from the main crowd a little ways to a sprawling fountain feature that dominated one side of the plaza.

"Who are you?" she asked curiously.

Alarm tightened his gut. "I beg your pardon?"

She leaned close and murmured conspiratorially, "I know my grandson, and he despises Jack Lacey. But a few minutes ago, he looked at you like you're practically the second coming of Christ. The resemblance really is striking, but you do look at least ten years younger than the senator, even after the nip-and-tuck I heard he had last year."

"Florida's relaxing. High humidity. New moisturizing regimen...," he mumbled lamely.

She laughed gaily and patted his arm. "Save it for someone who'll believe you, young man."

"What gave me away?" he asked low.

"Christian. Had he not looked at you like that, I'd have had no idea."

"What are you going to do about it?"

"It depends on why you're impersonating Jack Lacey."

Crap. "There's a security threat," he explained evasively. "I'd really appreciate it if you didn't say anything to anyone about our little switcheroo. We're hoping to draw out the person making the threats and apprehend him or her."

"Your secret's safe with me. On one condition."

"Which is?"

"Promise me that your intentions toward my grandson are honorable."

He stopped walking and turned to face her. "I beg your pardon?"

"I'm going to take it amiss if you break his heart. He's very dear to me, my Christian."

Stone started. "Mrs. Chatsworth, I don't understand—"

"Yes, you do. Christian was always a fine boy. He has become an exceptional man. His parents have not been kind to him over the years, and he deserves much better. Don't you hurt him."

Her words were a dagger to his gut. Hell, he'd already hurt Christian by forcing him out of his comfort zone and pressing him mercilessly to give up control in the relationship.

Shit. He'd insisted on everything being a one-way road where he called all the shots. He'd already run roughshod over the guy. What an asshole he'd been.

His attention jerked back to his companion. He said soberly, "Christian is, indeed, a remarkable man. I'm lucky to know him. I can't promise what will happen over the long-term between us, but I can promise you that I will always respect him."

She looked at him keenly and then nodded. "Fair enough. We have a deal."

Stone commented ruefully, "I see where he gets his negotiating skills from."

"Never underestimate a Chatsworth, Jack. Or whatever your name is."

"Stone. Stone Jackson. And thank you for rescuing me from the barracudas."

She smiled up at him. "They aren't exactly your type, now are they?"

Damn, this woman was perceptive. She must be where Christian got his mad skills at reading people.

"It's nice to meet you, Stone Jackson. And good luck."

Although with what, he wasn't exactly sure.

CHAPTER TEN

CHRISTIAN WASTED no time closing in on Stone when he and his granny returned to the gala. "What was that all about?"

"Impressive lady, your grandmother. You should go say hello to her. She thinks very highly of you."

"That woman doesn't think highly of anyone. She rules the Chatsworth clan with an iron fist and doesn't even bother with the velvet glove."

"She said you're an exceptional man."

Christian stared, nonplussed. "Shut the front door. She did not."

"Cross my heart and hope to die."

"Son of a bitch."

Stone tsked. "Mr. Chatsworth-Brandeis. Such language!"

Christian grinned crookedly and started to say something, but a man in a tuxedo that had fit twenty pounds ago approached, wanting his minute in the spotlight with Jack Lacey before he opened his checkbook. "Seriously, Christian. Go talk with her. She'd appreciate it. I'll be okay for a few minutes on my own."

"You're sure?"

"Go."

He studied Stone thoughtfully. What was that new tone in his voice? He would almost call it gentleness were it not coming from Stone… a man who was every bit as hard as his name suggested. Perplexed, he headed toward his grandmother.

She'd always refused to speak about his sexual orientation and had never publicly acknowledged that he was gay. She had paid for his education when his father had refused to do so unless he agreed to therapy to *fix* him. But he'd always thought she'd covered his education costs mostly to tweak his old man's nose. Had he misjudged her?

"It's lovely to see you, Gran. You're looking wonderful."

"I'm looking old," she replied tartly. "You, however, are positively glowing."

"It's the humidity—"

"*Jack* said it was his new moisture regimen."

Jesus H. Christ. *She knew.* "Gran, I really need your help with this—"

She waved a dismissive hand. "Never fear. We came to an understanding, Jack and I."

Oh, dear Lord. "Dare I ask—"

A tremendous explosion of sound and light made him duck violently. A huge burst of fireworks erupted, making hearing, let alone conversation, impossible. His grandmother squeezed his hand and waved him back toward Stone.

Good grief. Stone and Tucker were going to lose their shit over these fireworks. They were exploding way too low and close to be safe. Another burst of noise and light made him throw his arm over his grandmother's shoulders protectively. Jeez Louise, that was loud. What idiot thought it would be a good idea to launch the fireworks display from inside the same plaza as the viewers?

The thought had no sooner crossed his mind when a whistling noise passed very, very close overhead at a shallow angle. Surely *that* wasn't supposed to happen.

Someone screamed, and then everyone was pointing up, screaming and running every which way. A news helicopter was spinning around and descending toward the plaza in a slow-motion corkscrew.

A single instant of horror roared through him, but then hyperalertness kicked in, stripping away fear and leaving behind a stop-action time distension that had everything around him happening at a fraction of normal speed.

His grandmother very slowly threw both arms up in front of her face and turned to flee. Pieces of burning something—maybe bits of the firework charge itself—flew through the air, leaving comet trails of sparks in their wake. People rose from their seats at the tables, mouths opening on screams he couldn't hear, chairs tipping over in slow motion.

As for the helicopter everyone was pointing at... a great, billowing plume of smoke boiled out of it from where the rotors attached to the roof of the fuselage. He thought he spied a large black hole angling through the tail section, as well. Very slowly the aircraft spun around, the broken tail flailing for purchase against the air.

Had a firework gone astray and hit it? Regardless, it was coming down. Now. In the middle of the plaza.

Where's Stone?

And with that thought, time snapped back to full speed like a painful rubber band against his skin, and noise and chaos and panic erupted around him in all their ugly insanity.

"Gran, can you get to that building over there on your own?"

"I'm not in my dotage, boy. I still do Pilates three days a week."

"Thanks. I need to go help."

"Go find Jack. Make sure he's all right. I'll be fine."

People scattered in every direction. Overturned tables and chairs made a jungle of the middle of the plaza. And somewhere in this disaster, the man he loved was no doubt risking his life to do something heroic and suicidal because that was who Stone was.

He dashed forward into the carnage of the gala, searching frantically. As the main wave of partygoers cleared the center of the square, he abruptly had no trouble spotting the tall, muscular silhouette. Stone, followed closely by Tucker. Both men were rushing *toward* the area where the helicopter was coming down, herding people away from the danger. Of course they were.

Christian could only stare, aghast, too far away to reach him, as the helicopter's damaged tail departed the aircraft and careened wildly through the air, slamming into the side of a building with a huge crash of breaking glass.

The helicopter started to spin, picking up speed with every rotation until it was spiraling frantically toward the ground without any apparent means of support to break the fall.

With a tremendous crunch of collapsing metal, the helicopter slammed into the middle of the plaza. Pieces of metal and furniture and who knew what else went flying, propelled by the force of the impact and likely the turning rotor blades.

Stone threw up his arms and ducked as Christian reached out helplessly with his hands. It was an involuntary reflex, a desperate need to protect the man he cared about.

Too far away. He couldn't reach Stone to throw his body over Stone's, to protect him. He could do *nothing* to protect Stone.

The helicopter rolled onto its side. Rotor blade tips hit the ground and bounced violently, breaking off from the aircraft and flying wildly in every direction. By a minor miracle, all the blades flew over the heads of the crowd now flat on the ground and screaming.

Frantic, Christian took off running toward the mess and spied Stone and Tucker heading for the demolished copter. As he sprinted for all he was worth toward them, he saw the pair climb up onto the actual wreckage to rescue the occupants. Thank God. At least he knew Stone was alive after that rotor had disintegrated and done its best to decapitate everyone around it.

Women attempting to climb back to their feet and run in high heels and ball gowns were tripping and falling all over the place, and he stopped to help a half dozen of them to their feet before he finally reached the smoking hull of the dead helicopter.

"What can I do to help?" he called up.

Stone yelled down from his perch straddling the top of the wreckage, "We need something long and hard to use as a crowbar!"

Christian looked around and found some sort of tubular metal pipe from off the helicopter that seemed to fit the bill. He hoisted it up to Tucker and Stone. They used his pipe to jimmy open the door. Then the pair bodily hauled out a young man who was a reporter, if the digital movie camera still clutched in his fist was any indication. The guy was bruised and battered with blood running freely down one side of his face, but ambulatory.

Christian caught the young man as he slid down the roof of the helicopter to the ground. Christian yanked out his shirt and his pocket knife, sawing at the bottom of it until he could tear off a long strip. He grabbed the reporter's hand, shoved it against the gash on his head, and quickly bound the guy's hand tightly over the wound.

"Can you make it to that cluster of police cars over there?" He pointed to where the security detail had been staging this evening. "There's an ambulance parked over there, and the cop cars will also have first aid kits in them."

The reporter nodded.

"Keep pressure on that wound until someone can clean it and bandage it, okay?" Christian gave the guy a gentle push to get him moving in the right direction.

He looked up at the rescue operation going on over his head and jolted. Stone had disappeared. Only Tucker straddled the now gaping doorway. Stone must have jumped down into the helicopter. "What's he doing?" Christian called up to Tucker.

"Looks like the pilot has busted both legs!" Tucker called back. "We'll need help handing him down."

"I smell gas fumes, Travis. It's possible this thing could explode. Can you guys hurry with your rescue heroics already?"

The rescued reporter behind him yelled, "There's a wire in the tail throwing sparks into a puddle of fluid on the ground!"

He'd be damned if he would leave Stone behind to fry if this thing blew up. Grimly, Christian held his ground, waiting to help with the pilot. Somebody cried out in pain from inside the helicopter, and then Tucker leaned down inside the wrecked cockpit, grunting and straining.

The upper torso of a man in a flight suit appeared. He was unconscious and hung limp over the edge of the helicopter. Tucker eased the man down to Christian.

He turned around to catch the injured pilot on his back. He draped the man's arms over his shoulders in a fireman's carry and moved away from the crashed craft.

He took off in a heavy-footed jog and prayed Tucker and Stone were close behind him. But it wasn't as if he could spare the time or energy to turn around and look. It took an eternity to carry the pilot to the far edge of the square, well away from the crash site. A policeman came up with a bulky first aid kit and identified himself as a first responder. The cop radioed for the next ambulance on scene to be sent to his location, and then he went to work immobilizing the pilot's legs and neck.

Following the officer's instructions, Christian knelt and helped the guy stabilize the pilot's body. The flier's breathing was another issue as he gurgled and gasped for air with every breath.

"Collapsed lung," the cop announced. "We've got to get this guy help now. Help me lift him so I can carry him over to the one ambulance on scene."

It was hard to work around the various makeshift splints they'd applied, but they got the pilot draped over the cop's back, and the officer took off running much the same way Christian had.

With the pilot safe in a medic's hands, Christian turned his attention back to the crash site, searching frantically for Stone. He found him and Tucker herding the last of the partygoers away from the helicopter.

And that was when a spark finally caught up with the pool of jet fuel or maybe the collected fumes. It wasn't a spectacular explosion like on television. Rather it whooshed and suddenly, there was fire where there'd been none before. It flared up quickly and engulfed the helicopter in flames. Christian saw the outline of Stone's big body hunching protectively over an elderly man, no doubt to shield him from the heat as the gentleman shambled away from the accident.

Sirens howled and grew louder as police, fire, and rescue units streamed to the scene. The square was littered with debris from both the crash and the panicked flight of the partygoers, but everyone seemed out of range of any danger.

The bystanders milled around the edges of the plaza, looking dazed and disheveled. Christian spied more than a few bloodied people, but they all seemed alive and receiving first aid of one kind or another.

He probably ought to go looking for his grandmother, but she'd been at the farthest edge of the square from the disaster and moving away from the chaos the last time he saw her. Frankly, he was more worried about Stone's safety. That guy's heroic streak was a mile wide, after all, and tinged with a touch of self-destructive impulse.

He searched through the crowd until he spotted the familiar visage. Stone's tuxedo coat was off, no doubt draped over someone's shoulders, and at the moment he was bent down in concern over someone seated on the edge of a concrete planter box.

Christian sprinted for his side. He desperately needed to be close to Stone. Close enough where he could protect his lover if need be. To touch him to be sure he was really alive and unhurt.

He reached Stone's side and rasped, "Are you okay?" He was shocked at how hoarse his own voice was.

"Yeah. You?"

"I'm good."

For an instant their stares met, and raw, profound relief showed in their gazes. It was all there in their eyes: the unspoken attraction that went way deeper than simple lust. Awareness that they could have a future together. That they'd come perilously close to losing it all just now. A promise to do something about it with this second chance they'd miraculously been given.

"Thanks for carrying out that pilot. We couldn't have done it without you."

Christian responded, "I dunno about that. You and Tucker seemed to have things pretty well in hand."

"Time was the problem. We got him out twice as fast with you there to take him. That was the difference between us getting away from the copter before it caught fire and not."

"I'm not the hero, and you can stop trying to shift the glory to me. You are. You and Tucker."

Stone looked around the square. "There were probably a bunch of heroes out here tonight. For a crowd this size to disperse that fast and not have any serious injuries that I can see means a whole lot of people helped one another."

As a fire truck careened into the plaza, then steered up a set of shallow steps and over next to the burning helicopter, he added, "And here come a few more heroes. We need to let them know the passenger and pilot are out of the craft already."

"I'm on it," Christian declared.

He raced over to the nearest police officer and relayed the information with a request to radio the information to the firefighters immediately. It was taken care of and a brief thanks from the fire department relayed back to him. Indeed, as he looked on, the firefighters backed well away from the copter to spray it with water from a safer distance.

Tucker came up beside him. "We need to get Stone—Jack—out of here. The police are too busy to hold off the media, and reporters are going to be all over this place in a minute."

Aww, hell. The guy was totally right. He hadn't been thinking about their ruse at all in the past minutes of chaos and danger. "Let's go get him, Travis."

They ran over to Stone, who was comforting someone who seemed to be hyperventilating or maybe having an asthma attack. Christian and Tucker grabbed his elbows and bodily dragged him away from the scene. Christian paused long enough to tell a cop who looked like a supervisor that they were taking the senator back to his hotel, and then they were out of there.

The SUV wound past a phalanx of emergency response vehicles and then was clear of the inbound emergency response. Tucker accelerated onto a highway, and Christian finally breathed a sigh of relief. He closed his eyes in abrupt exhaustion and eventually opened them to find Stone staring worriedly at him.

He smiled, or at least tried to, and Stone reached over to hold his hand. "No one was killed, and our side won the battle. It was a good night."

Tucker responded soberly from the front seat, "Ooo-rah."

He just sat there, focusing on Stone's warm, strong grip and the reassurance it offered. They were all alive. They'd made it. Everyone he loved had survived the accident.

They were nearly back to the hotel before he roused himself to ask, "What the heck happened back there? It looked to me like a firework hit the helicopter and brought it down."

"Pretty much." Stone pulled a disgusted face. "Someone obviously thought it would be a great idea to shoot off fireworks from inside the damned plaza. Those were commercial-grade explosives and should have been staged from a lot farther away than that. It's a miracle not more people were seriously hurt."

"Agreed."

"How's the pilot?" Stone asked. "He didn't look great when I hauled him out."

"He was unconscious, had a punctured lung, and multiple broken bones. A cop and I stabilized the bone breaks and then the officer hustled him toward the nearest ambulance to get the guy some oxygen and a high-speed ride to a trauma hospital."

"Can we get an update on him?" Stone asked.

Christian smiled and pulled out his cell phone. "Observe one of the perks of being a United States senator."

It took him a second to find the phone number of the nearest major hospital to the crash site and to dial it. "Hello. This is Senator Lacey's office calling. The senator is worried about the helicopter pilot who crashed down on tonight's fundraising event. Can you give us a general update on his condition?"

He put the call on speaker so Stone and Tucker could hear, and they all listened to the good news that the pilot was stable and heading shortly into surgery to set his various broken bones.

Tucker went into his own room when they reached the suite to call his wife and let her know that he was safe before the story hit the national news channels.

Christian strode over to Stone, who held out his arms silently as he approached. He grabbed Stone and held on for dear life for a long minute. It was gratifying to feel the fine trembling passing through Stone's body too. It was nice to know the badass commando was at least a little affected by nearly having a helicopter crash on top of him.

"You okay?" Stone murmured against his neck.

"I will be now. For a minute there, before I spotted you in the crowd, I thought I'd lost you. And I confess, it flipped me out worse than I could have imagined."

Stone made a sound vaguely like humor. "I'm a tough old bird. I'm harder to kill than that. A dinky little helicopter smashing me flat wouldn't do the trick."

He laughed reluctantly. "You're such a jerk."

"I love you too," Stone retorted.

They froze.

Should he say it back? He'd already had the thought, but did he dare admit it? God, the power it would give Stone over him—

Did power dynamics in their relationship matter for a damn when Stone had nearly died?

He opened his mouth to reply. But too late.

Stone stepped back. Smiled crookedly. "Don't panic, Christian. I meant it metaphorically. Not literally. You can breathe now."

But could he? What if he really did want Stone to love him back?

He studied Stone's face intently, but under the Jack makeup, grime from the crash, and the completely closed emotional mask Stone had donned in the past few seconds, he couldn't read a damned thing. He had no way of telling if Stone was lying about his declaration being just words and not an expression of real feelings.

"Stone. We need to—"

The phone rang.

Of course it fucking rang exactly as he was about to tell Stone they needed to have a serious talk. Honest talk.

He stared at the phone, still ringing insistently.

"Need me to get that?" Stone asked.

Swearing under his breath, he shook himself. "No. This part is my job. You did your hero thing on the plaza. But this is the part of crisis management that I excel at. I've got it."

He picked up the phone. The reporter on the other end of the line was excited out of all proportion at rumors that the senator himself had pulled the passengers out of a burning helicopter.

"It wasn't burning when the senator and his security chief helped the passengers exit the craft," Christian corrected. Not that the journalist was going to listen to a damned thing he said. They smelled a sensational headline, and the truth could stand aside and get out of the way of it.

Stone flashed him a thumbs-up and retreated into the bedroom. Probably washing off the Jack face and changing into nonbloody clothes. That and shutting down his emotions and carefully locking them away in some mental drawer way the hell in the darkest corner of his brain.

Dammit, they'd almost had a breakthrough there. Mr. Emotionally Unavailable had almost been forced to admit to how he really felt about the two of them.

With a sigh, Christian picked up the next call waiting on hold. He spent the next hour repeating the same line over and over to journalists. "The senator is unharmed and prays for the safety of everyone else involved. He has no further comment at this time."

Sometime in the middle of the media frenzy, Stone strolled out of the bedroom, his hair damp, and wearing fresh clothes. He poured himself a stiff whiskey and sprawled on the sofa in front of the television to watch the news, muted of course, so Christian could give telephone interviews.

"Why don't you just record a message?" Stone finally muttered, after he'd repeated his stock responses for about the tenth time.

He rolled his eyes, wishing it were that easy. It was all about forming a personal connection with the reporter and then striking a calm yet concerned tone of voice that conveyed reassurance and empathy to each person who called. His superpower was reading other people and knowing exactly how to connect with each one.

Gradually the panic in the callers diminished as word got out of no fatalities and only the pilot having suffered serious but not life-threatening injuries. The journalist who'd been on the chopper was already making the rounds doing live interviews, a white bandage prominent on his forehead, and he milked the moment for all the coverage he could squeeze out of it.

A few channels started to speculate that the helicopter had been shot down. Which made him cover the receiver with his hand and ask Stone, "Is that possible? Could the chopper have been shot by a small missile or something?"

Stone shook his head decisively. "I know the sound of an incoming missile. I'd recognize it in my sleep. No missile flew into that plaza. It was a couple of firework mortars that took out the chopper. Period." He added, "You might want to have the press ask what the hell that bird was doing over the plaza, though. Surely that fireworks show had a permit from the city. Which meant air traffic control was notified and wouldn't have been routing any air traffic over that area."

Christian stared. "Are you suggesting that the helicopter didn't have permission to be there?"

"I'm not suggesting it. I'm telling you that's how it was."

"Fascinating." On his laptop, he typed the name of the reporter who'd been in the chopper and sat back, startled when he realized the guy worked for a notorious gossip publication known for making up the wildest tales. They were the people who routinely reported Bigfoot sightings and alien abductions.

His spiel changed in the next phone call, this one from a reputable news agency who found his questions about why the helicopter had been flying over an active firework display deeply interesting. The caller got off the phone quickly, no doubt to do a little more digging.

It would be morning before the television stations collected all the information and compiled enough cell phone footage to put together a coherent view of what had happened.

As the calls petered out, he leaned back, exhausted. He'd done his job and deflected the majority of the interest in the story away from Jack Lacey and onto an investigation of the reporter and pilot in the helicopter. Tucker came into the room, announcing that he was spending tonight on the sofa where he could be close if Stone needed anything. It appeared that Stone had himself an admirer.

"Thanks for everything you did at the fundraiser, Travis. You were a real hero."

"Stone was the hero. When he jumped down into that chopper with smoking and sparking like that—mad props to the guy—that was some dangerous shit."

A knock on the door made them both look up sharply.

A journalist had somehow managed to get past the hotel's security staff, and Tucker unleashed a hard-core Marine ass-chewing on the guy, chasing him all the way back to the elevator. Christian thought he heard the elevator door close before Tucker quit barking like a pissed-off elephant seal.

Tucker returned to the suite and snatched up a phone to give the hotel security staff a chippy piece of his mind about their effectiveness at protecting hotel guests. The worst of his outburst over, Tucker rang up room service and ordered a tray of snacks and sandwiches to be sent up to the suite, pronto.

Then the ex-Marine announced, "I'm getting a chair and parking in front of the damned door of the suite for the rest of the night. And neither of you are going anywhere. Understood?"

Stone and Christian exchanged amused glances. "Yes, sir!" Christian replied briskly.

Tucker nodded in satisfaction and replied more calmly, "Holler if you need anything."

Christian nodded his thanks at the man, who really was a boon to have around in a crisis.

He planted himself in front of the television to watch the results of his work intently. The evening news cycle passed and the media blitzkrieg of breaking news reports finally wound down. They'd weathered the storm, and no one was reporting that one of Senator Lacey's bodyguards had been impersonating him at the disastrous fundraiser.

He reached for the remote and turned off the TV.

"We good?" Stone asked.

"Mischief managed," he replied, relieved.

The suite was quiet, and they were alone at last. Their gazes met.

"You okay, Christian?"

"I will be."

"Combat stress takes some getting used to. It gets easier to handle the more you're exposed to it."

"No, thanks. I don't need scenes like that mess in the plaza to become a common occurrence in my life."

"Oh, that wasn't anywhere close to how bad combat gets. No one had any body parts blown off, and nobody died in my arms. There were no lakes of blood, and the only screaming was from scared people, not half-gutted people. Like I said before—it was a good night."

Stone's words conjured up all of Christian's fear for Stone's life from earlier. A shudder passed through his entire body.

He stood up and moved toward Stone slowly, his legs feeling a hundred years old all of a sudden. He said raggedly, "My first thought when the helicopter started to come down was of you. I was terrified for your safety. And I was scared shitless that you might die before we got to figure out what's going on between us."

"What is going on between us?" Stone asked seriously.

"It's more than I've wanted to admit to myself is going on, that's for darn sure."

That drew a short laugh of commiseration out of Stone.

By mutual unspoken consent, they moved into the bedroom. Christian wrapped his arms around Stone and hung on for a long time, again, absorbing the strength of Stone's embrace. Eventually, the shock and relief wore off a bit, leaving just the two of them behind.

Stone muttered, "When I heard that firework blow so close, I thought someone had shot me. And my first thought was how pissed off I was going to be if I had to die without ever telling you how goddamn crazy about you I am."

Christian's entire being froze. Stone felt the same way about him? Something opened up around him, not exactly unicorns farting hearts and rainbows, but *possibility*. Hope.

In his entire life, he'd never seriously believed he might find a man like Stone, who was his equal in intelligence, focus, and drive, and who actually might be able and willing to love him back.

By being gay, the dating pool was already vastly reduced in size, and then his impossibly high personal standards eliminated most of the rest. As if that weren't bad enough, within that tiny pool of possible life mates who met his high standards for ethics, intelligence, and general hotness, one would have to exist who would put up with his OCD tendencies, his high-powered job, his high-stress life, his need to control his world but also his need to relinquish that control in the bedroom, his sarcasm, his arrogance, and all his other many imperfections. And then to top all that off, he would have to actually *find* that person.

Had lightning truly struck?

Stone was kissing him, and all of a sudden he was kissing Stone back passionately, desperately. The adrenaline rushing through his blood turned to molten desire, and insatiable need to have this man was slowly driving him half-mad.

Stone seemed to be similarly affected, and they tore each other's clothes off, wool and starched cotton, silk ties, socks and underwear pooling on the floor around them.

And then it was just the two of them, chest to chest, belly to belly, heart to heart. Their lovemaking was frantic at first, but then, as their bodies joined and became one, they slowed, savoring this moment, languidly exploring the boundaries of pleasure with each other.

Stone seemed to understand that tonight Christian needed to be made love to tenderly in the same way Christian instinctively knew that tonight Stone needed the human connection with him more than he needed to breathe.

Face-to-face, gripping each other's cocks firmly, they stared into each other's eyes as their pleasure grew and grew, and then grew some more.

His craving for Stone knew no boundaries. He hung on with all his strength and rode the wave of building ecstasy, reveling in the almost lost look that came over Stone's face as he gave himself over completely to this magical thing between them.

He knew the feeling. This was new territory for him as well. He was unused to the silence inside his mind. Absent was the usual sarcastic little voice telling him he was a fake and not worthy of this man. There was something so right about being with Stone, so natural. It just felt right. Easy. Meant to be.

A sense of having found home came over him. Stone was home, the place where he could rest, recharge, and find solace.

Something was different about how Stone was touching him tonight. Sure, the usual intensity and physicality were there, but Stone took his time, was more thoughtful, seemed intent on showing Christian how much he appreciated him. It was… respectful. And it was mesmerizing as hell.

They met tonight as adults, sharing a mutual expression of caring for each other. It was tender within the collision of big, strong bodies. Emotional within the panted exclamations of pleasure. Loving within the lust.

A great yawning space opened up within him, and then Stone was there, filling every last corner of it with his humor and honor and determination, and all the other qualities that made Stone so very special. He absorbed them all into his soul, and in return gave all of himself back.

And then the sheer sexual sensory overload of the moment took over, ripping away all thought, leaving him raw and exposed and hungry. Pounding lust drove him harder into Stone's hand, pushing against the hard, immovable wall of his lover.

It was all about straining muscles, sweat-slicked skin, bodies slapping together, groaning pleasure, and then a grinding rush toward release. The explosion, when it overtook them, was especially epic, enhanced by the raw emotions left over from the earlier crisis.

They shouted into the pillows as their bodies convulsed in paroxysms of bliss that rocked Christian to the core. His world actually shifted on its axis a little, making room for the possibility of blinding pleasure that left him emptied to the bottom of his soul and refilled to the brim with Stone's soul. He collapsed back against the pillows.

Mind. Blown.

Stone panted beside him, also lying on his back, staring up at the ceiling. They were silent for a change. But then words would do paltry justice to what they'd just shared between them. Stone touched his forearm, sliding his fingers down it to grasp his hand. He managed a reassuring squeeze in response to the unspoken question.

They stayed like that a long time, lost in the feelings, without words, just being with each other.

Gradually, the tension and stress of the evening's crisis drained, and where it all had been, only the two of them remained. Whole. Unbroken. Together.

Chapter Eleven

STONE WOKE abruptly, startled awake by Christian mumbling in his sleep and tossing in the throes of what sounded like a nightmare. He put a comforting hand on Christian's shoulder, and Christian settled immediately at Stone's touch, moving on to something less disturbing in his dream.

Stone was still blown away by the sex they'd shared earlier. He'd never felt anything like that. It moved him. As in, emotionally. Hell, as they'd lain together in the afterglow, he'd actually teared up a little. The grizzled combat warrior had been overcome by the beauty and generosity Christian shared with him.

Since when was *he* Mr. Sensitivity?

Wide-awake, he looked at the bedside clock. Another hour till sunrise. Time enough to sneak out for a run on the beach, which he desperately needed. Not only did he still feel residual adrenaline from last night coursing through his veins in need of release, but he badly needed to get his head together.

Things were moving fast with Christian. Things he was completely unprepared for and hadn't seen coming. At all.

He slipped out from under the covers with all the stealth of his Special Forces training and silently collected running shorts, T-shirt, and running shoes. He dressed in the living room and then eased past Tucker, dozing in the chair outside the suite.

The elevator bell would wake the security chief, so he opted for the fire escape. He jogged down a few floors, then ducked into a hallway to catch an elevator the rest of the way down.

Free. For the first time since he'd started this circus of a job, he could disengage, stretch his legs, and clear his head. Except as he finished stretching and took off running down the beach, thoughts of Christian would not let go of him.

He remembered the stricken look in Christian's eyes as he'd talked about his fear of losing Stone last night. An image came to him of Christian's determination and courage as he'd hauled that pilot away from the burning helicopter. He recalled Christian's openness and honesty in bed last night. He listed everything he couldn't get enough of about the man, and the list took him several miles down the beach to compile. As he turned for the hotel, he was still adding things to the list, in fact.

Face it, buddy. Christian is perfect.

Stone's stride lengthened as joy flowed through his now warm muscles and the kinks of vigorous sex worked out. He reveled in his deep breathing, in the blood surging through his veins, in the glorious sensation of being alive.

Eventually it dawned on him that his body might feel great, but his head was generally a mess. The last few days had really done a number on him.

Not only was it bizarre living another man's life, but what the hell was he going to do with Christian? His life wasn't set up for another human being to share it. How much was he willing to give up to be with Christian, assuming Christian was even thinking long-term about the two of them?

God, he'd give a million bucks to know how Christian had planned to finish that sentence he'd started when the phone rang last night. The sentence that would have been his response to his accidental declaration of love for Christian.

It had just slipped out. Hell, he hadn't even realized it was true until the words were out of his mouth.

Love was a topic they'd assiduously avoided so far, and he wasn't sure it was a place either of them wanted to go. They both had demanding careers they'd thrown themselves into with abandon. Of course, maybe that was both of them compensating for the emptiness of their personal lives.

But after last night, did he have any choice except to bring up the subject? First Granny Chatsworth had forced him to admit how special a man Christian really was, and then the big jerk had to go and show it.

He'd shown it in his active, brave response to the crisis in the plaza, and he'd shown it in bed last night.

He'd thought at first that their emotionally intense sex had been the adrenaline aftermath hitting Christian hard. But it had shifted and become so achingly tender, he'd had an errant urge to weep while they'd made love. It had seemed as if Christian was trying to communicate silently to Stone all the things neither of them dared to say out loud.

Hell, he'd been shaken by the accident too. He had enough combat experience working with close-air-support aircraft to know how near a miss it had been. A thousand people had been in that plaza. They all owed that pilot a huge debt for keeping the helicopter airborne long enough to get everyone out of the way before it autorotated to the ground. What a clusterfuck it would have been otherwise.

Speaking of clusterfucks, it seemed they'd pulled off a second public appearance of faux-Jack Lacey successfully. But honestly, he wasn't sure their luck would hold for much longer. The bastard needed to get back here and resume his regularly scheduled life pretty damned quick or the jig would be up.

To that end, he paused a mile or so down the beach from the hotel and put in a call to Pere Cardiffe at Wild Cards. "Hey, it's Stone. What's the word on our missing senator?"

"The *Wrastle Castle* still has not made landfall. All our efforts to relay a message to the senator by way of the ship's captain have been unsuccessful."

"Meaning that the captain won't relay the message or that Lacey won't respond?"

"The latter."

Having lived in the bastard's shoes for a few days, he had a better understanding of the allure of fame and constant attention that must draw Jack to politics. Perhaps an appeal to jealousy and ego might sway the man.

"Has anyone tried telling him that a body double is doing a better job at being him than him? If you tell him a security guard is hogging all of his attention, media interviews, and women, he might come running back to Miami to stop it."

Pere laughed at the other end of the phone. "It's worth a try. At this point I have no better ideas. As long as the yacht stays in international waters, everybody's hands are tied."

"Please tell me this is the strangest job you guys have ever taken."

Another laugh out of Pere. "I don't know. We've got a weird one unfolding in Gibraltar. But you're right up there."

"Sometimes it sucks being the special one." Pere laughed yet again and Stone added, "Good luck baiting Lacey to get his ass back here."

"Good luck continuing to be him."

Stone snorted and disconnected the call. Jack Lacey could use a good old-fashioned ass-kicking for the hassles he was causing a whole lot of decent people. He pocketed his phone and continued back toward the hotel as the sun came up in a blazing ball of red.

His thoughts turned back to Christian and the intense lovemaking they'd shared last night. An overwhelming desire to do that again rolled over him. In fact, he could do that a whole bunch of times and never grow tired of it or of the man himself.

No doubt about it. He'd fallen, and fallen hard, for Christian.

He was almost back to the hotel when another runner came toward him on the beach, tall and athletic, moving with the efficient, ground-eating strides of a hard-core runner. With a start he recognized Christian.

As they drew near, he drew breath to give a cheerful greeting. He was feeling a million times better after getting some exercise. But then he caught Christian's thunderous expression and came to a full stop.

"What in the bloody hell are you doing out here all by yourself?" Christian ground out.

"Running," he answered cautiously.

"In the first place, Jack doesn't run."

"But I'm not wearing Jack makeup. I'm being me."

"At a distance, you still bear a striking resemblance to the man," Christian snapped. "And in the second place, what possessed you to come out here alone?"

"Why not? No assassin's going to be out looking for Jack on the beach, and certainly not at this time of day. Like you said, he doesn't run."

"And yet you're not the only person out here. You could be seen."

"I don't see how that's a problem—"

"That's because you have no idea how rapacious the press really is. Not to mention most of them hate Jack's guts."

"I don't see a mob of reporters anywhere, Christian. It'll be okay," he soothed. "Hell, it's barely sunrise. They're all still in bed asleep. I would tell you not to overreact if I didn't know how infuriating it is to be told that when you're freaking out a little. Just breathe for me. Okay?"

Christian took a step closer and confessed, "When I woke up and you were gone, I freaked out a little. Last night was a lot."

Was he talking about their sex, or about the mess at the fundraiser?

"Did you think I was running away from you?" he blurted, equal parts pleasantly surprised and dismayed that he'd upset Christian.

Christian mumbled something unintelligible.

He would take that as a yes. Stone said forcefully, "Jesus, Joseph, and Mary, man. I'm not running away from you or avoiding you! I'm out here trying to wrap my mind around what's happening between us. It's overwhelming to me... in a good way, I might add."

Their gazes met, Christian's troubled and his incredulous.

"For real?" Christian asked doubtfully.

"Don't be an idiot," he said fondly. He leaned in, grabbed Christian by the back of the neck and laid a quick, hard, smoking-hot kiss on him that was more tonsillectomy than smooch.

Forehead to forehead with Christian, he mumbled, "I don't know what the hell I'm going to do with you, and we have a lot of shit to sort out, but I'm not pulling a runner on you. I promise."

Christian went very still, absorbing his words.

It felt as if Christian was testing the truth of what he'd said. He relaxed against Stone. Please God, let him have heard the honesty in Stone's statement.

"Later," Christian said low. "After this is all over."

"Deal."

They kissed once more to seal the deal, and then Christian stepped back and looked around furtively.

Stone commented wryly, parroting back the man's words from the first time they met. "This is South Beach, dude. No one's worried about a little PDA between a couple of guys on the beach."

"Still. We can't be too careful."

"So, I still feel pretty good. You wanna go a few miles with me?" Stone asked.

"While I'd love to take you up on that because Lord knows I do need the stress relief, we'd better get you back to the hotel before someone sees you and thinks you're Jack."

Stone grinned as they turned to walk back toward the hotel. "I maintain that we should run back. That way, when the real Jack returns, he'll have to take up jogging to cover up for his absence."

Christian cracked up. "I'd pay good money to see him slogging up and down this beach."

"We should think up a few more things for me to do as him that'll torment him when he resumes being himself."

"Remind me never to well and truly piss you off, Stone. You've got a mean streak in you."

"Only where people who've treated you badly are concerned."

Christian grinned lopsidedly at him. "Maybe we can find another way to blow off a little of your stress besides running out here? And I could use a shower somewhere in there, while we're at it."

"Is that so?" Stone replied, a grin breaking across his face.

CHRISTIAN'S NEAR heart failure at waking up to an empty bed had mostly calmed by the time the two of them emerged from a steaming and very lengthy shower that involved a great deal of soap suds and slippery sex.

Stone was in an expansively good mood, and Christian was feeling pretty damned skippy himself. They sat down to go over the day's itinerary.

"Okay, so we can safely cancel your golf-tournament appearance after last night's fiasco."

"Thank God. As a golfer, I'm a pretty good tennis player," Stone admitted.

Christian winced. "Jack's actually not a half-bad golfer. My plan was to fake a wrist injury for you and have you drive the cart and drink beer."

"Well, hell. That sounds like the first fun thing I'd have gotten to do as Jack."

"If you were a womanizer, you'd have a deep appreciation for living in Jack's skin for a few days."

Stone snorted. "Even if I did swing that way, I think it's skeezy to use status and power to get anyone in my bed."

"And that's why I lo—" Christian broke off. Holy shit. He'd almost done what Stone had. "Metaphorical," he mumbled. "Metaphorical."

Stone leaned back, though, studying him speculatively.

He said hastily, "That leaves us with the casino fundraiser Saturday night to get through."

"Thank God," Stone replied fervently. "Only one more appearance."

"Tired of playing senator?" he asked.

"I've had my fifteen minutes of fame. I'm ready to return to my anonymous life, thanks."

"Introvert," he snorted.

"That's not a dirty word, you know."

"Maybe not if you sneak up on people and kill them for a living. But in politics you'd damn well better like being around hordes of people."

"The way I hear it, congressmen are pretty good at sneaking up on unsuspecting victims." He shrugged. "Like, oh, you. Jack dumped a hell of a mess in your lap without a word of warning."

Tucker hung up a phone and interjected, "The mess is about to get more complicated. That was Mrs. Lacey. She's flying in this afternoon. Show of support for her husband after last night's near miss and all."

Stone rolled his eyes. "Great. The last thing I need is a wife."

Christian muttered dryly, "What *would* you do with one?"

Stone scowled at him, and Christian broke into the grin he'd been holding back. "Never fear. You'll like your wife."

It was decided that Tucker would go alone to the airport to pick up Jill Lacey. There was too much potential for awkwardness if Jill and Stone's first meeting was in public. People might pick up on any formality or lack of displays of affection. Best to bring her fully into the conspiracy in the privacy of the hotel suite.

Assuming, of course, that she agreed to go along with the risky scheme at all.

Tucker duly left for the airport, and Christian made one more pass through the speech he'd drafted for Stone to deliver at the casino fundraiser. Although the appearances so far had been important, the really big fish would turn out in force on Saturday night. Not only did the speech have to strike exactly the right note to loosen purse strings, but it also had to sound like vintage Jack. Any number of people who knew Jack well would be at the event.

His current working plan was to hold Stone out of the main casino party until it was time for his speech, have Stone deliver the speech, and then have him get called away immediately afterward by an emergency. Everyone thought it was cool when senators had classified crises to deal with. It made the politician look important and observers feel like insiders to know that something was up before the rest of the world did.

His cell phone rang and Christian fished it out of his pocket. Now why was Tucker calling him on his personal line? "Hey, Travis. What's up?"

"I'm at the airport with Mrs. Lacey. She's being mobbed by reporters and paparazzi."

Alarm sliced through his gut. "Why?"

"Something about pictures of Jack and his lover. They're going crazy. Full-on feeding frenzy."

Oh, Jesus. Had someone gotten pictures of Jack and Chesty? That was the one variable he had no control over. He'd prayed that Jack's innate hatred of paparazzi and well-developed radar for when they were around would save them all. But no.

He closed his eyes in chagrin as the whole house of cards unraveled before his very eyes. Jack was ruined. His own career was over. His life was over. The scandal was going to be horrendous.

Belatedly he mumbled, "You know what to do. Pull her out and get her over here ASAP so we can coordinate damage control."

"Roger that." Tucker hung up the phone, and Christian slumped in his chair.

Stone wandered into the living room. "What's up?"

"Pictures of Jack and Chesty have hit the press."

"Aww, jeez. I'm sorry. Is there anything I can do? Maybe deny that the pictures are Jack, err, me? After all, fake Jack has been in Miami the whole time. The pictures will be coming out of the Caribbean, right?"

"True." A glimmer of hope flickered in his gut.

"You can have an analyst declare them to have been taken in St. Thomas or wherever they were snapped. A bunch of people can verify that I've been making public appearances here over the past few days."

He had a point. Maybe they should brazen out the ruse and dare the press to prove them wrong. "We'll need Jill to corroborate the story. Everyone loves her, and people will listen to her. If she calls the story a ridiculous lie, that will hold weight."

"More than if Jack, aka I, call the story a lie?"

"Oh, heck yeah."

"Wow. Jack must hate the fact that her credibility is higher than his."

"It drives him crazy."

"Doesn't give him the right to cheat on her," Stone commented.

"Amen."

Thank God Jill had arrived. This thing was getting bigger than him. He didn't have the authority to be making some of the decisions that were going to have to be made soon. This involved the Lacey marriage, and he needed Mrs. Lacey to be on board.

"Oh, no," he groaned.

"What?" Stone said quickly.

"We're going to have to tell her about Chesty."

"Surely she suspects that Jack fools around beyond Valerie."

"Their deal is that Jill tolerates the long-term mistress. But any other women are to be kept strictly under wraps."

"Oopsies. Ol' Jack is gonna get his pee pee whacked when he gets home, isn't he?"

Christian rolled his eyes. "Not my job to get in the middle of their shitstorm of a marriage."

Stone said evenly, "So let me be the one to tell her. I'm the outsider who'll be gone soon enough. Let her hate me."

He lifted his stricken gaze to Stone. He'd been trying so damned hard to pretend Stone wasn't going to waltz out of his life as suddenly as he'd waltzed into it. But the guy had just thrown it out like it didn't mean a damned thing to him to move on to the next town and the next job.

"Aww, man. I'm sorry—" Stone started.

He whirled and turned away, rejecting the upcoming lame attempt at an apology before Stone could insult him by uttering it. Behind himself, he heard Stone slip into the bedroom and close the door.

The door to the suite opened, and Christian moved over to hug Jill, but she screeched to a stop and demanded angrily, "What the hell have you done?"

"I don't understand—"

"The pictures, Christian."

"I haven't seen them. Jack and his girlfriend must have come ashore—"

"They're not of Jack and a woman. They're of Jack and *you*!"

CHAPTER TWELVE

STONE CAME out of the bedroom and stopped cold. An attractive woman, who was aging as spectacularly well as money could buy, was glaring at Christian. For his part, Christian looked remarkably like he'd been run over by a freight train. Tucker was looking back and forth between them like the two of them were aliens speaking in tongues.

What the hell had he walked into?

He stepped forward. "You must be Mrs. Lacey. I'm Stone Jackson. Pleasure to meet you."

She whirled to include him in her glare, and he recoiled. She did know that he had been impersonating her husband, right? He looked over at Christian questioningly. What was he missing here?

"What the hell have you done, Christian?" she demanded forcefully.

Egads. She *didn't* know what he and Christian had been up to. She was so going to fire his ass, and Wild Cards, Inc. would get a black eye over this mess. And then they'd have to fire him over the scandal. What on earth had he been thinking to agree to this madness?

Christian faced the boss's wife, his shoulders set defensively. However, he spoke with admirable calm. "You gave us an impossible task. Jack and Chesty absconded to international waters where we couldn't retrieve him, and we were forced to improvise—"

"*Chesty?*" An Antarctic winter couldn't have been any colder than that single word.

Stone felt rotten that Christian was taking so much heat for merely being the messenger bearing bad tidings, particularly since he'd volunteered to be the designated bomb dropper. He stepped into the line of fire beside Christian, physically moving up to stand with him.

"Chesty Hills, ma'am. She's the porn star Jack left the country with."

"Speaking of which, how did my husband manage to slip out of an entire country without you knowing?" she asked him sharply. "Weren't you supposed to be guarding him?"

"He insisted that I stay away from him, Mrs. Lacey. And he refused to let Tucker or me guard this suite's door. The two of them snuck out of here and used a stairwell with no security cameras to make their escape."

"Well. At least the bastard learned from the last incident with a woman and took precautions not to get caught this time."

He was stunned at her equanimity over the fact that her husband was currently on the lam with a porn star.

"Am I to gather that you've been pretending to be Jack in the interim?"

"That's correct, ma'am."

Not to be left out of the general ass-whupping, Christian dived back in. "That was my idea, not his."

She glared back and forth between the two of them for upward of a full minute, her mental wheels turning loudly in the silence.

The tension stretched out until Stone actually had to restrain an urge to squirm like a guilty schoolboy. A flush was climbing Christian's fair cheeks, so Stone would guess he felt about the same way.

Without warning, she began to chuckle. "Well, well, well, Christian. I have to give you full marks for ingenuity. And people are actually buying that this impersonator is my husband?"

Stone picked up one of Jack's cowboy hats off a coffee table and jammed it on his head. He put on his best Texas drawl. "Aww, don't get your britches in a hitch there, darlin'. I'm not half-bad at being ol' Jackie boy."

Jill Lacey literally fell into a chair and stared up at him in shock.

"Walk across the room and back," Christian encouraged him.

It was a bit of a struggle to get the swagger right without cowboy boots on, but he did his best.

"Put him in one of Jack's suits and a pair of sunglasses, add a little stage makeup to age him, and nobody can tell the difference," Christian declared.

"Except for the pictures the paparazzo shoved under my nose at the airport. The bastard wanted cash to keep them out of the press. I've got his card in my purse somewhere," she responded.

A single photographer, huh? He opened his mouth to ask her the man's name, but Christian cut him off, snapping, "You can't kill the photographer, Stone. This is the civilian world."

"Yeah, but it's only one sleazeball—"

"No."

"Fine," Stone groused. "But if you change your mind...."

"There will be no murders," Christian replied firmly.

"Party pooper."

He shot Christian his best pout.

Pointedly ignoring him, Christian turned to Jill and asked cautiously, "What kind of pictures?"

She, in turn, ignored him and instead stared down Stone. Man, she had that whole "mother guilting kid into confessing anything" look down to a fine science.

"You're gay, aren't you?" she demanded.

Damn, her gaydar was on point. "Yes, ma'am. I am."

"And you're hot and heavy with Christian, aren't you?"

Tucker made a surprised sound. For his part, Stone frowned. He and Christian had been exceedingly circumspect about their relationship. Neither one of them let their private lives interfere with their professional lives, after all. They'd never touched each other in public except for on the beach at dawn this morning. Hell, they barely even looked at each other in public. And there'd only been that one quick, furtive embrace on the beach—

—where they'd kissed. Passionately.

"Aww, hell," Christian muttered. "The beach this morning. I told you we had to be careful."

"Well, you weren't careful enough, boys," Jill interjected tartly.

Stone winced. He and Christian deserved that. But ouch. He'd been naïve to think that a man like Jack Lacey wouldn't be stalked morning, noon, and night. Christian had tried to warn him, but he'd refused to listen. This was his screwup.

Jill was holding out a business card. "The paparazzo wrote down the address of the website I can visit to preview the layouts that will go public if I don't buy the images from him."

Which was a fancy way of saying that if she didn't pay the guy's blackmail demand, he would send the pictures to whatever tabloid would pay him the most for the scandalous pictures.

There wasn't really any question of her paying off a blackmailer. Once that faucet was opened, it was nearly impossible to shut off, and besides, they had no guarantee the photographer wouldn't take their hush money and then turn right around and sell the damned things to the highest bidder anyway.

He looked over Christian's shoulder reluctantly as the pictures popped up on Christian's laptop. The quality wasn't great; they'd obviously been taken with a telephoto lens from some distance away. But they were clear enough. The passionate kiss was clearly between two men.

The next photo of him and Christian, foreheads pressed together, might be achingly romantic in any other situation. But it was damning as hell in this one. Worse, their faces were clear enough in this photo that there was no question it was him and Christian. Or rather, Jack and Christian.

Any chance Christian had ever had at protecting his privacy was completely, irrevocably blown. Stone rested a hand on Christian's shoulder, and it was like touching ice. Or maybe glass. There was a brittle quality to Christian's posture that made him feel as if he might shatter at any second.

"God, I'm sorry," Stone breathed. "I should've listened to your warnings. You told me they'd be watching me 24-7, and I didn't take you literally."

Christian looked up, but at Jill, not at him. "If we're lucky, these photos will smoke out your husband. I can't imagine him letting them pass undisputed and unrefuted."

Stone looked back and forth between Christian and Jill candidly. "This screwup is squarely on me. What can I do to make it right? Anything. Just name it. I'll do it."

Christian was the one who answered. "How do you feel about an impromptu press conference with your wife?"

Jill lurched. "Stop the wagon there, Nellie. You want me to go out in public with a man who's posing as my husband? What if somebody realizes he isn't Jack?"

"We feed them the same contingency line we've always planned to in that event. Someone's threatening your husband's life, and his security team felt a decoy in his place was the safest alternative."

"And when the donors are pissed all to hell that they've been tricked?" she demanded. "At this point, I'm half-tempted to let Jack go down in flames. But all my charity work will go down in flames too."

Christian nodded solemnly. "Here's the thing, ma'am. If you do nothing to disprove or refute these pictures, you're going to come under intense pressure to take action. Your conservative constituents will demand that you divorce Jack."

"No way!" she declared. "That bastard's been demanding a divorce for months, but there's no way I'm giving it to him until he wins this election. It's going to be his last term in the Senate, in case he hasn't shared that with you, Christian."

"Umm, no. But I can't say I'm surprised."

"One more election," she ranted. "All he had to do was behave himself through one lousy election season. But could he do that? No. He had to take off with a porn star right under my nose. I'll kill him. I'm going to grab him by his scrawny, shriveled wiener and cut that sucker off. Maybe I'll stuff it in his mouth and watch him bleed out."

Whoa. She was *pissed*. Not that Stone blamed her, but dang. That whole "hell hath no fury like a woman scorned" thing was *no joke*.

Christian said evenly, "I'm sure we can find a way to save your reputation so you can continue the charity work you so love doing."

She said a little more rationally, "If I try to refute the allegations that Jack is gay and the public believes them anyway, then I'll look weak and pitiful for standing by a man who suddenly likes boys better than girls. Hell, I won't only have to divorce Jack. I'll have to move out of Texas."

Stone couldn't fault her logic.

"Or I can go all in, stand with Stone—Jack—and we do what? Laugh off this whole thing as… what? A joke? A bet Jack lost and he had to kiss his aide full on the mouth?"

Christian tossed out a few suggestions for silly reasons why Jack might have had to kiss his aide. A dare, maybe. Or proving that he wasn't homophobic.

Stone looked back and forth between the two of them desperately trying to cover for a man they both despised. Abruptly, the insanity of it all was too much for him.

"Or," he interrupted, "we could have me appear as myself and explain that I'm a security guard and am involved with Christian in my off time. We can laugh it all off as a case of mistaken identity."

"But then you can't appear as Jack at the casino night," Christian objected. "Worse, they may expect you and Jack to appear together to prove that you're two different people."

"Maybe. But not definitely. After all, Jack is a sitting senator. The onus is not on him to prove these crazy allegations by a scum-bucket paparazzo."

Christian sighed. "Sadly, the public is more inclined to believe a salacious accusation from the media than it is the word of an elected public official."

He supposed he couldn't blame the public on that one. "But what if I go back to looking a lot more like myself and much less like Jack?" He warmed to the idea the more he thought about it. "I haven't shaved today. If I don't shave tomorrow, I'll have a good stubble going. I'll wear my own clothes. I can get you a bunch of official photos from my military days. Wild Cards, Inc. can verify that I work for them. I've got an official résumé picture on file with them too."

Jill nodded slowly as Christian murmured thoughtfully, "It could work. But it would make a casino-night appearance by you doubly risky. People would be checking to see if Jack was actually Jack or not."

"One crisis at a time," Stone retorted.

Tucker piped up. "If the would-be killer thinks we've duped him or her, that person could come after Jack—well, you—with a vengeance. Your profilers said the stalker could be volatile and prone to violent outbursts, remember? Recognition wouldn't be your main problem at the fundraiser. Staying alive would be the real challenge."

Stone shrugged. "We can deal with that when the time comes. I'm not entirely inexperienced with high-threat situations." He continued persuasively, "At this point I don't give a crap for Jack's reputation—no offense, Mrs. Lacey."

She snorted like a mad elephant about to trample him.

He continued, "I'm primarily concerned with protecting your good name and Christian's professional reputation. The two of you need to come out of this with the ability to do the work you are committed to. You just have to buy me one lousy day to get scruffy, Christian. I'll do the rest."

Of course, the six-hundred-pound gorilla in the corner was that by him and Christian publicly admitting to being lovers, it blew any chance Christian would ever have of keeping his private life private and separate from his professional life.

There was coming out and then there was coming *out*. A press conference on national television couldn't get a whole lot more high profile.

Jill looked back and forth between him and Christian. "I say we do it. As much as I... dislike... my philanderer of a husband, I'm not giving up my charities if I don't absolutely have to."

He winced. She obviously didn't have any idea how abhorrent it would be to Christian to parade his personal relationship all over the media.

The brittle quality clung to Christian more than ever, but as Stone looked at him questioningly, Christian met his gaze grimly and nodded once. "Agreed. Stone and I go public."

He tried to catch Christian's gaze again, to offer him silent support and sympathy, but Christian was having none of it and instead turned away to stare down at his laptop.

Even from across the room, Stone could feel Christian silently shattering into a million pieces. And something painful in his own chest ached in response, as if shards of Christian's splintered dignity were stabbing him too. And there wasn't a damned thing he could do about it.

The deadline for Jill Lacey to buy the photographs from the scumbag came and went.

Ominously, the phone stayed silent. No last-minute pleas for cash came from the photographer, so they could only assume the greedy little worm was now engaged in a bidding war with the tabloids for his pictures of Christian and Senator Lacey making out on the beach.

The dinner hour approached. "Anytime now," Christian murmured. "The phone's going to start ringing, and it won't stop until we put you in front of the press, Stone."

Stone said quietly, "If it's any consolation, I think you've got the right of it. Once this story breaks, it'll smoke out Jack. I can absolutely see him prancing out in front of reporters with Chesty on his arm to refute accusations of being gay."

"Oh, Lord. I hadn't even thought of that. At all costs he *cannot* be seen with that woman. Then Jill will have to divorce him immediately, and everything we've done to protect her will be for nothing."

Fuck. He hadn't thought of it that way. "Have you considered sending Tucker down to Barbados to meet the *Wrastle Castle* when it docks and stop Jack from committing career hara-kiri? Travis could make sure he's not seen with Chesty. Heck, he could plant a story that other people were on the boat. Maybe a single guy who'd claim to have been Chesty's date?"

"Yes, but if you have to go through with the casino fundraiser, we'll need Tucker here. If he's in Barbados, you'd be even more exposed to Jack's stalker. You heard what Tucker said earlier. The stalker's going to be royally pissed off at having been duped." Christian added strongly, "I *won't* leave you unprotected like that."

An entirely unfamiliar feeling seeped into his awareness. It was fuzzy. And warm. All cuddly and soft and—

And nauseating, dammit. Totally nauseating. Yeah, that was it. *Good Lord.* He didn't do warm and fuzzy.

Aww, who was he trying to kid? He totally loved feeling warm and fuzzy where Christian was concerned.

But only Christian.

His machismo restored, he said firmly, "In the first place, it's my job to take risks. In the second place, I'm very good at what I do. I know how to stay out of an assassin's sights."

"You're asking me to bet your life on it," Christian responded in what sounded like desperation.

"Indeed I am. Do you trust me?"

They exchanged a long look. Christian still looked doubtful, and Stone did everything he could to inject reassuring vibes into his gaze as he murmured, "I'm just trying to look out for the people I care about. Please let me do that."

Christian swore under his breath. "And you say *I'm* good at managing people. Ha! Bastard."

"I'll go tell Tucker to pack a bag and jump the first flight to Barbados."

"Impress on him how vital it is that Jack not be seen by anyone with Chesty."

"Got it!" Stone called over his shoulder as he went in search of Tucker.

THE FIRST phone call came at precisely 6:00 p.m. Christian moved over to take the call. *And so it begins.*

He picked up the receiver, but before he could say hello, a female voice screeched in his ear, "What the hell is that rat bastard doing? If he thinks he can get out of his promise to marry me before the end of this year, he can freaking forget it!"

"Valerie?" Christian guessed. What was this about Jack promising to marry her in the next several months? This was the first he'd heard of it. God knew, it would be career suicide to divorce his popular wife in the middle of a campaign for reelection.

But then, this afternoon was the first he'd heard of Jack asking his wife for a divorce too. That one made sense now. Jack needed out of his forty-year marriage to tie the knot with his mistress.

"Damn straight it's me. I wanna talk with him right this minute. Put him on the line."

"I'm sorry, ma'am. I can't do that—"

"Don't give me the runaround. I'm in no mood. No mood, I tell you. I've got half a mind to call my father and have him send his boys to break one of Jack's kneecaps. No, make that both kneecaps!"

"If you don't mind my asking, what's he done to upset you?"

"He kissed a man! On TV! As if anyone who's ever met him will believe Jack Lacey's gay! That's a hell of a way to dodge marrying me...." She devolved into swearing colorful enough to actually make Christian blush.

"There's been a misunderstanding, Ms. Micklethwaite. Jack was not on any beach today. Whoever took this alleged video, or whatever it is, has mistakenly identified the person in the picture. I guarantee you Jack did not kiss anyone on any beach today." *At least not in Miami*, he added silently.

Valerie was silent for a moment. "He's not trying to dodge marrying me?"

"I'm sure I wouldn't know anything about that, ma'am."

"He didn't kiss a guy?"

"No, ma'am."

"He still loves me?"

"Umm, as far as I know, his feelings haven't changed." Which was to say he had no idea what Jack's feelings were about any woman. He was still processing his shock that the man had asked Jill for a divorce. He'd honestly thought Jack was too afraid of his wife to actually go there.

"Oh." A pause. "I still want to talk to him."

"I'm so sorry. He's not here."

"You're lying!" Her voice rose toward a screech quickly.

"I give you my word of honor that he is not here and not avoiding speaking with you."

"He'd better not be. I'd hate to have to kill him. But I would if he dumped me."

"I can believe it, ma'am," he replied carefully. Damn. Death threats from his wife *and* his mistress in under two hours. Jack was having a hell of a bad day, and he didn't even know it.

Nope, he'd left Christian behind to clean up this mess and take the hits for him. Hell, if he weren't such a good guy, he'd be seriously considering putting arsenic in the senator's coffee.

Valerie hung up without saying goodbye. Jack had said before that she had a hot temper, but yikes. He silently wished Jack good luck and Godspeed with all that drama.

He didn't get a chance to set the receiver down before the phone rang again. This time it was a journalist, and he launched into the prepared response.

Once all the major networks he cared about had checked in with him, he stopped answering the phone. The smaller outlets and gossip publications could pick up the story or not from the big news agencies as they saw fit.

One phone call would no sooner be transferred over to voicemail than the damned thing would start ringing again. It made Christian want to scream. Every ring shouted at him of his betrayal of his employer, of his principles, of a lifetime of class and privacy.

He passionately hated having to expose himself to the world like this. If only he and Stone were really a couple in every sense of the word. Then, this mess could be bearable. He would walk through fire for Stone if Stone would agree to a real relationship and not just a hot fling for as long as this gig lasted.

In real danger of losing his mind, he resorted to turning off the ringers of every phone in the suite. Even his cell phone was exploding. He *really* didn't want to take those calls because they would be from friends. Possibly even family. Oh, God. He was going to be ill.

Burying his head in the sand wasn't going to change anything. Manning up, he forced himself to sit in front of the television and turn on the evening celebrity gossip programs.

The press was all over this story. The glee was palpable as commentators made arch comments at the conservative senator from Texas being exposed as gay. In their defense, he had to admit the hypocrisy of it was too rich for the media not to react exactly that way.

Not to mention that reporters loved nothing better than bringing down a rich and powerful public figure, particularly one who'd consistently been an asshole to them over the years. They might be going after Jack, but he was caught squarely in the crossfire whether he liked it or not.

Christian drove Tucker to the airport but didn't get out of the SUV lest someone recognize him and shove a cell phone camera in his face. When he got back to the hotel, he was touched to discover that Stone had arranged for hotel security guards to meet him at the loading dock, park the SUV for him, and escort him in a service elevator to the suite.

It was a bizarre sensation being the man in the media's bull's-eye. That had always been Jack's job. Christian had been the invisible aide standing in the shadows, well clear of the spotlight. And then Stone had been the guy at the podium, getting all the attention.

No wonder both of them had freaked out in their own ways—Jack by running off with a woman, and Stone by just running. He couldn't entirely blame either one of them for needing an escape. It was a suffocating sensation to always be looking over one's shoulder, trying to spot one's watchers.

He made it back to the suite, and Stone wrapped him up in a hard hug as soon as the door closed behind him.

"Jill?" he managed to gasp past the rib-crushing embrace.

"Spa," Stone muttered into the side of his neck. "God, I've been waiting all day to get you alone so I could apologize to you. I should have listened. You warned me the press was everywhere, but I didn't believe you. This is all my fault."

"What's done is done, Stone. Don't beat yourself up over it. You have to let go of it and move on. I'm going to need your undivided attention tomorrow. You'll have to do exactly what I tell you—"

The doorknob rattled, and he and Stone leaped back from each other as Jill returned to the suite. He lifted a bag of complimentary beauty supplies out of her hand and hustled it back to the master bathroom. It had been decided that Stone would move back to his own room since he was supposed to be himself again. They would all pretend Jack was spending time alone with his wife in the suite after the big scare at the gala with the helicopter crash.

When Christian returned to the living room, Stone was gone. He cursed silently. He hated every second they had to be apart. Which was to say, he had it *bad* for the guy.

"I like him," Jill commented shrewdly.

"Who? Stone?"

"Of course, Stone. You've fallen hard for him, haven't you?"

"What makes you say that?" he asked cautiously.

"For one thing, those pictures that got shoved under my nose. That's as hot a kiss as I've seen between any two people in a long time. And my dear boy, you positively glow when you're around him. I've never seen you happier."

He didn't have the heart to tell her that she was merely seeing the absence of misery because he wasn't having to deal with her husband 24-7.

"Go on. Get out of here already," she ordered him.

"I beg your pardon?"

"The story is that the two of you are lovers. So, go be lovers. If you made that poor man live out your cover story and be my husband for three days, the least you owe him is to live out his cover story for a couple of days."

A smile broke across his face, and he couldn't stop grinning like a love-struck idiot no matter how hard he tried. "Call me if you need anything, ma'am."

"I'm sure Jack and I will be fine in the suite by ourselves. I may need one of you to come down and eat the breakfast in bed that the two of us are going to order in the morning, though."

"Call me before you do that. We'll have Stone come down and make a brief appearance as Jack so the hotel staff can verify that Jack's in the suite with you."

"An excellent idea. That's why you're the best staffer on Capitol Hill, Christian," she said warmly. "I'm going to miss you when you get that fancy job over at the Justice Department."

He stared. "How do you know about that?"

"I heard you talking about it once on the phone. I always did wonder why a man like you, who disagrees with my husband on so many issues, agreed to work for him. I admire your commitment to your cause. It's a lot to put up with Jack Lacey for years to get to your goal."

"Thank you, ma'am."

"Scoot. That handsome young man is waiting for you."

He ducked his head and then all but ran down to Stone's room. He slipped into the suite and into Stone's arms with profound relief.

Stone was already looking more like Stone again. A five o'clock shadow darkened his square jaw, and the T-shirt that clung to his prodigious biceps was pure badass. Even the close, European cut of his black jeans screamed of a soldier or security type and not a middle-aged politician.

And that fire in his eyes. Oh no. There was no sign of Jack Lacey in this man.

He breathed, "I need you to be the soldier tonight. No civilization. No nice manners. I don't want there to be any confusion as to who I'm in bed with. Erase all memory of Jack Lacey from my mind."

"Jack who?"

They traded grins.

CHAPTER THIRTEEN

STONE WOKE up slowly, splayed out on his belly, a little hungover. There'd been a fair bit of Jack Daniels involved with last night's delicious depravity. He'd fantasized about letting loose with Christian, but he'd never dreamed the man would actually revel in it. They were both fit enough and strong enough that they couldn't really hurt each other if they turned their bodies loose on each other with complete abandon.

As it was, he was stiff and sore in places he wasn't accustomed to feeling discomfort. And it felt fantastic.

"You awake?" Christian murmured in a deep voice from over his back. He was sprawled like a weighted blanket over him.

"No," he replied. "I'm still unconscious. I think I'm still a little drunk."

"Good. You up for a little more?"

"I can't move."

"I don't need you to move. I need you to relax and do what I tell you to."

That moved him considerably further along the scale to full consciousness. "What do you have in mind?"

"Does it matter?"

A chuckle rumbled in his chest. "Fair point, well made. I'm up for anything you can imagine."

"Including bottoming for me?"

"For you, anything." Particularly when it included those big strong hands kneading at his shoulders and then working their way slowly down his back, massaging out every last kink and knot, leaving him a boneless mass half melted into the mattress.

Christian had him lift his hips and slid a pile of pillows under them. He nudged Stone's thighs apart and knelt between them. Stone's languor dissipated sharply as he realized Christian was serious about taking him this way. He couldn't remember the last time he'd bottomed.

Tension claimed him, but then the lingering aftereffects of the whiskey and Christian resuming the druggingly wonderful massage combined to lull him back into a state of deep relaxation.

Something warm and slippery circled his anus, and he moaned with pleasure.

"Like that?" Christian's smooth voice murmured.

He groaned as Christian dipped a finger inside him in time with another finger sensually tracing the underside of his penis. He tensed, but Christian's teasing fingers retreated and he went back to massaging him, this time focusing on his thighs and glutes.

"Stay half-asleep. That's how I want you. All relaxed and mellow."

"Done," he sighed. It was the strangest feeling to just relax and let Christian do whatever he wanted to him. Equally strange was the realization that he trusted Christian completely, totally, and without reservation.

Christian gave him a full body massage that taught him a few things about himself. Like the fact that he had a bigger hedonistic streak than he'd realized. And that a good foot massage was possibly the next best thing to sex. And that he had a few ticklish spots he'd been heretofore unaware of. But as soon as Christian discovered those, he was quick to soothe him back into a semisomnolent state.

Christian rose up over him. "Ready for this?" he murmured.

"Yeah, sure. Anything you want. I'm yours."

Huh. He meant it too.

And then Christian was spreading him and filling him with smooth assurance. The cascade of sensations was startling, and Stone tensed beneath him.

"Relax, big guy," Christian murmured, soothing his hands up and down Stone's back. "You're mine, remember? Just sit back and let me do the work."

Maybe he was still more drunk than he'd realized because that sounded like the best idea he'd heard in a long damned time. Or maybe it was because Christian had so thoroughly lowered his barriers to trust that he genuinely was good with bottoming for the man.

Christian was no less endowed than him, and Stone's body stretched to the point of discomfort around the invading heat. Very slightly, Christian flexed his hips. Stone tensed but then told his body to relax. Christian patiently moved a tiny bit again. He had to give the guy credit for being a considerate and self-disciplined lover. Eventually he was able to stay fully relaxed and open beneath Christian.

Sensing it, Christian withdrew more fully and filled him with a little more strength.

Mmm. That was nice. "Do that again," he mumbled into the pillow.

"Like this?"

"Uh-huh."

By slow degrees Christian increased the pace and intensity, and Stone's breathing accelerated to match. It was becoming a struggle to lie passively beneath Christian and not rock his own hips. But every time he started to move, Christian froze and waited for him to still.

It became an act of enormous mental discipline to hold himself still and open for Christian. As he gradually got the hang of it and released the need to react to his raging lust, something changed. Not only was he holding his body relaxed and open for Christian, but also his mind. Hell, his soul.

The entire moment became an act of emotional submission. And Christian had gently insisted that Stone give it freely and completely. He finally understood what Christian was asking for.

Everything.

And I want to give it.

"Take me, Christian," he gasped. "I'm yours. Fuck me until I can't walk. Split me in two. Make me whole. I surrender. Body, mind, and soul."

With a groan, Christian drove into him with all the power Stone could have hoped for. He reached over his head and pressed his hands against the headboard, pushing back so he could be filled even more deeply and fully.

Christian grabbed his hips to increase his purchase and took him without holding back anything. And it was, bar none, the most amazing sex he'd ever experienced in his life. Never, ever, had he given himself fully to another human being like this.

His orgasm, when it came, was so emotional it felt as if his heart had exploded too. His entire being turned inside out. "My God, I love this. I love you," he groaned.

Christian drove into him one last time and then came deep, deep inside him with a shuddering shout of his own. It was intimate as hell. Christian collapsed on top of him, their bodies spooning together perfectly.

"Am I crushing you?" Christian muttered.

"Nope. It's perfect. Don't move," he managed.

They lay like that for several minutes before Christian finally rolled away from him and sprawled on his back. "I can't even sit up," he announced. "You killed me."

Stone also rolled onto his back and lazily threw the pile of pillows onto the floor. "You're dead? Ha. I'm deader."

"That's not a word, and that did *not* feel like sex with a corpse."

He asked humorously, "Are you speaking from experience?"

Christian snorted. "Zombies aren't my thing. I like my lovers...." He paused and then said seriously, "Just like that."

The words sank into Stone's soul like summer rain into hungry soil.

"How about you? Are you okay?" Christian asked.

"I don't think I've ever been more okay than I am at this exact second."

Christian pushed up onto an elbow and stared down at him, more beautiful than any one human being had a right to be. "You're okay with bottoming?"

"It's a good thing I had no idea how awesome it would be with you or you'd have never gotten any good lovin' out of me."

"I suppose there's always been so much pressure on you to be macho and manly that it never occurred to you to swing the other way."

Stone frowned. "While I'm sure that's probably true and speaks to deep psychological shit heretofore undiagnosed in my fucked-up noggin, I honestly think it has more to do with not trusting anyone enough to share myself that way until now."

Christian leaned down and kissed him. It was a slow, lengthy affair that had Stone thinking frisky thoughts before the jangle of Christian's cell phone on the bedside table jolted them both.

"Don't pick it up," Stone muttered.

"Gotta. That's Jill Lacey's ringtone."

He groaned. "I'll go take a shower while you two formulate your diabolical plan for world domination."

"Remember not to shave!" Christian called after him.

"Roger that!"

CHRISTIAN ANSWERED his phone. "Good morning, Mrs. Lacey. What can I do for you?"

"I need Stone down here in a half hour to be Jack on a phone interview. And I'm hungry. I want to order that breakfast in bed we talked about last night."

"I'll have him there, ma'am. Order breakfast in about fifteen minutes. He likes his eggs scrambled, and he'll eat anything else you put in front of him." In the meantime, he would order breakfast in Stone's room to keep up the ruse of Stone Jackson being a different person than Jack Lacey.

The water cut off in the shower, and Christian poked his head into the bathroom. "Hey, babe. Can you shift to Jack mode for a quick phone interview with Jill?"

"Sure."

"Love you."

"Love you more," Stone called.

"Nuh-uhh!" he called back, grinning.

Breakfast arrived, and Stone made a point of chatting with the server before the young man left the suite.

Christian watched Stone intently as they shared the meal, trying to gauge his state of mind after last night. He still couldn't believe that Stone had actually surrendered to him like that. It was as humbling as it was exhilarating.

"You're quiet this morning, Christian," Stone startled him by saying.

He stirred sugar into his coffee. "Says the pot to the kettle."

"Yes, but I'm naturally taciturn. You're not."

"I'm just enjoying the afterglow of an amazing night with my lover."

"Ditto."

Christian had to smile. *Ditto.* That one stupid word captured their whole relationship in a nutshell. The feelings behind it were real, but Stone wasn't the kind of man to spell them out.

He could live with that. After what they'd shared, there was no doubt how Stone felt about him. He was a man who would show his feelings long before he would talk about them.

The phone interview itself was uneventful. Jill laughed in genuine amusement at the reporter's suggestion that Jack was gay and made a sly comment that her problem with him was his eye for the ladies, not his eye for the guys. Stone impersonated Jack's drawl to a T, responding charmingly that there was no other lady in the world for him but his lovely wife. Stone fielded a few questions about the helicopter crash and was modest when he was credited with saving the pilot's life.

Yet again, Stone was doing Jack better than Jack did.

The phone call ended, and Jill commented, "If you played for the hetero team, I'd seriously consider replacing Jack with you permanently, Stone."

Christian's eyebrows lifted. She sounded as if she might actually be considering dumping her philandering husband. Which would be disastrous for Christian. She was a huge limiter on Jack's worst excesses. Without her, Christian hesitated to imagine how difficult Jack would be to control. Or at least to prevent from self-destructing.

The Laceys' breakfasts arrived, and Christian was relieved to see a young woman pushing the cart into the suite. Standing in the door to the bedroom, he waved subtly to Stone to have him come out into the living room and put in a Jack appearance.

Hand over his lower face, Stone-Jack drawled, "Set it up over by the window, will ya, darlin'? The li'l lady likes to watch the ocean. Says it relaxes her." He waggled his eyebrows suggestively, and the maid giggled as she pushed the serving table over to the big picture window overlooking the beach.

It ended up taking both Stone and Christian pitching in to eat the gigantic breakfast Jill had ordered for Jack. Eventually, they consumed the evidence of her husband's presence.

Stuffed to the gills, Christian announced, "It's about time for Stone to go be himself."

As they walked down the hall so Stone could change into his own clothes, Stone muttered, "This is getting to be a bit of a mental ping-pong game, bouncing back and forth between two identities."

"Sorry about that."

"You're not the asshole who thought it was a great idea to boink Chesty."

"I'm the asshole who came up with the plan for you to be two people at once."

"I could've said no."

"Why didn't you?"

"Because I was desperate to do anything to stick around and sleep with you."

"I've worried a few times that my attraction to you was why I proposed the scheme in the first place. I wanted you to stick around."

"Just don't ask me to eat for two again, will you? My girlish figure can't take the pig-outs."

Christian grinned. The guy had a hot bod, all right, and it was anything but girlish.

It was time to walk Stone down to the mini press conference Jill had arranged. She'd called on a few reporters who'd been particularly kind to her over the years for an exclusive sneak peek at the man everyone seemed to think was her husband.

"Do you remember how to be you?" Christian asked Stone anxiously.

"Come again?"

"The only time you've been in front of a camera, you've had to act like Jack. You may fall into that habit. I need you to be vintage Stone."

"What the hell is vintage me?"

"Focused. Serious and observant but closed off. Not interested in chatting."

Stone stared at him in dismay. "I'm all those things?"

"Not at all. It's just a facade you put on from time to time when you're feeling insecure. And we need you to be nothing like Jack."

"Insecure?" Stone echoed.

Startled, Christian looked up. "Well, yeah. Was that too honest for you?"

"No. I'm an adult. I can take the criticism."

"I'm sorry—"

"Seriously. I'm good. Christ, I'm coming to realize you know me better than *I* know me. Like it or not, it's true that I get insecure and overcompensate."

"We all do."

"Stop trying to make it better," he ground out.

Not that he'd set out to piss the guy off, but now he really was sounding like vintage Stone.

Looking worried, Stone's face emerged from the neck of a tight black spandex T-shirt. "Do you need me to wear my pistol?"

Christian considered it for a moment. "No, let's not go overboard."

"No, let's not." Stone was sounding outright alarmed now.

Crap. Stone was overthinking this. He was going to psych himself out. "Relax. Say something funny or sarcastic."

"Holy shit. You do realize you just jinxed me into not having one even remotely clever thing to say, don't you?"

"Me? What did I say?" He feigned an overreaction in a desperate, and hopefully not transparent, attempt to rile up Stone.

"You're such a snob, sometimes."

Yes. Riling working. "I am not a snob! You're a… a hick."

"Ooh. Good one. I'm wounded to the quick. Beltway leech."

"Death mongerer."

"Political hack."

"Baby eater."

And that was how they arrived at the ballroom, which the hotel had provided for Jill's press conference: laughing and calling each other progressively more rude names. Hopefully it would help Stone be… well, Stone.

While Stone continued down the hallway to use a back entrance to the stage, Christian slipped into the main ballroom and paused in the shadows at the rear of the room. He'd been doing his damnedest not to think about what this moment was going to do to his life. But now that the moment had arrived, there was no avoiding it. He was throwing himself on his sword to save the Laceys, each in his own way.

He was a good employee. Loyal. And Jill really was a grand lady. She deserved at least one man in her life to stand beside her when the going got tough. Too bad it couldn't be her husband.

At the end of the day, his being gay wasn't a big deal. Right?

If only he could be sure that was how the world would see it. He'd never made any secret of it, and any employer he wanted to work for wouldn't discriminate against him on the basis of it. But the blurring of the separation between personal and professional, that was another story. In his kind of work, people didn't mess with that distinction. That way lay danger, blackmail, and corruption. And he'd obliterated that line in the sand.

He lurched as brilliant camera lights turned on him suddenly in the back of the ballroom. What the hell? This event wasn't supposed to start for a few more minutes.

Horror of the sudden exposure froze him in place. All these people staring avidly at him were going to pry into his personal life in the most invasive and insensitive way they could. They would mount him on a slide like a bug and stare at him through a microscope from every possible angle. *And I have to let them.*

He walked between the rows of reporters. The stage looked eerily like a hangman's platform, and reluctantly he stepped up onto it. He moved to the podium and could almost feel a noose dropping around his neck. He turned on the microphone. The noose tightened until he could hardly choke out words.

"Thank you for coming today," he started. He turned away from the mic, coughed, and cleared his throat nervously.

He started again, determined to force himself onward through this nightmare. "Thank you for coming today. We'll start with a formal statement from Mrs. Lacey. She won't be taking questions, but I assure you, she will clear up any confusion about the rumors being reported overnight regarding Senator Lacey."

A dozen voices shouted, demanding to know why Senator Lacey wasn't making a statement. And a few of them asked if someone was trying to kill Jack. Dammit, he thought they'd successfully killed that rumor.

Christian answered evenly, "Please be patient. Everything will become clear in a few minutes."

Someone shouted a rude question at him about how good a kisser the senator was, and he ignored it. But his stomach twisted violently and threatened to heave. That double breakfast had *really* been a bad idea. He stepped away from the podium without acknowledging the question.

He blinked to clear his vision from the bright camera lights. *Must. Not. Puke.*

He spied Jill, standing off to his right, and he moved over to her. "Are you ready?" he murmured. "They're in a rabid mood. They smell a scandal, and they're all salivating over it."

"We'll just have to take the bone away from the dog, then, won't we?" she answered lightly.

"Do you need a moment?" he asked gently.

"Is Stone here?" she asked.

"I walked down with him. He's staying out of sight until you do the big reveal. We have to give the media the theatric drama they're looking for, or else they'll keep digging."

"Cynical much?" she murmured.

One corner of his mouth lifted. She was every bit as cynical as he was. Particularly when it came to the press. Or her husband. "Okay, ma'am. Let's do this. I'll introduce you."

He went back out into the bright lights, waited through a momentary electrical crisis with someone's light box, and then made the introduction. Jill stepped out onto the stage, and he yielded the podium to her with profound relief. Even a few seconds in front of the press gave him the wiggins.

Jill read a brief opening statement poking fun at the allegations that Jack Lacey had suddenly switched sexual orientations. She'd insisted on writing it herself and had struck just the right tone to make any allegations that the photos were of Christian and her husband seem patently ridiculous.

She concluded with "I do, however, have a good idea of how this story got started, and I'd like to clear up the confusion once and for all. My husband recently brought on board a new security consultant who looks a great deal like him."

Christian felt Stone's presence beside him without having to turn his head to look. "Are you ready?"

"As I'll ever be."

Jill continued out on stage, "Mr. Jackson happens to be dating Christian Chatsworth-Brandeis, a man you all *did* identify correctly in the pictures. Gentlemen, I'd like to introduce you to Stone Jackson, my husband's new bodyguard."

"Go get 'em," Christian murmured.

Stone rolled his eyes and stepped out on stage. Shit. He was walking like Jack.

"Less swagger, *less swagger*!" he whispered frantically.

Stone's stride shifted to something more akin to marching. It looked stiff and unnatural, but at least it didn't look straight off a West Texas ranch anymore. Every light in the room trained on Stone.

He stepped up to the microphone and said uncomfortably with a slight hint of a British accent, "I'm not sure what all the fuss is about. I wasn't aware that it was newsworthy stuff for two guys to share a kiss on South Beach at sunrise."

A faint chuckle passed through the group of reporters.

"But you don't look gay," a woman in a pastel pink Jackie O suit said in a wondering voice.

"And exactly how does gay look, ma'am?" Stone bit out.

Perfect. He sounded irritated, and when he got irritated, he got intimidating. Indeed, Stone gripped the edges of the podium, unconsciously flexing his biceps in a heart-stopping display of muscle, and he leaned forward a little, staring down the unfortunate woman.

"Well, I'm sure I don't know," she huffed.

"Tell us how you met Christian Chatsworth-Brandeis!" someone shouted.

Stone frowned. "In a bar. Arguing over how to properly drink Jack Daniels."

"How long have you known each other?"

Stone's frown deepened into a dangerous-as-hell scowl. "I don't see how that's any of your business. I'm here today to let you know you got your facts wrong, and that's all. Christian Chatsworth-Brandeis is my boyfriend, not Senator Lacey's. If you need to know more about me, then I'd suggest you contact my employer, Wild Cards, Incorporated, in England. It's a high-end private security firm."

"Reenact the kiss!" someone shouted.

"Are you with *Penthouse* or something?" Stone demanded. "You're gonna have to pay for that shot, buddy."

The mainstream media reporters snorted, enjoying the putdown of whoever had asked the question. Must have been some scandal-rag reporter who'd slipped into the press conference.

"I expect you all have actual news to cover, and I have a job to get back to. It's been fun, ladies and gentlemen. Let's not do this again soon." And with that, Stone strode off the stage, looking every inch the dangerous security type.

He joined Christian and Jill in the wings and muttered a single word to them. "Move."

They turned as one and hurried to the exit.

"Go right," Stone ordered.

They hurried down a short hallway to the kitchen, wound through the maze of prep tables, and hustled into a service elevator at the back of the kitchen used by the room service staff.

The elevator door shut, and Jill demanded, "Why the emergency exit?"

"That guy who asked for the kiss was going to jump us in the hallway. He was pissed at my mouthing off and embarrassing him, and he had a look in his eye. He's going to dig for more dirt."

"I'll tell the hotel security guys to keep an eye out for him and keep him as far away as possible," Christian responded.

Stone's cell phone rang, and he dug it out. He listened to someone, and as he did so, his expression went dark, then black.

"What?" Christian asked as soon as he disconnected.

"Later," Stone bit out, glancing significantly at Jill, who was looking the other way.

Crap. What had Jack done *now*?

They delivered Mrs. Lacey to Jack's suite, and then the two of them headed down to Stone's room. The door closed behind them and Christian bit out, "Spill."

"You might want to sit down."

"Cripes. What's so bad I have to sit? What has he done?"

"Sit."

Scared to death, he sat.

Stone exhaled hard. "The *Wrastle Castle* has arrived in Barbados."

"Okay. That's good news."

"And Tucker is with Jack and Chesty on the boat right now."

"Even better news." Still, he felt a sword dangling by a thread over his head, and Jack Lacey was holding a pair of scissors.

"Apparently, Jack told Chesty a while back, when they first met, that he's had a vasectomy."

Christian frowned. "Not that I'm privy to every detail of his life, but I'm not aware of one. Jill couldn't have children, and Valerie had her tubes tied years ago."

"Well, Chesty's pregnant, and she insists the baby is his."

"Oh, dear Lord," he groaned. "Are you kidding me?"

"Wish I was. Apparently, she's livid. She's accusing Jack of destroying her career and her reputation."

"Fair. If he lied and he's the father, she has a right to be mad."

"Tucker says that when he boarded the yacht, Jack was locked in his stateroom and refusing to come out. Travis had to take a revolver away from Chesty. Pearl-handled derringer. An antique. Sweet little piece—"

"Focus, Stone. What else did Tucker have to say about Jack?"

"Oh. He's drunk. Been drunk for most of the past week. And seasick too."

Christian's gaze narrowed. "Can't say as I'm sorry to hear that."

Stone grinned. "Me neither."

"How fast can Tucker pour him onto a plane and get his ass back here?"

"Depends on whether a private jet happens to be sitting down there with an available crew," Stone answered. "He's working on arranging it now. The gang at Wild Cards is helping. They usually have a string or two they can pull and make the impossible happen."

Christian flopped into the nearest chair. "I need a drink."

He slugged a shot of whiskey far too elegant to be tossed back like rotgut but felt better when its burn hit his belly. It cleared his mind and made his rage at his boss manageable.

Jack had knocked up a woman when his wife and his mistress were breathing fire in his direction. What man *anywhere* made three women homicidal at the same time? The bastard bloody well had a death wish.

His cell phone rang and he tugged it out of his pocket. He saw the caller ID and put it on speaker so Stone could hear too. "Yes, Mrs. Lacey. What can I do for you?"

"Did the press conference work?"

"Too early to tell, ma'am."

"What comes next?" she fired off.

"Ideally, Stone will make an immediate appearance as Jack in the next hour or two. Someplace public but where we can hold back the press so they don't get too close a look at him. Honestly, Mrs. L, I'd suggest you be seen with him, as well."

"I know just the place," she declared. "Not to mention I'm in need of some serious retail therapy after all these shenanigans. On Jack's credit card, bless his cheating heart."

He winced. *Bless your heart* was the kiss of death from Jill Lacey. It was her Southern version of fuck off, you moron, but ever so much more politely offered up, of course. Because Jill was a lady.

"Y'all come on up so we can transform our boy. And then Jack 2.0 and I are going shopping."

Christian disconnected the call, laughing at the long-suffering look on Stone's face. "Thanks for taking one for the team, man," he teased. Stone had obviously been dragged on shopping sprees before and knew what misery lay ahead of him.

They got back to the Lacey suite, where Stone shaved, and the makeup artist put on his Jack makeup. Stone put on one of Jack's altered suits and stomped into a pair of the senator's lizard-skin cowboy boots.

Even Jill stared when he came out of the bedroom. The transformation was amazing.

A pair of security guards lent by the hotel were going to act as bodyguards for the day, and the upscale mall that Jill had chosen for the outing had already been notified to have its own security personnel hold back any press that tried to get close to Jack.

The suite went silent as everyone else left, and Christian collapsed on the couch. It was done. His life was ruined. He just hoped it hadn't been all for nothing.

CHAPTER FOURTEEN

THE CASINO night was starting downstairs, and there was still no sign of Tucker and Jack, even though their plane had left Barbados several hours ago. Which meant Stone was going to have to go through with appearing as the senator and risk his life for the bastard.

Christian broke the news to Jill about Chesty's pregnancy after the mall trip, which was a blessing. Jill was so furious she couldn't form words, and he'd been genuinely worried she might give herself a stroke the way her face turned nearly purple and the veins in her temples throbbed visibly. Stone had walked her into the bedroom and gently forced her to lie down on the bed and put her feet up. But as he left the room, she'd been reaching for her telephone with a murderous expression on her face.

Somewhere, in the back of his mind, he'd been certain Jack would show up at the last minute to save him from tonight's insanity. But there was no telling exactly when the plane would land and whether or not Jack would even deign to show up at the event.

Now that Stone was alone with only minutes to go before he made a major public appearance as another man—in front of people who knew the real Jack Lacey, no less—he let himself pace the suite in a futile effort to work off some of his stress.

Ominously, there had been no more emails from the stalker. The Wild Cards' profiler was concerned that the person was done talking and was now preparing to take action. The police and gun stores in the local area had been quietly put on alert, and the Wild Cards staff was watching every layer of the internet like hawks. But that was about all anyone could do until the stalker made his or her next move.

It was ironic that he'd been the one adamant to have Jack cancel the appearance, and now he was the one insisting on going through with it. Christian had tried last night to talk him out of it and then to seduce him out of it. But this stalker nutball had to be caught, and this was the most expedient way to do it. Not that he cared much at this point if Jack got shot.

But he did care a great deal if Christian got shot or not. He didn't want Christian working or making public appearances anywhere near Jack Lacey until whoever was planning to shoot at Jack was caught.

It scared him that Christian's arguments last night actually had the power to sway his decision. Not only did he respect the man's opinions, but when Christian had spoken earnestly about not being able to live with himself if something bad happened to Stone because of him, it had actually moved Stone. Emotionally. Complete with a torn-apart feeling in his gut. What the hell was up with that?

He wasn't a feelings kind of guy.

Apparently, he was now, compliments of one Christian Chatsworth-Brandeis.

Jill had already left for the party, with Christian acting as her temporary escort. They were going to spread a story that a crisis had come up in Washington and Jack had to deal with it before he came down to join the festivities. Fortunately, there was a full slate of other politicians to keep the crowd occupied and feeling schmoozed until Jack 2.0 put in an appearance.

Of course, that very slate of politicians was their biggest problem. Many of them knew Jack well enough to spot an impersonator. Stone was supposed to wait up here until just a few minutes before Jack's speech and only then go downstairs.

He checked over his bullet-resistant vest again, then cleaned and reloaded his pistol to pass the time. He picked up the deck of cards Christian had used earlier to explain poker to Jill and idly dealt himself hands. His left hand kicked his right hand's ass at seven-card stud before his cell phone rang, startling him and shattering the silence of the room.

Jeez, dude, get your act together. He answered the phone tersely with "Go ahead."

"Hey, it's me." He exhaled in relief. Just hearing Christian's voice made him feel better. "How are you holding up?"

"I'm tense, which makes me horny as hell. I would rather be in bed with you than playing fake senator. But otherwise I'm fabulous."

Christian laughed in his ear. "Glad to hear it. You're on in ten. I've sent the security guys up to get you."

"See you in a few, good lookin'."

"Right back at you, sir."

Sir? Oh, right. In case anyone was eavesdropping, Christian was talking to "Senator Lacey."

The knock on the door came, and two burly, expressionless men stood there. Stone noticed one of them surreptitiously checking the suite over his shoulder. They thought the crisis was a woman, huh? Even with Jack's wife entertaining his guests downstairs as they stood here? Wow. That was one hell of a low opinion they had of Jack Lacey. And fully deserved.

Both of the bodyguards were big men. He sighed. People who didn't know a lot about the security business seemed to think that bald, overmuscled giants in black rock band T-shirts were the way to go for protection. Size helped if—and only if—the security operative knew what to do with his body mass to protect a client with it.

Given that these two stepped back respectfully to let him out of the suite, his money was on them knowing absolutely nothing about blocking a real security threat. Shiny.

At least one of them had the good sense to step out of the elevator first when they reached the ground floor. They skirted the edges of the busy prep tables in the kitchen and dodged the ant line of waiters entering and exiting the space.

"Where to, Senator?" one of them asked loudly enough to turn a few heads in his direction.

Jesus H. Christ. The idea was to be anonymous, not shout out his identity to everyone in earshot. "Backstage," he muttered without moving his lips.

"You got it," the talkative one boomed.

Just shoot him now. He might as well walk out onstage and make a public announcement that he was ready to die if the assassin would please get on with it.

The noise was intense as he slipped into the wings of the main stage. The big ballroom was packed. Easily two thousand people milled around the various gaming tables, drinking, gambling, and shouting over the live band playing in the orchestra balcony. Why musicians always insisted on being thirty decibels too loud for the occasion, no matter what the occasion, he would never understand.

He felt Christian approaching and looked over his shoulder. Good Lord, that man wore a tuxedo like an Armani model. His breath actually hitched in his throat at the sight of Christian in stark black and snowy white. Their gazes met, and they shared an instant of private acknowledgment.

"Looking good," Christian breathed.

"Ditto."

A little louder, Christian asked, "Have you got your notes, sir?"

"In my jacket pocket."

"In about five minutes, the emcee will read an introduction and finish with 'From the great state of Texas, I give you Senator Jack Lacey.' That's your cue to walk out."

"Any news from Tucker?" Which was an oblique way of asking if there might be a last-minute reprieve from this suicide mission.

"Talked with him about twenty minutes ago. The eagle has landed, but it can't join us here immediately."

He turned to stare fully at Christian. "Why not?"

"Customs problems. Long lines and crowds." Christian shrugged, but Stone saw the stress lines around his eyes. Christian added, "I've got a helicopter standing by to airlift them directly to the roof of the hotel. It's possible they'll arrive soon, but I have no way of knowing when."

"We'll get through this," he muttered. "Not much longer now. Fifteen minutes, tops."

"I'll have you know that speech should take no less than seventeen minutes to read."

"Yeah, yeah. I know. Drawl and go slow."

"You'll do fine," Christian murmured. "I believe in you."

"I'm glad one of us does."

Christian reached surreptitiously between their hips to give his hand a quick squeeze.

"Any more hassles from the press?" he asked Christian. The ticked-off tabloid reporter had been making wild allegations, but the guy didn't seem to be gaining a whole lot of attention nationally. Thank God.

The emcee came out from the other side of the stage and took the podium. He had a series of announcements and thank-yous to go through before Jack would be announced.

A flurry of activity behind Stone made him and Christian both look over their shoulders. A deeply tanned man in shorts and a polo shirt was arguing with one of the hotel's security guards.

"Holy shit," Christian breathed. "It's him. He's here."

Jack Lacey had finally shown up. About damned time.

Christian raced over to a stage manager. "Have the emcee stretch it out, will you?"

The guy in all-black clothing nodded and gave a hand signal to the emcee, who launched into a lame joke that made the crowd groan loudly and laugh reluctantly.

Stone and Christian rushed to the senator, whose anger and volume was starting to climb as he tried to convince the security guards he was the real Jack Lacey.

"Come with me, sir," Christian said firmly. He grabbed the real Jack by the arm and bodily dragged him toward the kitchen. Lacey looked back and forth between Christian and Stone, a frown gathering on his brow.

"What in the Sam Hill is going on here? Why in the hell are you wearing my damned suit, Jackson, isn't it? The bodyguard, right? And those are my boots—"

"Quiet, Jack," Stone bit out.

Shocked, the senator complied for once. They hustled into an employee bathroom, and Christian checked all the stalls to make sure they were alone before locking the exterior door and announcing, "We've got two minutes at most."

Stone talked quickly to the senator. "I've been impersonating you for the past week so you wouldn't lose a crap-ton of campaign contributions. You're welcome, by the way."

Aware that they had only seconds to gain Jack's cooperation, Stone talked fast. "You need to go out and make your speech at the big fundraiser out there, and then you are going to be called away on an emergency. We have reason to believe your stalker may try to assassinate you here tonight."

"Nah. No way," Jack interjected.

Stone ignored the interruption. "If you want to go back to the party in a little while as yourself, as long as you do exactly what I say and you let the hotel security guys and me stick to you like glue, I can allow you to spend a little time in the crowd. It should provide you with enough cover to make the risk acceptable."

"Listen here, Jackson. You're a fucking bodyguard. You don't tell me what to do. If I want to—"

Stone cut him off, letting every intimidating impulse he'd ever experienced roar forth. He stood to his full height, swelled out his chest, and leaned forward to glare into the senator's eyes. "Let's get one thing straight. I don't work for you. I work for your wife. And she doesn't give a fuck what you want right now."

Lacey spluttered. "She's here?"

"Oh yeah," Stone replied coldly. "Been here a couple of days, covering your ass. She knows all about Chesty and the *Wrastle Castle*."

"Oh shit."

Christian piped up. "Valerie's in town too. She's spitting mad that she hasn't been able to speak with you all this time. I've been putting her off with excuses, but she thinks you're avoiding her."

"Hell yeah, I'm avoiding her! She wants me to marry her, for fuck's sake."

"Do you want to marry her?" Stone asked, curious about the man he'd been impersonating.

"Hell no. If I wanted to get hitched to her, I'd a' done it back before I ever ran for the Senate. She's not political wife material."

Stone snorted at that pithy observation.

Christian dived in. "Stone's plan makes sense, sir. Make the speech and then get under cover immediately. We've received a credible death threat that you need to take seriously. We have good reason to believe an attacker will strike tonight."

Jack laughed. He *laughed*. Stone stared at him in open shock. What in the ever-loving hell was wrong with the guy?

The senator slapped Christian a little too hard on the shoulder. "Son, the death-threat thing was a publicity stunt I cooked up with Valerie. She wrote and sent the emails to help boost public sympathy for me. We figured I might need a little help with my polling numbers when I ask Jill for a divorce."

"You can't divorce your wife before the election!" Christian exclaimed. "At least not if you want to win. Jill's more popular than you by thirty percentage points."

"Your mistress, Valerie, sent the threats?" Stone asked, still stuck on that bombshell.

Jack replied cheerfully, "That whole stalker thing was fake. No one's trying to kill me. Now let me make my damned speech. I'll just go upstairs and change into my tux—"

"No time, sir," Christian said. "You're due on stage, right now."

Lacey held a hand out to Stone. "Give me the fucking speech."

At the end of the day, the man was a sitting United States senator. Stone couldn't very well refuse to let Jack Lacey be himself if there was no threat to his life. He fished out the papers and passed them to Lacey.

Christian unlocked the bathroom door, and the three of them hurried back toward the stage.

"What's this I hear about you kissing Christian on the beach? I had texts coming in the whole damned flight back here to ask if I was gay or not. Jesus Christ. I'm not a fag!"

Clearly, he was a bigot, however.

"Sir," Christian hissed. "I told you that you can't use that word."

"Aww, c'mon. You're an okay fag. I hired you, didn't I? Got a bunch of votes for being progressive too." A pause. "Hell, you even turned out to be a decent staffer."

Stone spied shock in Christian's eyes. He wasn't aware he'd been hired as a publicity stunt, huh? Wow. That sucked.

They hurried to the stage, and the emcee spied Jack and Stone side by side. He looked back and forth between them in confusion for a second and then shook himself and announced, "Without further ado, from the great state of Texas, I give you Senator Jack Lacey!"

The senator strolled out onstage in his Bermuda shorts and polo shirt like he owned the place. The crowd applauded and cheered, but a note of confusion was present in the noise. This was a black-tie event, after all.

Jack had no sooner reached the podium than a voice shouted out from near the stage, "Why are you afraid to admit you're gay, Jack?"

Fuck. The tabloid reporter. Christian started to lurch forward, but Stone put a hand on his arm. "Let hotel security deal with that asshole. You don't need any more exposure to the media. And I'd lay odds that guy's got someone filming him in hopes that Jack will cause a scene."

Christian subsided, but Jack Lacey did not. He came around the side of the podium aggressively to confront the reporter. "Why, you little pissant. You wouldn't know what to do with a woman if her cunt jumped up and down on your dick all by itself."

"Jesus. I've got to stop him—" Christian started.

"Stone! Come on out here. Let's stop this bullshit once and for all!" Lacey called out loudly.

It was Stone's turn to lurch. He looked at Christian in alarm. The senator was going to expose their whole scheme. After all they'd done for the bastard, he was going to ruin them all!

"Talk about a security threat and that's why you did it…," Christian got out before Stone stepped out into the bright lights.

The crowd gasped.

He moved up beside the senator and took advantage of the ballroom's excellent acoustics to call out, "There was a security threat to the senator's life, and he graciously allowed me to impersonate him for several public appearances in the name of protecting his life. I apologize if the ruse has caused any confusion for anyone."

"Did you catch whoever was threatening him?" someone shouted.

Jack opened his mouth to answer, no doubt to declare that there was no threat. Stone shifted his cowboy-booted foot to step rather heavily on the senator's flimsily sandaled toes. Lacey sucked in a sharp breath.

Stone called back, "The threat has been neu—"

He never got the word "neutralized" out of his mouth.

He glanced over at Jack, and not one, but three red laser dots lit up on the man's torso. One came in from above at an angle centered over his heart, and another came in more from the side, also centered roughly on his heart. The third dot was lower. Groin high.

Stone's reflexes and long years of training took over. He leaped toward Jack, slamming into him and sending the older man flying. As Jack crashed onto his back, Stone realized that now he was standing in the exact spot Jack had been a millisecond before, and all three dots were lighting *him* up.

He had just long enough to think, *Oh, shit*, before a large, fast-moving object charged him from stage right.

Christian.

He came tearing out of the wings of the stage and laid a flying tackle on Stone that any NFL player would have been proud of. His arms wrapped round Stone's chest and slammed him to the stage boards at the exact same moment a gunshot rang out deafeningly loud in the confines of the ballroom.

Bang! Bang! Bang!

Stunned, Stone took only an instant to process what the hell had happened. "Where's Jack?" he demanded tersely.

"Laser dots were on your chest," Christian bit out.

"Gotta get to the senator!" Stone shouted at Christian over the cacophony. As Christian rolled one way, Stone rolled the other and pulled his pistol all in one move, landing prone on his stomach, weapon propped out in front of him. Those shots had come from different directions. Multiple shooters. Inadequate coverage to surround the principal, let alone properly cover him and move him to safety. Possibly more shots to come.

He spied a movement in the corner where the orchestra gallery met the wall. It was no more than a shadow, really, and a tiny flash of red, but it was enough. He took the shot, sending a double tap of two bullets up at the shooter.

"Get Jack offstage!" he shouted at Christian, who was now lying on top of the senator.

Someone from the balcony grabbed one of the band member's microphones and yelled, "Shooter down!"

Stone holstered his weapon and ran over to secure the senator. A pool of blood was spreading fast beneath Christian and Jack. *Which one was hit?*

His entire possible future life with Christian flashed before his eyes as he reached for the man he loved in slow motion. Courting romantically. A small wedding with family and friends. Maybe a couple of kids, someday. A little house on the beach. Lazy days and long nights stretching out in a lifetime of companionship and joy—

Christian rose to his feet, the front of his tuxedo soaked in blood. Stone grabbed him by both shoulders. "Don't move. I'll get you to a hospital—"

"I'm not hit. It's Jack."

Stone looked down as a doctor emerged from the screaming, fleeing crowd to kneel by the senator. He commenced tending to a wound in Jack's belly.

"Talk to me," Stone snapped at the doctor.

"Multiple gunshot wounds. None life-threatening unless there's internal hemorrhaging, which I can't tell from a superficial inspection. He needs to get to a hospital immediately."

"Ambulance is pulling around to the ocean side of the ballroom. It'll be here in one minute," somebody shouted.

Jill came rushing onto the stage, and Stone leaped forward to intercept her. He knew better than to let her see Jack like this. Everyone would need her to be strong for a while and make some decisions. And she would likely fall apart if she saw Jack's blood.

"Let me go," she ground out.

"Trust me, Mrs. Lacey. Doctors are with Jack. He's alive but injured. Right now, I need you to go with me to the ambulance. They're going to need some information from you so they can help Jack."

Christian closed in on Jill's other side, and the two of them gently but firmly escorted her off the stage and toward the line of french doors. The ambulance crew was already rushing toward them, pushing a wheeled gurney. More sirens were screaming their imminent arrival.

Stone threw the doors wide open for the medics, who rushed past them when he pointed toward the stage.

He followed as Christian guided Jill to the front seat of the open ambulance and crawled in beside her. That was when she broke down. She sobbed on his shoulder, and Christian held her tightly.

"Get it all out now," he soothed. "You'll be busy later."

She nodded and cried even harder. Stone backed away and ran for the ballroom, this time heading upstairs to the orchestra gallery. Police were already there.

"Stand back," one ordered him. "This is a crime scene—"

"Sitrep?" he asked tersely. "I'm on Senator Lacey's security team."

"We found a pistol on the floor backstage. And someone found a rifle on the beach outside with a laser sight on it."

"I saw three laser dots. The third weapon?" he demanded. "With the shooter up in the balcony. I'm the security guard who shot that person. I suspect you're going to need my weapon and to take me in for a statement. But first I'd like to see the shooter if I could."

He surrendered his weapon to the cops, who bagged it as evidence before escorting him over to where several more policemen were standing. A woman sat on the floor, glaring at everyone while someone tended to a wound not to be too delicate but on her right breast.

"Chesty?" he exclaimed. "Why?"

She looked up at him and scowled. "I'm not saying a word until I speak with my lawyer."

"Has she been read her rights?" he asked nobody in particular.

A cop spoke up. "Oh, yeah. A couple of times. She lawyered up before we even had a chance to tell her she could have one."

"Thanks, guys. If someone could take me to the station so I can get going on the paperwork, that would be great. I'd like to get over to the hospital to check on the senator as quickly as possible."

Which was to say, he wanted to get back to Christian to lend him his support.

The police were pleasant, particularly after they verified his identity and bona fides with Wild Cards, Inc.

The company's law firm had an associate in Miami who arrived at the police station before Stone had even finished writing out his official statement of what had happened.

He had to agree to stay in Miami until the police cleared him to go, but in under two hours, he walked out of the station a free man. The attorney gave him a ride to the hospital, and the radio on the way reported that Jack Lacey was in surgery and rumored to be in grave condition.

C'mon, you son of a bitch. Don't die. It was a purely selfish thought based on his fierce desire not to lose a client on his watch. Even if he hadn't been Lacey's bodyguard, the guy's death would still reflect poorly on him.

When he got to the hospital, he was admitted to the family waiting area as soon as he gave his name. Christian had apparently told the police to let him through the phalanx of reporters and the hospital security providing privacy.

Christian was staring out a window in the waiting room. There was no sign of Mrs. Lacey. Stone walked up behind him, and Christian must have seen his reflection in the glass, for he turned silently and stepped into Stone's arms. They embraced, hugging hard for a long time.

"How's Jack?" he asked.

"In surgery."

"How are you holding up?" Stone asked. "You're sure you weren't wounded? Shock can make people not notice even serious injuries."

"I'm fine. I promise. What about you?"

"I have on a bulletproof vest. And besides, I'm Superman. Bullets bounce right off me."

"That's not funny," Christian ground out. "When I saw those red dots pointed at you, and you were out there trying to protect that bastard alone...." A long pause, and then he whispered, "I died."

"But I didn't get hit. I'm fine."

Another long, hard hug.

"The dots weren't for me. They pointed at Jack. When I pushed him out of the line of fire, I momentarily took his place in front of the dots. Before the shooters fired, they changed targets and hit the senator."

"Ahh. That explains the delay from when I saw the dots until I heard the shots," Christian said hollowly. It sounded like he was in mild shock.

Fair. Civilians didn't often have to witness an actual shooting. Unlike him. He'd seen plenty of gunshot wounds, blood, and death in his day. Too much, maybe, if he'd gotten this immune to its horror.

"How's Jill?" Stone asked eventually.

"Pissed as hell."

"Really?" he blurted. "I'd have thought she'd be frantic."

Christian lowered his voice so only Stone could hear him. "She actually seems torqued off that he survived."

Stone whistled low. "Dang. She really was ready to kill him, wasn't she?" A horrible thought struck him. "Is it possible she was one of the shooters? The police did find one of the weapons backstage, and that was where she came from after Jack was shot."

"Surely not," Christian answered.

But Stone wondered, nonetheless.

Christian said grimly, "If he doesn't make it, this will be a fitting end for him. Did they tell you where he's hit?"

"It looked like his gut from when I saw him."

"That was the exit wound. Bullet went in just at the base of his penis. Hit the pubic bone and ricocheted out of his belly without hitting any vital organs."

"Ouch," Stone half laughed. "Talk about karma. What a bitch!"

"Please, God, don't ever say that in public—"

"Never fear, Christian. I understand what a nightmare a comment like that would be for you to handle. A guy on the radio reported that Jack was still in surgery and in grave condition. Any update?"

Christian's lips twitched with humor. "I might have taken a little liberty with the truth with the press. His life isn't in danger at all. But his penis is likely destroyed. It amused me to tell the press that grave condition line."

Stone grinned furtively, making sure no one else had come into the waiting room who might overhear. "That's cold, man."

Christian shrugged. "Guilty as charged."

"Does Jill know?"

Christian nodded. "She went to the chapel to have a few minutes alone. She's probably in there thanking the good Lord for making a eunuch out of her cheating husband. I'm supposed to fetch her if there's news."

"She's lucky to have you," Stone said sincerely.

"Things could get pretty crazy for a while. I don't know how much time I'll have…."

Stone got the message. He was being dismissed. Real life had overtaken their silly little fantasy of a future in which they could be together and happy. He needed to go back to being an invisible bodyguard, and Christian needed to give his full attention to the business of helping Senator Lacey's wife through this crisis.

A hot sword of agony slashed across his body, eviscerating him. His emotional guts spilled out onto the floor at his feet as he watched Christian grimly straighten his shoulders and put on his publicity face.

That was it. He was shut out. Whether or not he wanted to be done with Christian, Christian was done with him.

He witnessed death, lost friends, hell, brothers. But no loss he'd ever suffered compared to the pain of this one.

How was he supposed to go on? To lie down tonight, knowing he would always be alone, to get up in the morning knowing he would never find another man like Christian? How was he supposed to take his next breath?

His lungs burned as if he'd inhaled pure fire. His eyes burned; the back of his throat burned.

"No problem," he croaked. "I understand. You do what you have to do."

He turned around and walked out of the waiting room. And damned if he didn't feel something hot and wet on his face as he stepped out into the night.

CHAPTER FIFTEEN

CHRISTIAN STEPPED back into Senator Lacey's office in Washington, DC, with a heavy heart. He'd gotten into town last night and had put off coming here until this morning. The disastrous trip to Miami seemed like a distant nightmare, but then he stood in the doorway and looked at Jack's empty desk, and it all came back to him, far too real.

Senator Lacey was in Switzerland, where Jill had taken him and set him up in a long-term care and rehabilitation facility. She was due back in the office sometime today.

If Jack cooperated with his doctors and therapists and got lucky, he might be able to pee through his reconstructed penis in the next year or two. He would likely never have sex again.

In public, Jill was devastated. In private… not so much.

Jack was still technically a senator. But the reality was that he was in no position to do the job. Jill had quietly taken over doing all of the behind-the-scenes work of his office. The only thing she couldn't do was vote in his place. There was already talk—a lot of it—that she should run for Jack's seat herself next year.

He had no idea if she would run for office. She was pissed off enough at her husband to do it to spite him.

Christian had no energy for another campaign. This one had all but killed him. Well, losing Stone had technically been what did the damage. But that had been his fault. He'd been so hell-bent to keep Jack Lacey's campaign on the rails that he'd blown it with Stone.

Too much. This job had cost him too much. He had no love for the rat race anymore. He worked morning, noon, and night at it, though. Losing himself in the minutiae of government work was better than facing his cold, sterile apartment. Or facing sleeping in his big, empty bed.

Every morning, he still reached out instinctively when he woke up, looking for Stone's sturdy, welcoming warmth beside him. And every morning, he wasn't there.

An urge to go home, or maybe to head to the other end of the country and set up a quiet law practice, came over him yet again. And every time the urge to run came, it was a little stronger.

He couldn't live in this VIP and security-filled town without envisioning Stone every time he turned around. He caught himself hunting for Stone's familiar silhouette, the dark hair and sexy jaw at least a dozen times a day.

His therapist said to give it a few months. But it had been a few months, and it was getting worse, not better.

No doubt about it. He needed to leave this town. He'd lost his passion for the job over at Justice when Stone took all his passion away with him.

He couldn't blame the man for continuing his regular life. But God, he'd hoped Stone would consider changing his life around so they could be together. Hell, if Stone called tomorrow and asked him to move to London and become a house husband, waiting for him to come home in between security gigs, he would do it in a heartbeat.

But Stone had been dead silent since he'd walked out of that hospital waiting room and had never looked back.

"Good morning, Christian," Jill said behind him.

He whirled. "I didn't expect to see you at the office until later, ma'am. You should go home and rest. Get over the jet lag—"

"I flew back here in a private jet and got a perfectly lovely night's sleep." She dropped casually, "I got a call from the Justice Department while I was in Geneva."

His gaze snapped to hers. Was he being investigated for the mess in Miami?

She continued, "Apparently Stone Jackson forwarded your résumé to someone he knows there. They were impressed and called me to get a recommendation. I told them you were the most outstanding senior staffer in Washington, not to mention a man of sterling honor, whom they would be lucky to have on their prison reform task force."

He landed heavily in one of the chairs in front of Jack's—her—desk. She moved around behind the desk and sat down at it, running her palms over the burnished cherrywood as if to familiarize herself with it.

"I guess this is mine now," she commented.

He managed to make some inane gurgle that he hoped passed as a sound of agreement.

"Here's the thing, Christian. I would love to have you stay on, even if for a little while, to help bring me up to speed and get me settled in the job. I'm willing to shamelessly dangle a substantial raise in front of you and name you my chief of staff."

God, it was tempting.

Funny, though, ever since Stone had walked out of that hospital and taken Christian's heart with him, the appeal of clawing his way up the Washington ladder had dimmed.

A month ago, he would have been exultant over landing the chief of staff position, let alone having the Justice Department sniffing around about hiring him. Now he was only vaguely pleased. Mostly he was disappointed that he had no one to share his success with. And by no one, he meant Stone.

"Stay with me to the end of this term. One year. And then I'll do everything in my power to help you get that dream job of yours."

It wasn't a bad offer. Thing was, he wasn't even sure he wanted to stay in DC. He'd been having wild fantasies about moving to London. Maybe he could hook up with Stone between his bodyguarding jobs—

He broke off the thought. It was foolish to think about chasing after a man who'd walked out of his life without a backward glance. By the time Jack had gotten out of surgery and Christian returned to the hotel, Stone had packed up, checked out, and was long gone. A few calls had confirmed that Stone was already on a plane bound for London.

"Can I think about it before I give you an answer?"

"Of course. But I'm going to keep working on you to say yes."

He pulled out a tablet computer. "In the meantime, I took the liberty of building a rough itinerary for you."

"Whatever's on the morning schedule is going to have to be canceled. I have a very important meeting."

"With whom?" he inquired.

"It's private," she said cryptically.

"When does it start?"

A door opened and closed in the outer office. "Sounds like right now," she said.

He stood and opened the connecting door. The first person he spied was the Laceys' personal lawyer from Texas. What was he doing here?

And....

Valerie?

What on earth?

He turned his attention to the second woman and stared in shock. "Chesty?" he croaked. She'd obviously had a significant breast reduction, but now sported a definite baby belly. "How did you get out of jail?"

"Mrs. Lacey hired me an excellent lawyer and got the case moved to Texas. He argued that it was a crime of passion. Baby hormones made me distraught and I went temporarily insane. He got me two years' probation and a thousand hours of community service instead of jail time"— she stroked her belly—"seeing as how I'm pregnant, and Mrs. Lacey herself begged the court for clemency in my case."

It sounded a little fishy to Christian, but stranger things had happened. And Jack was so well known as a womanizer in Texas, Christian suspected that had weighted heavily in Chesty's favor with a jury. And he supposed Jill's plea for leniency would have also carried a lot of weight. A quiet, but hefty campaign contribution to the sitting judge probably wouldn't have hurt either.

God, he'd gotten cynical. It was definitely time for him to leave this job.

Someone moved at the edge of his peripheral vision, and he glanced to his right.

Froze.

Turned slowly.

Stared.

"Stone?" he breathed. The name stuck in his bone-dry throat.

"Christian." A heartbeat long pause. "You look like hell."

"It has been a little hectic around here," he replied. *Lame, lame, lame,* he chastised himself.

"Well?" Jill called out. "Bring everybody in."

Startled out of his stupor, Christian ushered the strange collection of people into Jack's—Jill's—office.

"Thank you all for coming today," she said, standing up and waving everyone to seats.

For his part, Christian took a seat off to one side where he could see everyone's faces. What in the ever-loving hell was going on?

"Clarence?" Jill said. "Do you have the papers?"

"Yes, ma'am." The lawyer passed her a thick sheaf of legal documents, and then passed similar sheaves to Valerie and Chesty.

Jill glanced through them quickly without reading them. "Everything's as the three of us agreed to?" she asked the attorney.

"Yes. Jack's estate has been liquidated and split equally between the three of you."

Christian's jaw dropped.

The three women started signing the documents and passing them around, and Christian managed to glimpse one of them on its way past him.

> *We, the undersigned, in recognition of our joint service to John J. Lacey these many years, Jill Lacey as his wedded wife, Valerie Micklethwaite as his long-term mistress, and Chelsea "Chesty Hills" Jenkins as the mother of his child, do agree to share equally in all the worldly goods given over to Mrs. Lacey in accordance with Senator John J. Lacey's power of attorney, executed this tenth day of....*

"What on earth?" he exclaimed.

Stone leaned forward, pinning him with a stare. "Haven't you figured it out yet, Christian?"

"Figured out *what*?"

The Texas lawyer leaped up hastily, gathered up all the documents and all but ran from the office as if he didn't want to hear the rest of this conversation. At all. What on earth? Christian turned his gaze from the door as it slammed shut behind the lawyer back to Stone.

Stone murmured, "The three of them. I'm guessing they were in it together from the beginning."

"I don't know what beginning you might be referring to," Jill objected. "We only met after Chesty called me to let me know she was pregnant with Jack's child."

Something exploded behind his eyelids. That was it. He'd officially had an aneurysm.

Valerie dived in, chewing gum furiously as she spoke. "He promised Jill he wouldn't divorce her until after he left the Senate. He promised me he'd leave her and marry me by the end of this year. He promised Chelsea she wouldn't get pregnant, and when she did, he promised he'd marry her. The way we figure it, he didn't plan to keep any of his promises."

"Why didn't you satisfy yourselves with blackmailing him?" Christian asked. "Why attempted murder?"

Chesty—Chelsea jumped in. "Oh, I tried blackmail. I got him out on that boat and demanded that he pay up or I was going public with the baby." Her voice took on a tone of disgust. "All he said was that maybe his bitch of a wife would finally divorce him."

"Did he indicate that he would marry you or Valerie after that?"

Chelsea, actress that she was, rolled her eyes dramatically. "He said he was never marrying any woman again and that we're only good for one thing."

Christian shook his head. The man obviously had *no* sense of self-preservation when it came to the female half of the species.

Christian frowned, looking around at the women. "So, you set up Jack and knocked him down? Took him for everything he's worth, and even took his job away from him?"

Three pairs of female eyes blinked innocently at him, as if they had *no* idea *what* he was talking about.

Sonofabitch.

"What I want to know," Stone drawled, "is which one of you took the groin shot."

Chelsea blushed. "My daddy used to take me hunting with him when I was little. I could knock the eye out of a squirrel at fifty paces. But I'm not admitting to anything, mind you. I swear I never would intentionally shoot the father of my baby and have no memory of having done anything like that."

Christian rolled his eyes. *That* was a lie.

"Nice shot," Stone commented dryly.

Chesty merely shrugged.

Christian shook his head to clear it from the fog of fuckery enveloping them all. "Were all three of you sending the threats?"

"That was Jack's idea," Valerie offered. "He thought it would get him sympathy from the public. He thought Jill might try to ruin his reputation when he asked for the divorce."

Christian stared at her as shock numbed his entire body. "How did you disguise the origin of the messages? Even the FBI couldn't figure out where they came from."

Valerie grinned. "My family might engage in certain extracurricular activities from time to time. I have connections, if you get my drift."

Oh, he got her drift, all right.

He looked around at all three women. "The three of you shot Jack?"

"I have no idea what you're talking about," Jill replied mildly. "Bless your heart, but that's downright crazy talk."

"Does Jack know?" he asked weakly.

Jill leaned forward and said coolly, "That's not the real question now, is it? The more salient question would be whether or not Jack would do anything about it if your wild speculations happened to be true."

"Look. I'm a lawyer. An officer of the court. It's my duty to report all crimes."

"And what crime would that be?" Jill asked evenly. A note of steel had crept into her voice.

Stone spoke up. "As you know, Christian, I sign an ironclad nondisclosure agreement with each of my clients. But that wouldn't prevent you from taking an educated guess about a recent job I took... if you'd like."

Christian stared hard at Stone, who stared back as if begging him to figure it out.

"Is it possible you escorted several ladies to, oh, I don't know, Switzerland, recently?"

Stone nodded. "I can't reveal the destinations of my clients."

"Did your most recent clients perchance ask somebody else to sign certain legal documents... maybe enacting power of attorney for one of them?"

Stone's chin lifted in a slight nod. "No idea," he said aloud.

"Was some sort of agreement struck that, in return for somebody pressing no criminal charges and filing no lawsuits, someone might be allowed to live out one's days quietly and without any more shootings?"

Stone broke into a big smile. "You are so smart! But I think you're way off base on this one. The police never identified the other shooters, and seeing as how Chesty can't remember any of the whole day Jack was shot, we'll probably never know. There was even speculation at her trial that she might have been hypnotized."

Christian snorted. "No sane jury would buy that."

Jill grinned. "Who says all juries are sane?"

Valerie said pleasantly, "I hear the sanitarium Jack's in is a nice place. Picturesque valley in the Alps. Lots of pretty young nurses he can fantasize about while he fades into obscurity."

"Who else knows about all of this?" Christian asked.

Jill frowned theatrically. "I have no idea what you're talking about. Only the people in this room have heard your wild theories, and I'd be obliged if you could keep it that way. Unless, of course, you have any proof...." She trailed off expectantly.

Christian fell back in his chair, utterly speechless. In point of fact, he had no proof at all. And not one of the women had said anything today that would directly incriminate herself.

"You want me to look the other way on this?" he finally demanded. "I can't in good conscience do that."

Jill said soberly, "I'm sorry if you feel like you've been put in an awkward position. But I'll ask you one more time. Do you have any proof whatsoever of what you seem to believe happened?"

"No."

"Then what good would it do you to go to the authorities with your theory. Would anybody believe you? Especially when Jack himself is prepared to say it's not so?"

He released a long, slow breath. The woman was not wrong. "Here's the thing," he said heavily. "I don't believe I can continue working for you, Mrs. Lacey. You may have no conscience, but I still have mine."

Her jaw tightened, but she nodded. "I understand. I'll be happy to write you a glowing letter of recommendation on behalf of the exemplary service you gave to my husband."

"Thank you," he said stiffly.

He stepped out into the outer office and released the breath he hadn't realized he was holding. He'd done the right thing. Why, then, didn't he feel the least bit satisfied with the outcome of it all?

The Texas attorney had sorted the documents into three piles. As Valerie and Chelsea came out, the lawyer gave a stack to each woman, and stowed the remaining copy in his briefcase. Stone escorted the lawyer, Valerie, and Chelsea out. The door closed quietly.

God, it still hurt as bad as the last time he'd had to watch Stone walk out of his life. His heart felt as if it had turned to ice in his chest and stopped beating, locked in still, silent agony.

The door opened again and a man stepped inside.

Stone.

He stared.

"You?" he finally choked out.

"Phone call for you," Stone said, holding out a cell phone.

What the—

Christian took the phone and put it to his ear.

"Mr. Chatsworth-Brandeis? This is Peregrine Cardiffe from Wild Cards, Inc."

"Mr. Cardiffe?"

"Peregrine, please. Or just Pere."

"What can I do for you, Pere?"

"I have a problem, and I'm hoping you can help me out."

"How?"

"One of my top field operators came home from an assignment in Florida a few months ago, completely wrecked. He hasn't been the same, since, and he's showing no signs of pulling out of this tailspin he's in."

"What do you want me to do, sir?"

"He's been offered a position as chief of security to a young congressman from Colorado. He was recommended by a gentleman named Travis Tucker."

"Was he, now? And did he accept the job?"

"He has declared he won't take it unless he has a compelling reason to stay in Washington, DC. I'm hoping you might be able to help him come up with one."

"Indeed. Well, thank you for letting me know."

"Oh, and I had a word with an old friend from my university days. He's at the US Justice Department now. I'm assured you're exactly the candidate the prison reform task force is looking for. You should expect an offer within the week."

"Really?" he blurted. "Are you kidding me?"

"Really. I never joke about such things."

Christian realized he'd pulled the phone away from his ear and was staring at it. He put it back up to his ear and mumbled, "Umm, thank you."

"My pleasure. I'm counting on you, Christian." The line went dead.

He handed the phone back to Stone. "Do you know what he said to me?"

"I caught the gist of it," Stone said cautiously.

"Is it true? Have you been offered a permanent position here in DC?"

Stone nodded slowly. "I have."

"Are you going to take the job?"

"That depends."

"On what?" Christian's stomach broke out abruptly into a full gymnastic routine just beneath his ribs. He could hardly breathe with it flipping and turning and spinning like it was.

"On you, Christian. Are you going to take the job at Justice?"

"It's my dream job."

"Is that a yes?" Stone pressed.

"I guess it is."

"Then I'm accepting my job offer too," Stone said firmly.

"Are you sure? I mean, I thought you like to travel. Be a rolling stone. Gather no moss—"

Stone laid a finger on his lips to stop the spill of words and stared deep into his eyes. "I've never been more sure of anything in my life. I want you. And I'm willing to do whatever it takes to have you. Including settling down, buying a little place for us, and building you a picket fence if that's what you want."

His jaw dropped.

"And," Stone continued, "now that you're going to be working for no less than the Department of Justice itself, we wouldn't want any hint of scandal to follow you from your previous employer."

"Heaven forbid." A pause, then Christian added fervently, "From this moment forth, I wash my hands of Jack Lacey and all his women."

Their gazes met in rueful understanding and Stone murmured, "Ditto."

Christian smiled. No person could possibly pack more meaning into fewer syllables than this man.

But then Stone said, "I figure the best way to protect your reputation is to get you safely into a long-term relationship with a respectable man."

His stomach stuck a perfect landing as he stared at Stone. "Are you *really* sure?"

"Positive. How about you? Are you in?"

He didn't have to think about it. Didn't hesitate for a second. "Yes, I am. Absolutely."

A slow smile of relief and wonder unfolded across Stone's face. "Glad to hear we're on the same page, Prep School."

"Cow-pie kicker."

Smiling broadly, he took one small step forward into Stone's arms and one giant leap into their grand and glorious future. Together.

New York Times and *USA Today* bestselling author, CINDY DEES started flying airplanes while sitting in her dad's lap at the age of three and got a pilot's license before she got a driver's license. At age fifteen, she dropped out of high school and left the horse farm in Michigan where she grew up to attend the University of Michigan.

After earning a degree in Russian and East European Studies, she joined the U.S. Air Force and became the youngest female pilot in its history. She flew supersonic jets, VIP airlift, and the C-5 Galaxy, one of the world's largest cargo airplanes.

She also worked part-time gathering intelligence. During her military career, she traveled to forty-two countries on five continents, was detained by the KGB and East German secret police, got shot at, flew in the first Gulf War, met her husband, and amassed a lifetime's worth of war stories. Cindy has turned many of her experiences into novels of military romance and suspense.

Cindy's hobbies include professional Middle Eastern dancing, Japanese gardening, and medieval reenacting. She can also be found often on various social media, hanging out with her friends and fellow readers.

Winner of a Golden Heart and Holt Medallion for writing, Cindy is a five-time finalist and two-time winner of the prestigious RITA Award for Romance Fiction, two-time winner of RT Book Review's Best Harlequin Romantic Suspense Novel of the Year, and is a Romantic Times Lifetime Career Achievement nominee.

She has published over sixty novels, including thrillers, adventure novels, epic fantasies, and many stories of military romantic suspense.

Also from Dreamspinner Press

BESTSELLING AUTHOR & TWO-TIME LAMBDA FINALIST

RHYS FORD

BACK IN BLACK

McGINNIS INVESTIGATIONS
BOOK ONE

www.ingramcontent.com/pod-product-compliance
Lightning Source LLC
Chambersburg PA
CBHW071006280626
47160CB00015B/1421